DEAD OF NIGHT

BY

PANDORA PINE

Dead of Night

Copyright © Pandora Pine 2018

All Rights Reserved

First Digital Edition: October 2018

For Mary and Judi. You've both changed my life in more ways than you'll ever know.

PROLOGUE

Ronan

Heavy pounding on a wooden door woke Ronan O'Mara from a sound sleep. He struggled to open his eyes. It felt like they were glued shut. Throwing his legs over the side of the bed, he was surprised when they encountered what felt like hard-packed dirt rather than the soft throw rug that sat at the side of his king-sized bed.

Finally prying his gummy eyes open, Ronan quickly realized he wasn't in his plush bed in his row house in Salem, Massachusetts. He was in some kind of a cabin.

Hovel might be a better way to describe his current lodgings. A homemade quilt was lying on what felt like a horsehair mattress. Looking down at the floor, he saw that his bare feet were indeed sitting on top of a dirt floor. The small room was lit by the embers of a dying fire.

The pounding on the door continued. "Ronan! We know you bide here!" a deep voice shouted.

"I'm coming!" Ronan called back. Thankfully, the voice sounded familiar. Nothing else here was, that was for sure. Grimacing as he walked over the dirt floor, Ronan grabbed the handle to the cabin door and gave it a jerk to open it. Standing on the other side with a flaming torch in his hand was his boss, Captain Kevin Fitzgibbon. "What the hell is going on, Cap?" Ronan could hear the confusion in his own tone.

"You must come now. It is time," Kevin said simply.

"Come where?" Ronan looked past Fitzgibbon to see a full moon high in the sky. "It's the middle of the night.

"We do not have time to converse. Dress quickly," Fitzgibbon commanded.

Looking down at himself, Ronan saw that he was wearing some kind of long white nightshirt that reached his ankles. What the hell was going on here? "Fine."

Shutting the door in Kevin's face, he went back inside the cabin. Did he even have clothes here? Wherever *here* was. He walked to the small table positioned near the fireplace and saw pants and a shirt hung over the back of chair. "Guess these belong to me."

The fabric was rough against his fingers, not what he was used to wearing at all, but there was nothing for it. He slipped into the shirt and pants, even found a pair of socks which were more like hose, and a pair of shoes that reminded him of what the pilgrims wore when disembarking from the Mayflower. "What the hell is going on here?"

Ronan supposed, for the second time, that there was nothing for it. Fitzgibbon was waiting for him outside with a torch. *A torch!* The man didn't look like he was in the mood to be trifled with either. He put on the pilgrim shoes and headed out the door.

"Where are we going?" he asked as Fitzgibbon started leading them toward the woods.

"You know where we are going. Silence!" Fitzgibbon ordered.

Not liking his friend and boss's tone one bit, Ronan obeyed. Things were crazy enough at the moment without further alienating the one person in this strange place that was familiar.

Speaking of familiar, where the hell was Tennyson? It was on the tip of Ronan's tongue to ask, but with the mood Fitzgibbon was in, he figured it would be best if he shut up and waited to see how this played out.

As they continued to walk through the woods, Ronan could smell fresh rain and decay of the forest floor. The scent of woodsmoke caught his attention, setting him on high alert.

"Kevin, where are we going?" Ronan grabbed his robed arm and pulled the bigger man to a stop.

"See for yourself." Fitzgibbon pointed ahead to a clearing.

Ronan stepped past him and saw a towering bonfire in the center of a clearing in the middle of the forest. There appeared to be a man tied to a post in front of the roaring flames.

"Jesus Christ! Why are you just standing here? We have to help that person." Ronan took a step forward, intending to run to the man tied to the pole when Kevin grabbed his elbow in a vice-like grip. "You wish to bring more trouble down upon yourself, I see."

"What?" Ronan didn't understand. "There's someone tied to a pole in front of an inferno. It's up to us to save him."

Fitzgibbon wore a curious look on his face. "We have been through this Ronan, either give evidence against the Witch Grimm or we fashion a noose at dawn for *you* as well. Choose now. The time is upon us."

The Witch Grimm? *Oh, sweet Jesus...* It hit Ronan all at once where he was and what was going on. The reason his shoes reminded him of something the pilgrims wore was because, unless he missed his guess, they only landed in the New World seventy-two years ago. Ronan had a feeling if he asked Fitzgibbon what year it was, after giving him yet another puzzled look, Kevin would tell him it was 1692.

"We go." Fitzgibbon grabbed his arm and began dragging him toward the raging fire.

Ronan could feel the heat of the flames against his face. As he got closer, Tennyson came into view. He was wearing a dark robe. The look on his face was unreadable until he caught sight of Ronan. Recognition lit in his dark eyes.

Ronan wanted to call out to his husband. He wanted to break free from Fitzgibbon's iron grip, but in the time that it had taken them to walk from the edge of the forest to where Ten was being held something else had taken over Ronan. It was an emotion he wasn't used to feeling, stone-cold fear.

He didn't know what this was, a dream, visitation, vision, but whatever it was, it was real. There was nothing dream-like about this situation. There were no fairies dancing around the fire. No buff naked men were offering to take him to bed. He wasn't giving the winning answer on *Final Jeopardy*. This was happening. This was real.

Fitzgibbon marched Ronan to where a group of similarly robed people were standing a distance from Tennyson.

"It is about time, Brother Fitzgibbon," a man Ronan did not recognize said.

"Brother O'Mara was not ready when I arrived, Preacher Black." Fitzgibbon shot Ronan an angry look.

"It is of no consequence. Your lateness merely bought the witch a few more minutes of life upon this earth." The preacher wore a look of satisfaction.

A few more minutes of life? Ronan felt his stomach lurch. He sucked in a deep breath. The last thing he wanted to do was start throwing up.

"Are you prepared to give your evidence against the Witch Grimm?" Preacher Black asked.

Ronan blinked a few times against the bright light of the fire. Why did that name sound so familiar? Who the hell was Preacher Black? He opened his mouth to buy some time when the answer came to him. Gideon Black.

Ronan and Tennyson had helped out friends of theirs, Niall Gallagher and Tobin Woods, with a haunting a few months back. Through them, they'd met the spirit of Mariah Goode, one of the victims of the Salem Witch Trials. Preacher Gideon Black was the man who'd pronounced sentence against her.

Now, it seemed he was asking Ronan to give evidence against Tennyson.

"The man asked you a question." Fitzgibbon gave him a shove from behind.

Meeting Tennyson's eyes across the expanse separating them, Ronan didn't know what to do. There was acceptance and love in Tennyson's dark eyes. His mind flashed back to an impossible scene. Tennyson was standing in front of the fireplace in the cabin begging Ronan to save himself if Black arrested him. Tears were flowing from his eyes as he told Ronan they'd be reunited one day.

"Yes," Ronan said, his voice weak. "I am here to give testimony against the Witch Grimm."

The hooded figures, who until this moment had their backs to him, turned. Ronan could see their faces now. Carson, Truman, Cassie, Cole, Greeley, and Jude were staring at him, their faces expressionless.

"Do you accuse him as a witch?" Preacher Black asked. His blue eyes blazed with glee.

"I do." With those simple words, Ronan knew he'd sealed Tennyson's fate.

"I commit Tennyson Grimm, a known witch, to the flames!" Gideon Black proclaimed.

The last thing Ronan heard before the blackness took him was Tennyson screaming.

"Tennyson! Ten, no! NO!" Ronan shouted, twisting and turning.

"Ronan!" Tennyson shook his shoulder. "Ronan! Wake up!"

"Ten?" Ronan sat bolt upright in bed. He reached for Tennyson who was still holding on to his right shoulder.

"I'm here. Are you okay?" Ten sounded terrified.

Was he okay? Reaching over to turn on the light, Ronan was relieved to see he was lying in his king-sized bed in his and Tennyson's Salem townhouse. Gone was the 1692 bonfire, although Ronan would swear he could still smell woodsmoke, somehow. "Yeah, I'm okay. It was just a bad dream."

"What happened?" Ten asked, still sounding a bit shaken.

"We ran out of lube!" Ronan kissed the side of Ten's head and bounced out of bed on his way to the bathroom. Even now, wide awake and back in the present, the dream was too raw to talk about. He was afraid that if he told Tennyson what happened, it would somehow still have power over him. Which was ridiculous, wasn't it?

1

Ronan

May…

Hours later, Ronan still felt like the nightmare had its claws sunk into him. Tennyson had fallen easily back to sleep after Ronan had come back to bed, but Ronan had been awake for the rest of the night, staring up at the ceiling, going over and over the dream in his mind.

Now, he was standing in the kitchen of their Salem, Massachusetts home with a cup of coffee in his hand watching Dixie, their Papillon puppy, do her business in the rain. Tennyson was out grocery shopping without him.

After his and Tennyson's encounter at the fledgling Black Cat Inn out on Witch Hill Road with some of the victims of the Salem Witch Trials, back in March, it wasn't any surprise to Ronan that he had a dream like the one he'd had last night. Somehow, though, while he'd been stuck in the grips of the nightmare, it hadn't felt like any other dream he'd had. There was none of the usual confusion or totally impossible scenarios of his regular dreams. Not to mention the fact that he remembered every detail as if he'd lived them.

Ordinarily, Ronan dreamed about fucking Chris Hemsworth. Hard. While the God of Thunder urged him on and called him dirty names. When Ronan woke up from those kinds of dreams he only remembered them in snatches and knew, to his deep regret, that he hadn't lived one moment of those crazy interludes.

This bonfire/witch hunt dream was something else entirely. From his time with Tennyson, Ronan knew that what he'd seen last night could have been a vision. Carson Craig, Tennyson's best friend and partner at West Side Magick, the psychic shop where they worked, never had his first vision until a few years ago. Was it possible he was coming into psychic powers of his own?

"Fuck me blue," Ronan muttered under his breath. He'd been there to witness the struggles first-hand that Tennyson, Carson, and his brother, Cole, went through dealing with their gifts of sixth sense. He hoped to fuck last night wasn't his induction into the psychic friends network.

"Can you hear me, Bertha?" Ronan called out to Carson and Cole's deceased mother. "Is that what this is? Am I getting superpowers too?"

Bertha Craig had passed away three years ago after a brave battle with breast cancer. She was Tennyson's mentor and helped out from time to time on the cold cases Ronan and Tennyson worked on for the Boston Police Department. Bertha was also slightly obsessed with Ronan's ass.

Unfortunately for Ronan, if Bertha was answering his question about becoming one of the cool psychic kids, he couldn't hear her. So, that meant, for the moment anyway, that he wasn't adding mediumship to his bag of tricks.

Ronan supposed he could rule out what happened last night as being a visitation. Usually, a visitation was a spirit's way of communicating with someone in the physical world. Since everyone in his dream, with the exception of Preacher Gideon Black, was still alive, Ronan felt pretty safe ruling this option out. Black didn't seem to want to speak to Ronan. He was more intent on playing his role as judge, jury, and executioner in the perverse drama.

His attention shifted back to Dixie, who had just scampered back up the deck steps and was daintily shaking off each paw. His little pixie was definitely not a fan of going out to do her business in the muddy backyard. Ronan opened the door for her, scooping her up in a clean towel. "Hello, my little love."

Dixie barked but let Ronan rub her down with the soft towel. He set her down on the kitchen table, dropping into one of the chairs. "What should Daddy do, hmm?"

The dog tilted her head to the side before barking sharply.

"Oh, you think I should talk to Other Daddy about the dream, huh? I was gonna talk to Uncle Carson and ask him if last night was a vision." Saying it out loud to the dog, Ronan could hear that the idea sucked.

Barking sharply again, Dixie started licking Ronan's face.

Under the circumstances, Ronan would take that as a vote for *not* talking to Uncle Carson.

Now all he needed was a way to bring up the dream to Tennyson and explain to his husband that he'd lied to him. Piece of cake, right?

2

Tennyson

Psychic Tennyson Grimm loved grocery shopping by himself. Still a few weeks away from Memorial Day Weekend and its influx of summer tourists, the aisles of the Salem Market Basket were relatively quiet for a Saturday morning. Tennyson assumed it had to do with the rain. Most people were probably sleeping in.

Ten would have liked being one of those lucky bastards doing that very thing, but he didn't tend to sleep very well next to his lying dumbass of a husband.

"Now, Tenny, that's no way to talk about my favorite boy-toy," Bertha Craig said from in front of the Lucky Charms. She folded her arms over her chest and raised an eyebrow at him.

Raising an eyebrow right back, Ten stepped around her and grabbed a box of Cheerios. "He lied right to my face, Bertha," he muttered low enough so that none of the nearby shoppers would hear the crazy psychic talking to himself. *Again.*

"That dream must have scared the hell out of him if he lied to you about it," Bertha remarked casually.

"Scared him? What the hell are you talking about?" Ten hadn't considered what Bertha was saying at all. He just figured Ronan was being a dumbass. *Again.*

"He's told you all about fucking Chris Hemsworth. Lordy, the things I'd do to that poor boy if I got my hands on him." Bertha shook her head, her eyes losing focus.

"But you digress?" Ten prodded, his lips barely moving as he spoke.

"Yes!" Bertha crowed. "Tennyson, he tells you about the dirty ways he manhandles Thor's hammer and the ways he wins *Final Jeopardy* in a landslide. If he's spilling the beans about dreams like that, this one had to be a doozy for him to keep it to himself. Plus, I might have a little inside intel..." She offered Ten a bit of a smirk.

Inside intel? What the hell was this? A C.I.A. briefing? "Spill it, old lady." Ten grabbed a canister of Quaker Instant Oats and pretended to read the box.

"I was spending a little quality time with your shirtless hubby this morning hoping that since you were gone he might use that quality alone time to spank the monkey."

"Jesus Christ save me from your horny dead woman hormones!" Ten angry-whispered.

"Well, it's a good thing for you that I was there perving on your man. I never took you for such a prude, Tenny! And don't say it's because you grew up a repressed midwestern Baptist. Some of the horniest men I knew were midwestern Baptists. Good times…" Bertha sighed like teenage fangirl.

"Focus, Hot Pants. Why was it a good thing that you were there perving on Ronan and Mary Palm?" Ten felt the irresistible urge to giggle, right there in the cereal aisle. Mothers with screaming toddlers were pushing their carts past him reaching for boxes of Cheerios, while their little terrors grabbed for everything in sight with their sticky little mitts. His little miss was sure as shit *not* going to be a supermarket terror with grubby hands.

"Of course not, Tennyson." Bertha rolled her blue eyes. "Your child will be the only perfect angel in recorded history with impeccable grocery store manners. 'Father, may I please have every item in the store. I realize it's horribly out of our household budget, but be a dear and load up the carriage, posthaste. There's a love.' Oh, please. She'll be a horrible brat just like all those other snot-nosed goobers." Bertha cackled.

Tennyson pinched the bridge of his nose. "For the love of Teddy Roosevelt's moustache, woman, why the hell was it good that you were perving on my half-naked husband this morning?" he shouted, his patience at the breaking point.

Everyone in the cereal aisle stopped to stare at him screaming at no one. A young mother turned her shopping buggy around and left, while a young man with bloodshot eyes slapped a hand down on Tennyson's shoulder. "Let go and let God, man." He pulled a rumpled business card out of his pocket. "Next AA meeting is at 2pm over on Essex Street. Hope to see you there."

Tennyson nodded at the complete stranger. He could hear Bertha laughing her ass off. Grabbing the handle of his cart, he wheeled it past her. She was bent double, her face beet-red, laughing so hard that she would have been peeing her pants if she were still alive. "You know what? I don't care what your inside intel is. I'll just go home and ask my husband what happened last night."

"He thinks he had a vision," Bertha managed between fits of the giggles.

That stopped Tennyson dead in his tracks. A vision? Why the hell would Ronan have thought he'd had a vision?

"I had a feeling that would grab your attention." Bertha grinned wickedly. "He thought about going to Carson about this, but after a soul-searching conversation with Dixie, he decided to discuss the matter with you."

"My husband decided to come to me with this dream situation *after* an in-depth discussion with our dog?" Tennyson wasn't exactly sure he *wasn't* the one dreaming at the moment. He was half expecting to wake up any moment now with Huge Jackman nudging the crack of his naked ass. He and Ronan were going to have a good laugh about this after his husband was done fucking him into the mattress.

"You're *not* dreaming, Tennyson. Although I would like to meet Huge Jackman…" Bertha's eyes went wide and she shook her head as if she were mentally trying to get back in the game.

"Check, please," Ten muttered. He still had half of his grocery list to get through, but all he could think about was getting home to Ronan. To talk about the dream, *not* to interview Huge Jackman on his knees.

Bertha had made a good point. Ronan had never been shy in the past in telling him about his wild and crazy nocturnal adventures. Why would last night be the dream to change things? Ronan being afraid of what he'd seen or done would be a good reason for keeping what happened to himself. It might not have been that he didn't want to share what happened with Ten, but more along the lines of Ronan needing to sort out what happened and why for himself before telling Ten about it.

Ten knew damn well he had the tendency to be like a dog with a bone with certain things. If Ronan had told him he didn't want to talk about the dream rather than lying about them being out of lube, Ten would have hounded Ronan until he'd either made up a lie or talked about something he wasn't ready to talk about. So, Ronan had taken the quick way out and just fibbed from the outset. Not that Tennyson appreciated being lied to, but he could see Ronan's reasoning.

Pushing the cart forward, Ten was no longer enchanted with the nearly empty grocery store. All he wanted to do was speed through his list and get home to his husband.

3

Ronan

Ronan was showered and shaved by the time Tennyson pulled up in front of the house with his Chevy stuffed full of groceries. He raced to the front door with Dixie hot on his heels. Scooping her up, he opened the door just as Ten was coming up the stairs, his hands full of reusable grocery bags. "Hey, babe." Ronan brushed a kiss against Ten's right cheek as he breezed past.

"Hi, Snookums." Ten snorted, setting the bags down on the kitchen table.

"So, I, um, lied to you last night about my nightmare." Ronan nibbled on his bottom lip. This was going to go one of two ways. Ten was going to play dumb and make Ronan work for his forgiveness or he was going to play the role of ice queen and tell Ronan he'd known his husband had been lying all along. Ronan's money was on ice queen.

Ten grabbed a box of Cheerios out of the first bag and moved across the kitchen to put it away. He didn't say a word.

This didn't bode well at all. Ronan held his tongue, curious to see how Ten would deal with the situation.

"I had an interesting visit from Bertha in the cereal aisle." Tennyson turned to face Ronan. The look on his face was full of concern rather than the anger or disappointment Ronan was expecting to see.

Ronan let out the breath he wasn't aware he'd been holding. "Bertha?" None of what Tennyson said made any sense.

"Apparently she was taking advantage of my being out of the house in hopes you'd spend a little quality time with yourself." Tennyson held up his right hand and waggled his fingers before making the universal hand gesture for jacking off.

"She was hoping I'd have a tug of war with cyclops so she could watch?" Ronan burst out laughing. Thankfully self-abuse was the last thing on his mind after the dream last night. "Who knew she was such a dirty old woman? The next time I do that, I'm gonna call out her name instead of Chris Hemsworth's. That'll teach her."

"I think that would only encourage her." Ten walked over to Ronan, setting a hand against his cheek. "Bertha heard you ask her if what you saw last night was a vision. I know it's not playing fair to come to you with that inside intel. After our talk on the last day of the cruise I promised to do better with talking about what's going on in our marriage rather than taking the easy way out by using my gift, but this information was given to me."

Ronan nodded. He knew Bertha went to Tennyson with the best of intentions. He also knew Tennyson wasn't reading him.

On the last day of their honeymoon cruise to Bermuda, Ronan had told Ten that he sometimes felt like he was on uneven footing with his husband thanks to Tennyson's sixth sense. He was hoping Ten would try to use Ronan's body language and his words to figure out what was going on with him instead of instantly using his gift to read him. Over the last few months, Ten had made great strides in that area of their marriage.

"I had planned on telling you all about the dream when you came home and I did ask Bertha for help, so I'm not upset that she came to you." Ronan opened the refrigerated bag and started unpacking the meat. He needed a minute to put his thoughts in order.

"It wasn't your usual He-Man sex dream or one of those ego-driven things where you answer every question on *Jeopardy* and Alex Trebek asks for your number at the end, was it?" Ten chuckled.

Ronan snorted. "No and Alex only did that *once*." Taking a deep breath, he felt his mood sober. "Ten, this felt so real. Like, when I'm with Thor or on *Jeopardy*, in my dream-mind I know it's bullshit. This was so real. I felt like my words and actions had real-world consequences. Like I could actually do damage." Ronan shivered. His hands came up to rub against his arms.

Ten's dark eyes narrowed on his husband. "Come, sit." He guided Ronan to the dining room table and eased him into one of the chairs. "Tell me everything you remember."

Nodding, Ronan took a deep breath. He wasn't anxious to relive what happened, but he knew he had to tell the whole story to Tennyson. "Pounding on a wooden door woke me up. I was in a rustic cabin with a dirt floor and when I opened the door, Kevin was there telling me I needed to come with him. He led me through the woods to a clearing where a man was lashed to a pole in front of a raging bonfire. I went to go help the man, thinking I was still a cop and Kevin stopped me, telling me that I needed to make my choice to either give evidence against the Witch Grimm or have a noose waiting for me at dawn."

Tennyson took a sharp breath. "The Witch Grimm? As in me?"

Ronan nodded. "Kevin grabbed me and pulled me along through the clearing, closer to you. Our eyes met and you recognized me. He kept dragging me along until we got to a group of hooded people standing a distance away. It was all of our friends, Carson, Tru, Cole, Cassie, Greeley, and Jude. There was one other person standing there who I didn't recognize until Kevin said his name."

"I'm afraid to ask who it was." Tennyson's voice trembled.

"It was Gideon Black, Ten." The look in Ronan's eyes was dire.

"Oh." Ten's mouth dropped open. "Gideon Black, as in the man who sentenced Mariah Goode to die as part of the Salem Witch Trials?"

"The very same," Ronan agreed. "He asked me if I accused you as a witch and a strange thing happened."

Ten leaned closer to Ronan. "What strange thing?"

"I had a flashback." Ronan could see the image in his mind clear as day, like it was an *actual* memory rather than a memory of his dream.

"What do you mean you had a flashback?" Tennyson wore an incredulous look as if such a thing weren't possible.

"That's what made me wonder if this was a vision." Ronan met Ten's eyes. The look in them was full of curiosity and something Ronan would classify as fear. "I flashed back to the cabin I woke up in. We were both there and you were begging me to save myself if Black had you arrested. Then you said we'd be reunited one day."

Ten's head tilted to the side as if he were thinking about something. "What were we wearing?"

"What?" Ronan couldn't believe his ears. "I tell you I had a dream about you being burned at the stake and your asking me about your fashion sense in 1692? This isn't an episode of *Queer Eye,* Ten!"

Reaching out for Ronan's hand, Tennyson rubbed his thumb against Ronan's skin. "I'm not asking to find out how fab I was in the seventeenth century, but your rant answered my question. We were both dressed like it was a Salem Witch Trial costume party, yes?"

Ronan nodded. He felt worn to the bone. "My shoes had the buckles on them like the pilgrims wore."

"I don't think what happened last night was a vision. I'm one hundred percent sure you're not coming into superpowers like mine and Carson's."

"I'm not?" Relief surged through Ronan's exhausted body.

"That doesn't mean you're not *my* superhero." Ten winked.

Feeling instantly energized. Ronan perked up. "Oh, really? Do you want to see me go faster than a speeding locomotive?"

Ten burst out laughing. "Hardly! Why don't I show you what I had in mind?"

"You got it, Lois Lane." Ronan was still feeling a bit off-kilter about the dream, but that wasn't going to stop him from playing Superman for a little while.

4

Tennyson

The original fears Tennyson had about Ronan's dream had been put to rest. What Ronan had was most definitely *not* a vision. It wasn't a visitation either as he'd wondered. What it could be, however, was something else entirely. Something a bit more interesting and maybe more far-reaching.

Unfortunately, or fortunately, depending on your point of view, Ronan was trying to work his pants off which wasn't leaving Tennyson any brainpower to think about this new scenario.

"Jesus, a little help here, Ten. What did you do, paint these jeans on for fuck's sake?" Ronan laughed. "You were going to the grocery store. Who were you thinking you'd meet in these ass-huggers?"

"I was thinking my husband was a lying dumbass and if a good-looking, *younger* man offered to thump my melon, I wasn't gonna say no." Ten laughed when Ronan slapped his ass.

"Oh, so that's what we're calling it now, thumping a melon?" Ronan managed to drag Ten's jeans down past his cock, but left his briefs pulled up.

"I bought a cantaloupe. You thump the end to see if its ripe." Ten rolled his eyes dramatically.

"Hmm, and did some young stud thump you in the produce aisle?" Ronan licked Ten's cock through the material of his boxer briefs.

Ten hissed, loving the drag of the dampened material against his hardened flesh. He managed to shake his head no. Even when Ronan was being a dumbass there was no one else he ever wanted thumping him in the produce aisle or anywhere else. "Ronan, please."

"Please, what?" Ronan licked him again. "You called me a lying dumbass and then tried to get thumped by a total stranger in the grocery store. There has to be some payback for that." He blew a breath against Ten's wetted dick.

Ten felt his cock twitch. Ronan had a point. "You're right. I was a bad boy." It didn't make any sense to point out that Ronan was a bad boy first. His husband's sweet mouth was so tantalizingly close to his aching dick. The name of the game now was to get his dick into *that* mouth, not to antagonize his husband further. "I think you should punish me by sucking my cock to within an inch of my life."

Ronan barked out a surprised laugh. "That sounds like a punishment to you?"

"Yes." Ten plastered a serious look on his face. "That would teach me a lesson for sure."

Ronan lifted a curious eyebrow. "What lesson would that be?"

"Bad boys get their dick sucked. Good boys get fucked against the kitchen counter." Tennyson tried to look properly chastised. He wondered if Ronan was buying it.

"Do I look like I was born yesterday, Tennyson?" Ronan was wearing his resting bitch face.

Nope, not buying it. Oh, well, "A" for effort, as the saying went. Ten looked down at his drooling dick and then up at his smirking husband. "Of course not, Ronan, but if you don't do something about *that* soon, I'm going to have to take matters into my own hands."

"Hmm," Ronan rocked back on his heels. He went for the button of his jeans. "I'd like to see that."

"You would?" Ten's eyes went wide as Ronan pulled his own erection out of his pants.

Ronan nodded. His right hand sliding from the tip of his cock slowly down to the base.

Ten swallowed hard. His eyes were glued to Ronan's hand which continued to glide up and down his shaft.

"You gonna watch or participate?" Ronan's voice was barely above a whisper.

Getting down on his knees in front of Ronan, Ten parroted his husband's speed. When Ronan's hand slid up, Tennyson's hand slid down. He reached out to set a hand against the clean-shaven side of Ronan's face. "God, this is sexy as fuck."

Ronan bit his lip and nodded. "I love watching you take care of yourself." Leaning forward, Ronan nibbled at the hollow of Tennyson's shoulder where it met his neck. He could feel Ronan's tongue lashing against his pulse point. "I thought you wanted to watch?" Ten panted.

"Hmm, you're right." Ronan pulled away. "I forgot you were being punished for being a bad boy. I saw all that skin and just had to taste it. It slipped my mind that you were going to offer what's clearly *mine* to some troglodyte melon thumper."

Unable to help himself, Ten burst out laughing. He had a mental image of a bearded caveman dressed in animal skins trying to figure out which end of a melon to thump and in the end trying to gnaw it open with his teeth.

"Something funny?" Ronan asked darkly. "Keep it up and you won't get to finish at all…"

Tennyson sobered instantly at that suggestion. "I would only offer myself to you, Ronan." Tennyson shivered in the warm room. He got the impression he'd spoken those words before, but not to *this* Ronan.

"You love it when I'm possessive, don't you, babe?" Ronan growled.

If Ronan believed his shiver had to do with desire, Ten was content to let him believe that until he had time to do a bit more research on the matter. He bit into his bottom lip and nodded. Ten could see how crazy the idea had made Ronan. His blue eyes were nearly black with need. Ten knew it wasn't going to take much to push Ronan over the edge. "I'll be yours until the earth stops spinning," he whispered, feeling his own cock pulse in his hand.

"Ten!" Ronan cried out, his own dick jerking in release.

Those weren't the words of a lovesick fool, they were the words of a man who knew he'd live another life with his destined soulmate.

5

Ronan

"I sure as shit hope Bertha Craig liked that little performance earlier this morning!" Ronan announced as he picked up Tennyson's empty dinner plate and brought it to the sink.

"What?" Tennyson practically howled. "You did that for her? I thought you were punishing me for what I said about finding a guy to help me pick out a cantaloupe?"

"Oh, please." Ronan rolled his blue eyes. "Like you'd ever leave me for someone else. Face it, you won the husband lottery with me."

Tennyson was the one rolling his eyes now. "If your ego gets any bigger, we'll need to move. There won't be any room for the baby when she comes."

Ronan laughed. "You know that little girl is gonna inherit my swagger."

Tennyson sighed, sounding like he knew that exact thing. "God help us all."

Ronan opened his mouth to remind Tennyson that it was two weeks to the insemination date, when the doorbell rang. "Are you expecting company? I'm not."

Ten shook his head, looking uneasy.

"What? Should I not open the door? Is it bill collectors? Mormons? Yankee fans?" Ronan was especially concerned over the last one. He could deal with a lot, but Yankee fans just rubbed him the wrong way even now that the curse was broken and three World Series trophies resided at Fenway Park.

"Just open the door, drama queen." Tennyson sounded like Ronan was riding his last nerve.

"Yes, my liege." Ronan bowed dramatically and hurried to the door. The absolute last people he expected to see standing there, with the possible exception of the ghosts of Yogi Berra and Lou Gehrig, were Lyric Vaughn, Madam Aurora, and several other women who were complete strangers. "Lyric, is everything okay?"

"Ronan, my friends and I need to speak with you. May we come in?" For the first time in the years Ronan had known the DNA analyst, Lyric looked nervous.

"Yes. Please come in, ladies." Ronan held the door open wide. He counted seven women including Lyric and Aurora.

"Tennyson, how nice to see you again," Madam Aurora greeted.

Tennyson hugged his former arch-nemesis.

Ronan's eyes bugged out of his head momentarily. When Tennyson moved to Salem at eighteen years of age, after being kicked out of his home in Kansas for being gay and psychic, he'd gone to Madam Aurora looking for a job at her psychic shop across town. She'd turned him down flat fearing that one day, his own talents would far surpass her own.

Last year when Tennyson had somehow managed to shut down his gifts completely, it had been Madam Aurora who'd helped Tennyson discover the key to opening them back up. She'd also helped him cultivate the ability to shut them down and reopen them at will, allowing him to have downtime without spirits constantly interrupting his alone time with Ronan.

"Allow me to introduce my sisters," Lyric began. "This is Andromeda, Mina, Gia, Corazon, and Hazel." Each woman raised her hand as Lyric called out her name.

"Please have a seat, ladies." Ronan indicated the sofa and the accent chairs scattered around the living room. "How can we help, Lyric?"

"We're being hunted and killed one by one," she said simply.

Ronan sucked in a harsh breath. This couldn't be a coincidence. Last night he had a dream about Tennyson being burned as a witch and now seven members of the Salem Witch community were sitting in his living room claiming there was a modern-day witch hunt afoot.

Looking over at Tennyson, he could see his husband was wearing a skeptical look. This was a role reversal to be sure. Walking into the hallway, Ronan grabbed his flip pad and opened it to a blank page. "Tell me the story from the beginning," he urged.

Lyric nodded and took a few breaths as if she needed a minute to put her thoughts in order. "Last year, Jessa McIntyre died in a house fire. A few months after that Athena Mathieu was killed in a car accident. Two months after that Kendra Watts died in a 'domestic accident.'" Lyric made finger quotes over "domestic accident."

"In the year before that, three other members of our coven died in seemingly ordinary ways," Madam Aurora said.

"What seemingly ordinary ways were those?" Tennyson asked.

"Drowning, drug overdose, and suicide," the raven-haired beauty named Andromeda said.

Ronan looked up from his notepad to study the women. "What did you mean by domestic accident, Lyric?"

"Kendra was hanging a plant from a hook in the ceiling and slipped off the stool. She hit her head on the tile floor and died from a fractured skull. Her husband found her there hours later." Lyric swiped tears from her eyes.

"These all seem like normal deaths to me, aside from the fact that these women all died far too soon. What makes you think this is all part of a witch hunt?" Tennyson asked.

"You mean aside from the fact that we're all witches?" Redheaded Hazel asked. Her green eyes glowed with indignation.

This really wasn't like Tennyson at all. If someone asked who'd be the true believer and who would be the skeptic here, Ronan would have voted himself the skeptic. "What are you getting with your gift, Ten?"

"The women all believe in what they're telling you," he said. "I'm not getting any feeling of malice and none of the dead women are here to speak for themselves."

Madam Aurora arched an elegant brow. "Do you really think we're here for *your* help, Tennyson? If it were possible to talk to the spirits of our dead sisters, I would have done that myself."

"Wait a minute. What do you mean you can't talk to the spirits of your sisters? Six women are dead and you can't talk to *any* of them? Why?" Ronan thought that was curious too. Almost more curious than the fact that these six women had died under mysterious circumstances.

"We don't know," Corazon said. "We should be able to get through to at least one of our sisters." She twirled her dark hair around a finger. Her anxiety was obvious.

"Is it possible something or someone is keeping their souls from you?" Ronan asked.

"I told you he wasn't just a pretty face." Lyric smirked at Gia, who rolled her eyes.

"It's possible," Aurora agreed, "but we didn't want to go there yet. We wanted to see if you could dig anything up first."

Ronan sighed.

"Fine! If you don't want to help us! We'll do it ourselves." Gia was halfway out of her seat and heading toward the door when Mina grabbed her arm. She whispered gently to the younger woman, who reluctantly sat back down.

"I didn't say I *didn't* want to help. I was just thinking that it would be complicated on two fronts." Boy would it ever be complicated. Ronan felt a headache coming on.

"What do you mean, Ronan?" Andromeda asked.

"First of all, I'm a member of the Boston Police Department. Unless your sisters died in Boston, it will be harder to dig into their deaths because they would be out of my jurisdiction."

"Don't you have a friend who's a private investigator?" Lyric asked.

"Yeah, that's where things get really complicated." Ronan felt another world-weary sigh coming on and tried to hold it back. "Jude is a P.I., but he's not exactly what you'd call a friend to the Wiccan Community."

"So, he's a fucking bigot?" Corazon half-screeched.

"Now, I didn't say that. Without going into too much detail, Jude had a very personal dealing with a member of a witch community that didn't go so well." Ronan shook his head.

"What the hell does *that* even mean?" Gia asked.

"A witch killed his father," Madam Aurora supplied. "A rather nasty affair too."

"Jesus Christ," Ronan muttered under his breath. "So much for keeping things private."

"His father's killer was not a member of our community, Ronan. She wasn't even Wiccan." Aurora directed a pointed stare at him.

Ronan had no idea that not all witches weren't practitioners of Wicca. "Somehow, I don't think that's going to make a difference, Aurora. Right or wrong, I think he's still in a phase where he's painting you all with the same brush. I'll talk to him, though."

Lyric stood. The other women stood with her. "I came to you, Ronan because I knew I could trust you to help us. My sisters weren't sure you were the right person to turn to."

"How do you all feel now?" Ronan looked over the collection of women standing in his living room. If the unimpressed looks on their faces were any indication, he hadn't passed the test.

"You haven't done anything yet to earn our trust," Andromeda said, turning her pixie nose up at him. "Blessed be, Ronan. Tennyson."

As one, the women turned to leave. Lyric lingered in the living room. "Thank you both for welcoming us into your home. I'm sure you weren't expecting seven witches to show up on your doorstep unexpectedly."

Ronan took Lyric's arm and walked her to the door. "I don't know what's going on here, Lyric, but make sure you and Katie are taking all necessary precautions. If anything happened to either of you or baby Astrid…"

"We've had an alarm installed on the house and Katie keeps her gun within reach at night. I've blessed the house and have asked my spirit guides for added protection." Lyric straightened her shoulders. "I'm scared, Ronan. My sisters are too. This has been building for a long time now. I can't help but feel like something is coming. Something sinister and vile. If we're not careful it could get us all." With that, Lyric pecked Ronan on the cheek and walked out the door.

6

Tennyson

Ten was in the kitchen making two cups of tea when he heard Ronan shut the front door and arm the alarm. He'd headed for the kitchen knowing there was going to be a storm brewing between them the minute they were alone again. He planned to diffuse the situation with chamomile and cookies.

"What the hell was that?" Ronan boomed from the living room.

At least his husband was predictable. "I'm in the kitchen, Snookums!" Ten set the tea and cookies down on the table and took a seat.

"What is wrong with you treating those women like that? They came to us for help and you…" Ronan stopped in his tracks. "Oh, cookies." He took a seat and reached for an oatmeal raisin and took a bite. "Wait a minute, you did this so I wouldn't be able to yell and stuff my face at the same time, right?"

Ten shrugged a shoulder. Of course, Ronan was right, but he wasn't going to say that out loud. "I get that they came to you, Ronan, and that you feel a responsibility to help, but there's nothing going on to help them with. Just a random series of unfortunate coincidences."

Ronan was in the process of reaching for his second cookie when Tennyson made his pronouncement. His hand stopped cold. "A random series of coincidences? Who are you? You don't believe in coincidences. Ever. Why now?" Ronan sat back in his chair. His full attention was on Tennyson.

Reaching for his steaming mug of tea, Ten took a sip. Ronan had a point. He never believed in coincidences. "Like I said earlier, I don't feel anything off in this. The women think that there is something going on, but we've never heard about any of these deaths in the news or read about them in the Salem paper. Don't you think we would have?"

Raising an eyebrow, Ronan shook his head. "No, I don't."

"What do you mean, that this is some kind of massive cover up? Come on, Ronan, there isn't a conspiracy theory at the root of everything."

"I'm not saying this is a conspiracy theory. If there is something going on here, it's well crafted. Like Aurora said, the deaths all look commonplace. Tragic, but run of the mill, until you consider the fact that the victims have one common bond that links them."

"They're members of the Salem Witch Community," Tennyson said.

Ronan nodded. "Would you have given the story more credence if the women had all been Salem schoolteachers? Nurses from Northshore Medical Center? How about stay-at-home moms?"

Ten sighed. "Are you trying to say I have something against the witches?"

"Do you?" Ronan challenged.

"Of course not!" Tennyson rolled his eyes. "I went into this interview like I do with any other that we conduct for the Boston Police Department. I opened my gift wide and asked my spirit guides for help. I didn't hear one word from the spirits of the six dead women. I didn't hear anything from my spirit guides about the situation. Lastly, I wasn't getting any psychic urges that this was a bad situation. I don't mean to sound like a dick here, Ronan, but you know that old saying, 'Where there's smoke, there's fire?'"

Ronan nodded.

"There aren't even matches or kindling here." Ten reached across the table to set his hand on Ronan's. "Look, I know you want to help Lyric. I just don't think you're going to find anything."

His eyes narrowing, Ronan seemed to be studying his husband. "What do you think got them all riled up and scared enough to come to me?"

"What do you mean?" Ten asked.

"Aurora said herself that they didn't come here looking for your help, Ten. The women came here hoping that I could help them. Lyric said the last woman died two months ago. Why not come to me then? Why today?"

Tennyson hadn't considered that. There had to have been some sort of catalyst that made the women decide that it was time to seek outside help. "Do you think there was some piece of evidence they were holding back from you?"

Ronan laughed. "That's usually your forte, isn't it, Nostradamus?"

"Yeah, it usually is, but I wasn't getting anything from them."

"Do you think they were employing those blocking exercises you used to talk to Carson and Cole about?"

Ten shook his head. He'd originally met Carson and Cole Craig after they'd begun to develop their psychic powers. Tennyson had been brought into West Side Magick as their mentor, to help them learn how to use and harness their new-found powers and abilities. Ten had been teaching them blocking exercises so they weren't always hearing peoples' thoughts or seeing spirits everywhere they went. "No, I was getting other things from them loud and clear. Corazon and Gia each wanted to kill you on a few separate occasions and Andromeda was fascinated by my gifts and our relationship."

"Well, that aside," Ronan rolled his eyes. "Do you remember the Justin Wilson case?"

"How could I ever forget it? A serial killer was targeting teenaged street kids. Are you feeling okay, Ronan?" Tennyson shot his husband a concerned look.

"I'm fine. The point I was trying to make was that the killer was at work for a long time without being detected. Do you remember why?" Ronan reached for another cookie.

Where Ronan was going with his line of thought all made sense now. "The bodies were all being dumped in different towns. Different jurisdictions. No one thought to connect the dots until we put the pieces together."

Ronan nodded. "Just like Lyric and her friends did. There might not be anything to this, Ten, just a random set of awful coincidences, just like you said. But if it's something more than that, if someone is deliberately targeting these women and I sit on my hands and do nothing and someone else is hurt or worse..." He stared up at his husband with a pleading look in his blue eyes.

Tennyson knew he was a goner when Ronan looked at him with *those* eyes. Those were the puppy-dog eyes that would get him a hundred babies, a new Mustang, and yes, free rein to investigate a possible modern-day witch hunt. "Where do we start?"

"There's the Starsky to my Hutch!" Ronan leaned across the table to plant a wet kiss on Tennyson's cheek. "I'll call Lyric in the morning and get the names and death dates of her six friends, then I'll pull the police reports. There might not be anything probative in there, but at least I'll have all the facts."

Tennyson nodded. "Ronan, why is this so important to you?"

"Do you remember when we were out at The Black Cat Inn with Niall and Tobin?" Ronan's voice had taken on a somber tone.

"The day we met the spirit of Mariah Goode and nine of the other women who were killed during the Salem Witch Trials?" Ten asked.

"Right," Ronan agreed. "I didn't want to be there that day. I thought the women were ridiculous for still being angry and bitter over what happened to them three hundred years ago. I was bitchy to Lyric and she called me out, accused me of being hateful like Jude, remember?"

Ten did remember. It had been out of character for Ronan to act like that, especially when it came to protecting people who were weaker than he was and unable to defend themselves.

"I took a good, hard look at myself after that day. Mariah's story was heartbreaking. What the people of Salem put her through because she was a single woman trying to survive by any means possible. What Gideon Black put her through in the name of religion, when he was just as guilty as the other men darkening her doorstep under the cover of darkness…" Ronan trailed off. "Why couldn't Salem have come together to help her, Ten? Would I have been just as harsh on her? Calling her names and then calling her out as a witch because she sold her body to put a roof over her head?"

"It was an ugly time, Ronan. People did what they had to do to survive. That's what Mariah was doing. Then, when the witch hysteria started, that survival instinct ramped up to a whole other level. Some people accused neighbors from sheer jealousy, others to get rid of rivals, others to deflect suspicion from themselves. I like to think you wouldn't have shamed her or called her out, Ronan, but in those times, it was eat or be eaten."

"Survival of the fittest," Ronan muttered. "We know what it's like to be discriminated against our whole lives. So do the witches. No one understands what Wicca is all about. Hell, most people think its pointy hats and spells whispered over boiling cauldrons. Midnight flights with broomsticks and black cats, you know, all that Halloween bullshit Salem uses to sell itself to tourists."

"You're right," Ten agreed.

"If someone is coming after the Witches of Salem, they're going to have to come through me," Ronan vowed.

A full-body shiver tore through Tennyson. He knew Ronan meant every word he was saying. He could only hope this time around, it was the witches suffering from mass hysteria and there wasn't something deeper going on here.

7

Ronan

Monday morning found Ronan at his desk in the South Boston Headquarters of the Boston Police Department. His expensive cup of coffee sat to his right, steam escaping through the little vent, while his computer booted up.

Ignoring the dozens of cases in his Work In Progress file, Ronan pulled up the email he'd gotten earlier in the morning from Lyric Vaughn and printed it out. He'd sent her a text message at zero-dark-thirty asking for the names of all of the women who'd died and in which towns their deaths had occurred.

He fast-walked to the printer to grab the two-page document hoping that none of his co-workers would waylay him before he could get there. In his experience, there was no one nosier that cops. Well, unless it was psychics. Thankfully, all the cops around him had their heads down too. It was a rainy spring Monday in Boston. Everyone looked like they could use another couple of days off to recover from the weekend.

Walking back to his desk, Ronan saw the one person who could derail his plans to research the witch deaths before it even got off the ground: his boss, Kevin Fitzgibbon. Kevin was striding toward his desk looking like he hadn't had his morning coffee yet. *Fucking great…* "Good morning, Cap."

"Don't you good morning me, Ronan!" Fitzgibbon looked like he was ready to kill someone.

His brain on rewind, Ronan tried to figure out what the hell he could have possibly done to piss off his boss this badly only five minutes after the new work week had begun. He plastered on a fake smile knowing full well Fitzgibbon would enlighten him without Ronan having to ask what crawled up his ass and died.

"Dog shit!" Fitzgibbon shouted.

"Uh, dog shit, Cap?" Ronan was totally confounded now.

"Yes, Ronan," Fitzgibbon's voice was full of snark. "You know your little princess eats her Kibbles and Bits and then her tummy goes grumble, grumble and oopsie it's time for her to make poopsies."

Ronan's mouth hung open. He wasn't sure if he should laugh or call 911. Knowing either option could get him fired or punched in the jaw, he kept his lips zipped.

"What? No clever comeback? You're a criminal, Ronan!" Fitzgibbon accused in a harsh tone.

Ronan shook his head no. Ten would kill him if he came home with the contents of his desk in a box. Not to mention having to kiss his pension good-bye.

"Your dog is shitting on my sidewalk!" Fitzgibbon growled. "This is the third time in three days I've had to scoop your fucking dog's poop! You are in violation of Salem City Ordinance Section 8-36! I should arrest your ass right now!"

"No, she isn't!" Ronan shot right back. "Dixie shits in our back yard. I should know, I'm the one who has to go around with the bags scooping it up while Ten cuddles the furry little shit factory. It squishes in my hand and some of it is still warm." Ronan dry heaved. It was like he could actually feel the consistency now, sitting in his office. "For a tiny dog, her shit smells so bad I have to wear nose plugs like those Olympic swimmers." Ronan rolled his eyes. "Arrest my ass? Aren't you out of your jurisdiction, captain?" *And out of your mind?* Ronan added to himself.

"It would be a citizen's arrest then!" Fitzgibbon crowed before frowning. "Well, who's poop am I scooping then?"

Ronan raised an eyebrow. "Uh, how about your own dog's? Lola is Dixie's sister, remember? They're the same size and they eat the same food. I would assume their shit looks the same too. Maybe Greeley isn't walking her properly and is blaming her mess on my sweet little princess."

"Sweet little princess?" Fitzgibbon squawked. "Five minutes ago, you were calling her a furry little shit factory!"

"Yeah, well, that was when I was thinking about having to clean up after her. Now, you're besmirching her good name. Greeley's been a bit different since he finished his first semester at Salem State. Or have you been too busy playing Sherlock Holmes over the dog shit on your sidewalk to notice?"

Fitzgibbon's mood instantly sobered. He slumped into the chair in front of Ronan's desk, the one Tennyson always sat in when he was in the office. "I'm worried about him, Ronan. He's been quiet and withdrawn. I wondered for a minute if he was back on the drugs."

Ronan's brows drew together. Greeley Hanks, now Fitzgibbon, had been through a lot in his eighteen short years on this planet. Put into the foster care system at an early age, he was turned out of his adoptive home when he came out to his parents. He turned to hooking as a way to survive and then to drugs when he was raped and nearly made the first victim of a serial killer.

When Ronan met the boy for the first time, it was while Greeley had been in rehab getting himself clean and sober. The kid had never looked back, becoming an instant member of their family. Never in Ronan's wildest dreams would he ever consider Greeley turning back to drugs.
"What about his grades or boy trouble, Cap? It has to be something else. Have you tried talking to him?"

Kevin sighed. "Grades aren't out yet and he won't talk to me about anything right now. He just shuts himself in his room with Lola. I'm not even sure if he's going back to work for Cassie over the summer."

"I'll tell you what, tonight's Ten's late night at the Magick Shop. I'll send Greeley a text offering to take him out to Lobster Charlie's. That's his favorite place. He won't say no to dinner there. I'll see what's going on with him."

"Lobster Charlie's is my favorite place too," Kevin sulked.

"Yeah, well bad boys who come into the middle of the precinct and accuse me of being a criminal and threaten to effect a citizen's arrest do *not* get to go to Lobster Charlie's. Now, if you will excuse me, captain, I have very important work to do." Ronan turned from his boss and typed Jess McIntyre's name into the search box of the database.

Fitzgibbon didn't need to know that the very important work he had to do this morning didn't have anything to do with cold cases or the Boston Police Department.

8

Tennyson

Since it was Tennyson's late night at West Side Magick, he had Dixie with him. The little dog walked around the place with her ears perked up, her head held high, like she owned the place. Ten kept a pink princess dog bed for her in the new part of the shop where Tobin Woods had built him and Cole their own reading rooms. Carson kept the original room in the store where his mother, Bertha, used to conduct her readings.

"Speak of the devil and she shall appear, Tenny!" Bertha Craig cackled.

Dixie gave a friendly bark and hightailed it over to Bertha's spirit.

"Hello, peaches. How are you today?" Bertha got down on her haunches and gave the dog's ears a scratch.

"That's not funny, you know," Tennyson grumped.

"What, calling your baby, peaches? I figured it was better than kumquat." Bertha burst out laughing.

"No," Ten whined. "I meant calling yourself the devil. You talk like that and you'll end up manifesting something you won't like and we might not be able to deal with by ourselves."

"Lighten up, Tennyson." Bertha stood up and walked over to Ten who was watching her with a cautious eye. "Who peed in your Cheerios?"

"Come with me. I don't want anyone to overhear us." Ten headed for his reading room.

"We're in a psychic shop with other psychics who can read your thoughts, and I'm dead. Who are you afraid is going to hear us?" Sighing, Bertha followed along behind Tennyson.

Dixie gave a sharp bark and followed on Bertha's heels.

When the door was shut firmly behind him, Ten walked to the table and took a seat. He loved this new space. Right now, it had a large bronze statue of Buddha in one corner, but he hadn't figured out how he wanted to decorate the rest of the room. He had his eye on a Tibetan gong. Ten took a deep breath to center himself.

"Whatever this is, it looks like it's serious." Bertha's usual snarky tone was gone.

"Witches," Ten said softly.

"Again? I thought they all went into the light that day out at the Black Cat Inn?"

Ten shook his head. "These aren't the same witches and those women were victims of the Salem Witch Trials, Bertha. They weren't actual witches. You know that."

Bertha nodded. "So, if it isn't those women making a return engagement, who are you talking about?"

"Jesus, Bertha, they aren't the Rockettes." Ten rolled his dark eyes. "One night only…"

"I'm sorry, Tennyson. I should be treating this matter with more reverence. Which witches are you talking about?"

"Members of the Salem Witch Community. Living members. Seven of them showed up at our house last night." Just remembering them parading through his living room was enough to give him the beginnings of a migraine.

"What did they think you could do for them?" Bertha sounded confused.

"They didn't come to see *me*. They came to see Ronan." Ten could hear the snark creeping into his voice.

Bertha frowned. "Handsome? What the hell can he do for them that you can't?"

"Investigate their deaths," Ten said with a shrug.

"Deaths?" Bertha shook her head. "I thought you said *living* members of the witch community came to see you. Did one of them have a premonition that they were all going to die?"

"They are alive. No one had a premonition, at least not that they told me. No one was psychically leaking that information either." Now that he thought about it, no one was leaking anything psychically. Usually, in a group that size, there was one weak link, but he'd gotten nothing from any of them aside from a general feeling of unease and suspicion.

"Then I don't understand." Bertha's brows drew together as if she were trying to puzzle this out for herself.

"It seems that six witches have died over the two years or so, under what sounded to me like tragic, but unremarkable circumstances." Ten shook his head.

"Explain what you mean by unremarkable?"

"One died in a car accident, another in a slip and fall accident, a third one died as a result of suicide." Tennyson felt awful about these deaths, but he just didn't see what there was for him or Ronan to investigate.

"And the women think their sisters were murdered?" Bertha asked.

Ten nodded. "Right, and they're hoping Ronan can help figure out by whom and why before someone else gets hurt. They actually think they're being hunted." Ten's voice was barely above a whisper. It scared him just saying that word out loud.

"What was it your beefcake friend Tobin said about history? That if we don't understand it then we're doomed to repeat it." Bertha seemed to be silently studying Tennyson.

Leave it to Bertha to bring up all 6'6" of Tobin Woods. The man looked like he could play linebacker for the New England Patriots. He was all muscle and even though he was thirty-two years old, could still pass for twenty-five.

"For your information, Tenny, I wasn't thinking about sliding down that delicious boy like a fireman's pole." Bertha shot him a so-there look. "I was thinking about the way people come into our lives for a reason. Something about that particular line stuck with me and I remember Ronan repeating it at some point too, so that means it stuck with him as well."

"What are you saying? That Carson, Cole, and I chose Tobin to be our general contractor on this expansion here at the shop so that he could say those very words to us three months later?" Ten shook his head. "That seems like a bit of a stretch."

"If you don't want my help, what am I doing here? I could be spending quality time with my grandbabies. Those kids are running now and driving Truman to drink. They do this thing where they see him coming and they break formation into three different directions so he can only catch one of them at a time. It's genius to watch. Like those veloci-thingys from *Jurassic Park*."

"You mean Velociraptors?" Ten asked, chuckling. He'd seen Brian, Stephanie, and Bertha do the same thing and it seemed to him like they'd coordinated the maneuver between them.

"Whatever." Bertha waved a distracted hand at Tennyson. "The point I am trying to make is that people come into our lives for all kinds of reasons. What was Handsome's response to the Witches of Salem wanting his help?"

"He was ready to dive right in." Ten sighed. He was really sounding like a total queen about this whole thing.

"Oh." Bertha's mouth formed a perfect "O." "I get it now. You don't want him working on this." She sounded stunned by her realization. "Why, Tennyson? This isn't like you at all."

"I can't put a finger on it. Something in this just isn't right. There are members of the coven who are psychic. Madam Aurora for one. She can't reach any of the women's spirits. I couldn't either."

"Good Lord, not that grey-haired menace again." Bertha rolled her eyes.

"She *loves* Ronan. Aurora was practically purring like a cat drunk on too much milk when he spoke to her."

"Jealously doesn't become you, Tenny." Bertha bit her bottom lip.

"That's what I mean, Bertha. I'm not a jealous man. Ronan doesn't like women that way. None of these six dead women can be reached. Something isn't right here and I haven't even told you about Ronan's nightmare yet."

"What nightmare?" Bertha was instantly in Mama Bear mode.

"He had a dream that he had to accuse me as a witch or face a noose of his own. Then the dream ended with me being burned at the stake." Ten hated recounting the dream for her.

"Jesus, Tenny. That sounds terrifying." Bertha shivered, odd, since she was dead and didn't get cold.

"The worst part was that all of our friends were there too, Carson and Tru, Cole and Cassie, Kevin and Greeley. Even Jude was there. The last of the onlookers was Preacher Gideon Black."

"The bastard from the actual Salem Witch Trials. I remember the name."

"Then Ronan said in the middle of the dream he had a flashback to a scene where I was telling him to accuse me as a witch if it meant saving his life because we would be reunited someday."

"That changes everything," Bertha said carefully.

"I know." Tennyson hadn't wanted to say too much about his suspicions, but it was obvious now Bertha was on the same page with him.

"Have you mentioned this to Ronan?" The look in her eyes clearly indicated she already knew the answer to that question.

Ten shook his head no. "I could be wrong. It could have just been a bizarre, very detailed dream. We had hot wings for dinner that night and spicy foods affect him differently…"

"Denial isn't just a river in Egypt." Bertha shook her head.

"I'll keep an eye on him. If anything else happens, I'll tell him. I promise, Bertha." It was a promise Tennyson would keep, come hell or highwater.

Bertha opened her mouth to respond when there was a knock on the door.

"Come in, Carson!" Ten called.

"Oh, hey, Mom!" Carson smiled at his mother. "I wish I could stay and talk, but we've got a situation. Ten, you need to come now."

Whatever was going on, Ten couldn't read it in Carson. Damn those blocking exercises.

9

Ronan

Lobster Charlie's was hopping for a Wednesday night before Memorial Day. Every stool at the bar was taken and there had been a line of diners crowded into the lobby of the restaurant waiting for a table when Ronan and Greeley arrived. Ronan was glad he'd called ahead and made reservations. The teenager was sulky enough as it was. Ronan knew having to wait for a table would only have made his mood worse.

Once they were sitting at a table by the windows, Ronan took the time Greeley was using to read the menu to study the teenager. There was definitely something different about the boy over the last few months. The problem was that Ronan had been so busy working, spending time with Tennyson, and getting ready for Emilyn's impending pregnancy, that he hadn't spent any time with Greeley either.

After the waitress took their order, king-sized lobster roll and fries for Ronan and a baked-stuffed lobster and shrimp combo for Greeley, Ronan knew the time had come to get down to business. "How did the end of your first semester finish up?"

Greeley shrugged and took a sip of his Coke.

Ronan frowned and tried again, "Are you registered for the summer session?"

Similar shrug only no sip of soda this time.

"Boy trouble?" Ronan asked. "It sure as hell isn't girl trouble."

Greeley raised an eyebrow, but stayed silent.

This wasn't like the kid at all. Greeley had been through his struggles, but for him to sit here, almost defiant in his attitude, was blowing Ronan's mind. "Listen, your father is worried that you're back on drugs."

Greeley's mouth hung open. He took a deep breath as if he were about to start a fight in the middle of the restaurant.

Ronan held up a hand to stop him. "Just give me a minute before you blow your top, okay?" He didn't wait for a response before pushing on. "You haven't been the same happy guy we all know and love. Everyone's noticed it and your father was brave enough to come to me about it after he tried to talk to you about what's going on. Tried unsuccessfully to talk to you, according to the Cap." Ronan raised an eyebrow. "Now you can respond, but if you get us kicked out before I can sink my teeth into that lobster roll, there could be hell to pay."

A ghost of a smile quirked Greeley's lips. It was there and gone in an instant. If Ronan hadn't been watching him so closely, he would have missed it completely.

"You know you can tell me anything. No matter what it is, we'll figure it out together." It killed Ronan seeing Greeley like this, a shell of his former self.

Greeley nodded. He looked like he was thinking over what Ronan had said. "Do you remember last fall when we went to Kansas and I helped out on the Shannon Bradley case?"

Ronan nodded, but stayed silent.

"Then, when we were on the cruise ship and I got to interview the passengers who'd been at the murder mystery night. I really enjoyed that, Uncle Ronan. I did well at school. I know I've earned all A's, but…" Greeley sighed as if the weight of the world was on his shoulders.

"But, what?" Ronan kept his tone curious, rather than accusatory like he'd do with a suspect in an initial interview.

"What if I don't want to be a drug and alcohol counsellor? What if I want to be a cop like you and Dad?" Greeley's green eyes looked up to lock with Ronan's.

"You're not on drugs?" Ronan's face split into a smile. "No little purple-haired turd broke your heart? You didn't fail out of Salem State? You don't have a raging case of VD?" Ronan felt like laughing out loud.

Greeley snorted. "No, Uncle Ronan. I can honestly say no to all of those things, except the purple-haired guy. All he wanted was to fool around, but I wasn't having any of that. He wasn't even that cute." He rolled his eyes.

"I'm confused then. If all you're wanting to do is maybe change your major, then why are you acting like someone died? Jesus, kid we all thought something was *seriously* wrong with you." Ronan felt relief coursing through his body. All of the worst-case-scenarios that had been playing through his head all day seemed to be for naught.

"I kind of think law enforcement is my destiny, but there's no way Dad will let me go to the academy." The sad look was back in Greeley's eyes again. "There have been so many officer deaths in the news lately and every time there's a new story that breaks, Dad gets all upset and will say, 'See kid, this is why I don't want you to be a cop.' I've been biting my tongue, but I don't think I can anymore. The deadline for registering for summer session is in two weeks. I need to shit or get off the pot as Bertha would say."

Ronan burst out laughing. That sounded exactly like something Bertha Craig would say. He had to admit though, Kevin had a point. It seemed like now, more than ever, members of the law enforcement community had extra-large targets on their backs. In recent months, two members of the Massachusetts law enforcement community had been killed in the line of duty.

"Are there any Criminal Justice classes you could take during the summer session that would fill a graduation requirement?"

Greeley nodded. "They offer Fundamentals of Law Enforcement. It's a freshman level class."

It seemed to Ronan like that might be a good place to start.

"Will you talk to him for me, Uncle Ronan? I know the reason we're here is that he sent you on a fact-finding mission. Could you report this back to him? That way if he blows up at you, maybe he'll listen to me when he gets home."

Ronan had to admit it was a good plan. He didn't mind if Fitzgibbon lost his mind yelling at him, but that kind of angry dad tantrum was the last thing Greeley needed to be a part of. "I will, kid, but there's something I need you to think about too, okay?"

"Anything. Lay it on me." Greeley's full attention was on Ronan.

"In the last two years, I've been shot four times, your Dad's been shot once. Ten's been kidnapped. You've been kidnapped. Then there's what happened to Mark Abruzzi…" Ronan trailed off. He spent a minute saying a silent prayer for the teenager and trying to get that last image of the boy out of his head. "Please tell me you understand why your desire to go into this profession could upset Kevin."

Greeley's eyes turned serious. "I met a lot of parents this semester. Don't tell Dad, but I compared them all to him. Were they strict like he was? Did they hand out money like water? Did they spoil their kids or not care at all?"

"What conclusions did you come to?" Ronan was interested to see what Greeley had seen through his own eyes.

"Dad is pretty strict, but it comes from a place of having seen what's out there. God, Uncle Ronan, there's a lot of drugs on that campus. Not that I want to narc on anyone, but that shit was everywhere. I'm glad we moved to Salem so I could live at home. A lot of the parents gave their kids money for drugs. Others bought booze." Greeley shook his head. "I didn't want to hang out with those guys."

Ronan knew Fitzgibbon would be so proud of his son for making those decisions.

"Dad's always talking about the guys he went through the academy with. It's like they're brothers." Greeley's eyes got a little misty. "I want that. I'll never have brothers of my own. It's like you and Uncle Ten say about how it takes more than DNA to make a family. I want to build my own, but the guys at college are kids and I'm…" Greeley looked up at Ronan as if he were hoping Ronan could supply the next word.

"You're a man." Ronan sighed. He knew this conversation with Fitzgibbon was not going to go well. "You had to grow up fast with being in the foster care system and then being out on the street. You might only be eighteen years old courtesy of the date on your birth certificate, but you're more like twenty-five or maybe closer to thirty thanks to all of the life experiences you've lived through and have overcome."

Greeley nibbled his bottom lip. "Do you think that's why I had a hard time making friends? Why I didn't really feel like I fit in?"

Ronan nodded. "I think that's it exactly. If you were with a group of young men and women who were at the same place in their life as you, ready for responsibility and to buckle down and to get on with a career, I don't think you'd have any of those problems again. It's why you get along so well with all of us."

Greeley chuckled. "You're my family. You have to like me."

"Not true. Being family means we have to *love* you. Liking you is a function of your personality and how you treat us."

"I haven't been so good at that lately," Greeley's eyes turned down.

"The good news is that tomorrow's a great time to fix that. Starting with your father."

Greeley's eyes grew misty. "He's been so good to me and I've been nothing but a little shit these last few weeks."

"That's the best thing about our family, we're really good at forgiving each other." Ronan was about to elaborate on his point when the waitress arrived, setting down a huge plate in front of Greeley before placing his own in front of him.

"I might need a little more forgiveness here, Uncle Ronan." Greeley nibbled on his bottom lip.

"Oh yeah?"

"I might have ordered the most expensive thing on the menu on purpose." Greeley wore a guilty look on his face.

"You picked up the fine art of passive-aggression from your Dad, I see." Ronan shook his head.

Greeley burst out laughing. "He's one hell of a role model. So are you, which is why I want to follow in your footsteps."

Ronan nodded, feeling humbled by the young man's heartfelt words. "You know Kevin is going to say there are other ways to help people without having to strap on a gun and carry a badge, right?"

"I know and I don't have a counter-argument for that. This is what I feel like I'm being called to do. It doesn't have to be in Boston. I could work here in Salem or for a university police department.

Ronan shivered in his seat, his thoughts casting back to Officer Sean Collier, a member of the MIT Campus police force, who'd been killed by the Boston Marathon bombers. "A cop is a cop, Greeley. No matter what uniform you put on, we're all at risk when we leave the house."

"I understand, Uncle Ronan."

Ronan didn't need to be psychic to see that the young man sitting before him truly did understand. "I'll talk to your father, but I can't make any promises as to how he'll take that news."

"Thanks. I appreciate it." Greeley forked up an enormous baked stuffed shrimp and set it on Ronan's empty bread plate.

"What's this?" Ronan grinned, not wanting to look a gift shrimp in the mouth.

"I figure I owe you at least one, since you're paying for this meal." Greeley smirked happily.

Ronan burst out laughing.

He was about to come back with some corny joke about having forgotten his wallet at home when his ass vibrated with an incoming text message. "Hold that thought." Digging his phone out of the back pocket of his jeans, Ronan saw the message was from Tennyson. [Magick Shop 911]

"Eat up, kid. We need to get to the store. Ten needs us." Shooting a quick message back to his husband, Ronan couldn't help but wonder what had Tennyson sending up such a mysterious distress signal.

10

Tennyson

Tennyson felt bad about sending Ronan such a cryptic message. He didn't want to deliver this kind of news over text. It would be much better coming in person. Every minute it took Ronan to get to West Side Magick seemed to take an eternity to pass. He knew his husband was only across town having dinner with Greeley, but it seemed to be taking longer than it should have for them to have gotten here.

The tinkling of the shop bell sent Tennyson's stomach plunging to the floor. He looked up to see Ronan striding into the store. His blue eyes roamed over everything and everyone standing there. It was easy to see Ronan was in cop-mode.

"Ronan!" Corazon cried, running to him and burying her face in his chest.

The burly detective wrapped his arms around the sobbing witch and held her tight. His eyes sought out Tennyson's. The unspoken question, "What happened?" was telegraphed in his blue orbs.

"Gia is dead," Lyric Vaughn whispered from behind him.

Tennyson watched as all of the witches who'd been guests in their living room last night gathered around Ronan and Corazon. Greeley walked over to him.

"What's going on, Uncle Ten?" Greeley's voice was a near-whisper.

"These women are members of the Salem Witch community. They came to Ronan last night because they think they're being hunted. I didn't believe them because the members of the coven who've died have done so under accidental circumstances. Earlier this evening, one of the women who came to see Ronan last night was found dead.

"What happened, Ten?" Ronan asked. His eyes were glassy and his voice was thick with emotion. He was still holding Corazon.

"I was in the reading room talking to Bertha when Carson came to get me. He'd been in the bakery when breaking news came on the television about a jogger being found dead on a running trail in Salem. He asked me if the name Gia Hernandez meant anything to me and I knew instantly that it was one of the women who'd been at our house last night. Soon after the news broke, Lyric and the others came here to see you. That's when I sent you the text."

Ronan nodded and set Corazon away from him. He quickly made the sign of the cross. "Have you been able to speak with her spirit, Aurora?"

"No. It's just like with our other sisters. I'm not getting anything." Aurora sounded more angry than disappointed.

"What about the rest of you? Ten? Carson? Cole?" Ronan spun around looking at each of the other psychics as he called out their names.

"I'm not connecting with anyone," Carson said. "which is odd because there is usually someone around wanting to chat with me or who enjoys the positive energy of the shop. "I haven't seen Mom in an hour or so. What about you, Cole?"

Cole's attention focused on the bell over the shop door. His blue eyes went fuzzy for a few seconds. "I'm not getting anything either. There are no spirits in the shop and I'm not getting any information about what happened to Gia. It's as if..." Cole trailed off, shooting Carson a confused look.

"It's as if what, Cole?" Ten asked. He was curious to know if his friend was getting the same kind of feeling about what was going on as he was getting himself.

"I feel like my gift is bumping up against a wall that I can't get through." Cole looked more confused saying the words out loud.

"That's exactly what I was getting too," Ten agreed. "It reminded me of Superman not being able to use his X-ray vision because the room he was trying to see into was lead-lined." Tennyson didn't like this at all. It meant that his initial feeling about this situation with the witches being nothing to worry about was all wrong. There was also a second, more disturbing thing at play here.

"We're being blocked by a power far greater than our own," Madam Aurora said.

"Blocked?" Ronan looked around the room, his eyes lingering the longest on the psychics. "What do you mean blocked? Like those exercises Ten is always cautioning Carson to use so he can't see that the mailman is having an affair with the crazy cat lady who lives next door to us?"

Ten nodded. "It's that but on a much bigger level."

"Why am I getting a bad feeling about this?" Ronan's brows knit together. "Define 'much bigger level.'"

"Think cup of ice water versus the Pacific Ocean." Madam Aurora raised an eyebrow at Tennyson.

Ronan wore a look in his eyes like his head was spinning. "So, along with restricting the flow of information, whoever is doing this is keeping the spirits of the dead women from speaking with you too?"

"That's what I'm beginning to suspect," Ten admitted. The kind of power it would take to do that and keep itself hidden was staggering. Terrifying too if it was being used for evil intent.

"Jesus," Ronan muttered under his breath. "As much as I hate to say this, I think I know someone who might be able to shed some light on this."

Tennyson knew exactly who Ronan was talking about: Jude Byrne. They'd met the wise-cracking, oversexed P.I. during the course of the Tank Hutchins case. He'd become a friend and part of the family over the last six months. Back in March, he'd been instrumental in helping to save the life of Niall Gallagher who'd been having a bit of trouble with the spirits of several of the victims of the Salem Witch Trials. He'd used some kind of Navajo weapon-word to get the accused witches to stop their attack on Niall.

"Ah, Ronan? May I have a word with you in private?" Without bothering to wait for an answer, Tennyson walked toward Carson's reading room. He knew the talents in the room would be able to listen in on this conversation, but it wasn't them he was worried about. It was the witches.

"I know what you're going to say." Ronan offered him a somber look.

"You do? So, you're the psychic now?" Ten raised an eyebrow.

"Jude hates witches. We have a roomful of witches. Therefore, Jude will not want to help the witches." Ronan reached out for Tennyson's hand. "Am I close? Is that what you were going to say?"

"More or less," Ten agreed.

"The only other time that you've ever come up against anything remotely close to this same situation with being blocked is with Jude. Maybe if you ask him about it, or how to defeat it, he might shed some light on it for you."

"For me?" Ten asked. "He's your bro from another ho? Remember?"

Ronan shrugged. "Face it, Ten, people like you better than me. I'm the grumpy bastard while you're all rainbows and unicorns."

A smile ghosted across Tennyson's face.

"A young woman who was just starting out her life is dead. Maybe it was just a freak accident, but maybe it is part of a larger, more sinister, conspiracy. I get that a witch killed Jude's father, but right now, my responsibility is to the living. His should be too. If there is a way to break the block or a way to circumvent it, then we need to know about it now before another young woman pays with her life." Ronan was all business.

Ten nodded. He knew Ronan was right. "I'll call him in the morning and see if he'll meet me for lunch."

"Thank you. If he gives you any trouble, just threaten to sic me on him." Ronan's lips quirked into a brief smile.

"I'm sure that will have him quaking in his boots." Ten shook his head. "Ronan, just keep one thing in mind here."

"What's that?" Ronan asked.

"Whatever protection Jude has in place is there for a reason. He might not be so anxious to give anyone the key to break it. Not even to his friends. He's keeping something close to the vest."

"I know he's hiding something from his past. I've been hoping that he'd get to a point where he knew he was safe with us and would open up, but that hasn't happened yet."

"It doesn't mean that it won't, but asking him about this thing in order to help the Salem coven isn't going to earn us any bonus points as friends here either." Ten had a feeling this conversation was going to do more harm than good.

"If nothing else, he'll know you're coming to him out of a place of love. You're not being a busybody here, you're trying to help people." Ronan pulled his husband close.

Ten allowed himself a minute to relax into Ronan's warm embrace. The mounting anxiety he was feeling melted away. He knew it would be back.

11

Ronan

Ronan might not have been blessed with Tennyson's gifts, but he knew his husband well enough to know he was frightened about what was going on with the witches. He might not have lent much credence to their story last night, but he definitely believed there was something going on now. Ronan knew that as well as he knew his own name.

After he'd been able to peel his husband off his chest, he'd asked him to get everyone into the reading room. While Ten was doing that, Ronan flipped the "Closed" sign on the shop and headed over to West Side Sweets to grab some provisions. Cassie, Cole's pregnant wife, took his order and was working to fill it quickly.

"Uncle Ronan?"

Ronan startled and spun around to see Greeley standing behind him. "Damn kid, you scared the life out of me. This old cat only has about five lives left in him to begin with."

Greeley rubbed his hands against his arms as if he were cold. "This whole thing is giving me a hinky vibe."

"Me too. Once all of the psychics agreed that they couldn't read anything and that there were no spirits in the shop, even I could feel the energy in the place change. It reminded me of when a weather front moves in and you can actually feel the pressure change." Ronan didn't like this at all. He couldn't imagine what it was like for Ten and the others who were more sensitive to these kinds of changes.

"I felt that too," Greeley agreed. "How do I help?"

Ronan turned around to study the teenager. He was wearing a throwback Aerosmith tee and a pair of faded jeans. His hands were shoved deep in the front pockets. His hair was cut short, with the bangs spiked up. He looked so young and innocent standing here like this. Christ, if Ronan didn't know better, he'd think Greeley was a fresh-faced sixteen-year-old boy who'd never known a minute of adversity in his life, when the truth of the matter was, up until he'd met Fitzgibbon last year, all he'd known *was* adversity. He had more empathy in his right little finger than most people had in their entire body. "Use your empathy to keep the tempers in the room from getting frayed. I don't have a lot of information to pass along."

"That's why you're bringing the food?" Greeley grinned and reached for the bags Cassie was setting on the counter.

"You're a fast learner, kid." Ronan went to reach for the coffee fixings, but Greeley beat him to it. "How much longer do you have to go with my baby nephew, Cass?"

"You mean with the newest member of the New England Revolution? All this little man does is kick me twenty-four/seven. I've got eight weeks to go until this little guy makes his debut."

"What if he isn't a soccer player? What if he thinks your insides are his MMA octagon?" Greeley laughed.

"God help us all then." Cassie rolled her eyes. "Are you going to be available to work here before classes start back up?"

Greeley nodded. "I was just going to ask you when you needed me."

"Now!" Cassie laughed. "But 5am tomorrow morning will have to do."

"You got it, Cassie. See you then!"

Ronan grabbed the stack of cups and the carafe of coffee. If only the situation in the reading room could be solved as easily as Greeley's summer job.

When Ronan opened the door to the reading room, he could sense instantly that the energy had changed. Again. He had a feeling it had to do with the stranger standing at the back of the room. He was instantly back in cop-mode assessing the man who looked to be about 6'3". He had sandy blond hair tied back in a pony tail, but his vivid blue eyes were the show-stopper. He was dressed in perfectly creased black suit pants and a black cashmere sweater that Ronan was sure cost more than an entire week's salary. "Who's Mr. GQ?" Ronan asked as he set the coffee on the table.

"In the name of the Goddess, you are a caveman." Andromeda shook her head and reached a dainty hand out for a cookie. "Ronan, this is Callum Churchill."

"Oh! *Nobody's Witch*!" Ronan grinned. Callum Churchill had written a book about his ancestor, Abigail Churchill, who had been a victim of the Salem Witch Trials. Ronan had been lucky enough to meet her spirit at The Black Cat Inn when he and Tennyson had been helping out Niall Gallagher and Tobin Woods. "Abigail is just lovely."

"You mean the way I portrayed her in my novel?" Callum's blue eyes sparkled with Ronan's compliment.

"No, when I met her in person back in March." Ronan grinned, setting a cup of coffee in front of Tennyson. Abigail had been an ally to Niall and Tobin, and as far as he knew, was still watching over the young couple.

"Oh, you mean my Great Aunt Abigail. She's my mother's aunt." Callum smiled indulgently at Ronan as if he thought the man was simpleminded.

"No, I most definitely did not meet your great aunt." Ronan laughed. "I met Abigail Churchill at the Witch Hill Road house out on Gallows Hill right after our friend, Niall Gallagher, bought it. There were some spirits haunting the house that were giving Niall and Tobin Woods some trouble out there. Abigail was kind enough to warn Niall of the danger. I met her when she appeared to us one day."

"*You* met my great-great grandmother ten times removed?" Callum laughed. "The one who's been dead since 1692? *That* Abigail Churchill?" Callum looked as if he was certain Ronan was somehow touched in the head.

It was Ronan's turn to shoot Callum a look like he was a few eggs short of a dozen. "You realize that you're in a room with four psychic mediums and other sensitives, right? My husband can see and speak to dead people, but Abigail appeared to us all that day as clearly as I see you now." To prove his point, Ronan walked up to the snotty author and poked his shoulder with his index finger.

"Take your hand off me!" Callum demanded.

"It was a *finger* and you're lucky it wasn't a different one." Ronan smirked before turning to Tennyson. "Why is he here?"

"As Salem's resident warlock I thought it wise that we bring Callum up to speed on the situation," Madam Aurora answered, raising an elegant brow. "I believe you have information for us all, Ronan."

Ronan hated it when Aurora read his mind. He'd gotten used to Tennyson doing that over time. It didn't feel like such an invasion of privacy when his husband poked around inside his head, but a total stranger? It gave him the creeps. "I do have some information, but not much that we can use to open an actual investigation."

"Then precisely what good are you, Ronan?" Callum Churchill asked.

If one of the women who'd come to him last night asking for his help weren't lying in the Essex County Morgue right now, Ronan would have shown the preppy SOB, with his five-hundred-dollar sweater, exactly what good he was, but Gia deserved better than him acting like a macho asshole. "The problem I ran into with my preliminary investigation is that all of deaths were deemed accidents, with the exception of the suicide. The police reports aren't as detailed in these kinds of situations. I didn't find any kind of evidence in the existing files that would allow for an investigation to be opened should the town of record choose to open one."

"Whatever do you mean, *choose* to open one? These policemen work for us. We pay their salaries!" Callum folded his arms over his chest. An offended look was plastered on his face.

Ronan could feel his temper rising with every perfectly pronounced word out of Churchill's mouth. He took a deep breath, trying to keep his temper at bay. "We may be paid by taxpayer money, but we have to operate by the laws of the Commonwealth of Massachusetts. If I can't show that a crime was committed then I can't bring a charge. More to the point, I only have jurisdiction to arrest someone in the City of Boston. I could certainly go to the Salem Police if I had evidence of a crime committed here, but that doesn't mean they have to investigate. It doesn't mean they have to open a case and look for suspects."

Callum made a disgusted noise and looked away from Ronan.

"What about Martha's suicide?" Aurora asked.

That had been the hardest of the deaths for Ronan to deal with. It brought back memories he wasn't ready to deal with yet. He might never be ready to deal with those memories. "From everything I read, it was a straightforward suicide."

"Whatever is straightforward about suicide, Mr. O'Mara?" Callum's words dripped with annoyance.

What the hell was wrong with this guy? The snotty attitude he could take, but not the disrespect. "It's *Detective* O'Mara, Mr. Churchill. Everyone in this room has been through enough tonight with the death of Gia without me going into detail about Martha and her death scene and autopsy photos. Whatever happened to her was good enough to convince a trained medical examiner that she had willingly taken her own life. In my fourteen years on the force, I've seen staged suicides, this looked nothing like those."

"So, you're saying our precious girl killed herself?" Callum's voice had taken on an incredulous tone.

"No, I'm saying that if someone else did this, that someone was an expert. Maybe even a doctor. Which brings me back to Gia." Ronan turned to Tennyson. "What information is the news releasing about her death at this time?"

"Just that she was found on a jogging path, but they didn't say if there were signs of foul play." Ten wore a grim look on his face.

"Ladies, did she go running alone or was this out of the norm for Gia?" Ronan had a feeling he knew the answer. Whoever was behind this was a predator and would have been good at identifying routines and picking out the weakest witches in the group.

"She always ran alone after Sophia was picked up for kindergarten," Corazon wept.

"Sophia?" Ronan felt his heart sink. He'd had no idea Gia was a mother.

"That child was the light of her life," Callum said, sounding human for the first time all evening.

"Okay, so if someone was looking to harm her it would have been easy for them to have learned her routine," Ronan said more to himself than the others. "All we can do now is wait for the police report and autopsy."

"So, you sit and do nothing while we are hunted down and killed like rabid dogs?" Callum's voice was full of venom.

Ronan sighed heavily. "Tell me what you'd do in my place, Mr. Churchill? Go rogue? Wear a green hood and have me call myself The Arrow? What? You tell me. I'm all ears." Ronan held his hands out to the author knowing full well that he wasn't going to have an idea worthy of using.

"It seems to me we've come to a crossroads, doesn't it, detective? You know full well what needs to be done here in order to get justice. It is the precise reason the women sought you out. They needed a champion who would color outside the lines. You failed them. Gia is dead." Callum moved from his place near the back wall and walked toward the door.

"Now hold on just a minute-" Ronan started.

Callum held his hand up to indicate he wasn't finished. "Good night, Mr. O'Mara. Pray we all survive to see the rising sun." The warlock walked toward the door of the reading room. All of the witches followed behind him. Lyric Vaughn shot Ronan a sympathetic look, but she walked out the door after him.

"Well, shit." Carson shut the door behind them. "The only way that could have gone worse was if they burned *you* at the stake, pal."

Ronan had been thinking the same thing.

12

Tennyson

Something smacking against Tennyson's naked back woke him from a dead sleep. Cracking an eyeball open he could see the time on the digital alarm clock read 3:24am. Before he could register what had hit him the last time, Ronan kicked him.

"No!" Ronan shouted, thrashing out with his arms this time.

Nightmare, Tennyson thought. He rolled over and shook Ronan's right shoulder. "Ronan? Ronan, wake up!" He shook harder.

"Ten?" Ronan's voice was thick with sleep. "Tennyson is it really you?"

Flipping on the light, Ten turned back to Ronan who was looking shell-shocked. "It's me. See?" Ten reached for his hands which were shaking. "I'm right here."

Ronan blinked a few times before he grabbed Tennyson and pulled him into his arms. "You were dead. They burned you. I had to watch. You made me turn you in *again.*" He gasped for air. "Why did you make me do that?"

All Tennyson could do was hold on tight while Ronan cried and mumbled the same questions over and over. What stuck out to him was that Ronan used the word "again." "What do you mean I made you turn me in again?" Ten asked when Ronan had calmed down a bit more.

"We weren't in Salem, but everyone was there. Carson and Truman and Cole and Jude. Preacher Black too." Ronan shivered.

"Do you know where we were?" Ten was afraid to ask the question. To be honest, he was more afraid of the answer. "Or when?"

"I'm not sure, but I heard the word 'inquisition' and I could speak and understand Spanish. You called me mi amor."

"I remember enough Spanish from high school to know that means my love." Christ, the Spanish Inquisition? Was that really where Ronan's *Magical Mystery Tour* had taken them this time?

Ronan nodded. "What the hell is going on here, Ten? These dreams are a little too real to be just dreams. Is something else going on? Something you're not telling me about?"

Ten hated keeping things from Ronan. With everything that was going on with the witches visiting and then Gia dying, he hadn't had the chance to talk to Madam Aurora about what he thought was going on with Ronan. "I do think there's something going on here. I'm not an expert, but I think what you might be experiencing are past lives resurfacing."

Ronan's brows knit together, but he didn't say a word.

It was fascinating to watch his husband's mind work. Ten could see Ronan was thinking over what he'd just said. His skeptical husband had come a long way in the last sixteen months. The Ronan O'Mara who'd walked through the doors of West Side Magick over a year ago would not have responded to the ideas of past lives in this calm manner. That Ronan would have responded with choice words and probably a slamming door.

"Past lives? As in plural?" Ronan's voice was filled with wonder.

"You said the first dream took place in Salem, but this one did not, right? Do you think we were backward in time from the Salem dream or was it more modern?"

"It seemed earlier to me. I'm no historian, but I know I heard the crowd murmuring about the Inquisition. Were witches hunted and killed during that time? By the church?" Ronan sounded like he had no idea if such a thing were possible.

Ten nodded. "Everyone was hunted in that time, but the Catholic Church didn't like to be associated with witch hunts so it was done on the down low." Ten took a shaky breath. "Was I only being accused of witchcraft?"

Ronan shook his head. His blue eyes filled with tears. "No, there was another charge." Tears dripped from his eyes.

Ten swiped at them with the pads of his thumbs. "Homosexuality, right?"

Nodding, Ronan buried his face against the side of Tennyson's neck. "You made me promise I'd tell them about you."

"See, that was something the church could kill you for back then. That way the witchcraft didn't have to come up at all." Ten wiped away more of Ronan's tears.

"Dirty fuckers," Ronan muttered against his neck. "Using religion as a torch to light your pyre."

"Shit, they barbequed me again?" Ten chuckled against Ronan's soft, dirty-blond hair.

"Not funny," Ronan squawked.

"You're right, it isn't," Ten agreed. "How many of us died over the centuries like this?"

Ronan held on tighter. "How many men like me sent their lovers to the flames? I was your Judas, Ten. How did I live with myself? How did you find it in your heart to forgive me?"

Tennyson's heart clenched in his chest. It seemed they'd been destined to be star-crossed lovers throughout time. "Well, I think that knowing you lived was probably enough for me. That, and knowing we'd meet again."

"You said that in this dream, just like you did in the first one. You told me we'd be reunited. Shit!" Ronan pulled back from Tennyson. He swiped angrily at the tears still falling from his eyes. "We were reunited. In Salem, and I was your executioner there too. Jesus Christ, Ten! How many other times did this happen? How many more times did I betray you? Is it going to happen again now? Here?" Ronan gasped for breath.

"It's okay. Breathe." Ten set a hand against his husband's pounding heart. "I don't know that much about this. I was hoping the first dream was just a dream."

"What do you mean?" Ronan's eyes narrowed.

"There were elements of that dream that led me to think this could be a past life resurfacing, but then I told myself I was just being over-sensitive. That it was just a dream. I promised myself I'd take action if it happened again." Ten wore a guilty look on his face. If he'd asked Aurora about this sooner, they might have been able to avoid Ronan having another nightmare.

"What kind of action are we talking about? Are you gonna douse me with holy water?" Ronan shivered.

Ten snorted. "No, we're going to have to go see an expert on this."

"Please tell me it's not that Churchill dick. I had just about all of him I could take in the fifteen minutes I was with him tonight."

"No, it's not Callum Churchill. I didn't even know he was involved in the Salem Witch Community until he walked into the shop tonight. You showed remarkable restraint. I thought he said at least three different things that should have earned him a fat lip." Tennyson pressed a kiss to the side of Ronan's head. "The expert in all matters past life is Madam Aurora."

"Of fucking course, it's her. Your arch-enemy to the rescue again." Ronan rolled his now dry eyes.

"She isn't my arch-enemy anymore and what's more, she was never yours. Aurora likes you."

"Everyone likes me." Ronan's shit-eating grin was back in full-force.

"Oh, please! Earlier tonight you said I was all rainbows and unicorns and that you were a grumpy bastard." Ronan never gave himself enough credit. People might have thought he was irritable, but they trusted him to keep them safe. In Tennyson's mind, that would be the more important thing.

"Yeah, that was just so you'd talk to Jude about his psychic-blocking magic." Ronan managed a smile.

"Are you saying you were buttering me up?" The hand sitting against Ronan's heart couldn't feel it pounding so hard anymore. At least this banter was calming him down.

"Yes! I'm so good at it you didn't even know I was doing it!" Ronan crowed.

"Just like I'm so good at cheering you up that you didn't even notice *I* was doing it?"

"Huh. Oh yeah, I guess I am feeling better. Very tricky." Ronan reached over to shut the light off. He pulled Ten down to lie on his chest. "Why now, Ten? Why are these past lives coming back now?"

"I'm not sure, babe." Ten pressed a kiss against Ronan's heart. He had an idea, he just needed more information before he told Ronan his theory.

13

Meeting with Kevin Fitzgibbon about Greeley wanting to drop out of college to join the police academy was about the last thing Ronan wanted to do. The only thing worse, in his mind, anyway, was trying to talk to Jude Byrne about his deal with the witches and how to crack his own personal Da Vinci Code in order to help keep said witches safe.

Just because he wasn't looking forward to the task at hand didn't mean he wasn't prepared for it. He'd stopped at West Side Sweets before making the hour-long trip into Boston. He'd grabbed Kevin's favorites: passionfruit muffins and mint chocolate chip cookies. There was no sense taking any chances with something this important to discuss. A little bribe could go a long way.

The captain was sitting at his desk, squinting at the computer screen when Ronan knocked on his door. His heart was knocking so hard against his ribcage that he could feel the beats in his toes. He was more nervous about this conversation than he was about chasing down gun-wielding murderers.

"Oh, good. I was wondering when you'd stroll in." Now that Greeley was out of school for the summer and Jace Lincoln was out of his life, Fitzgibbon had gone back to his old habits. He was in the office before the sun rose into the sky and his lips rarely formed a smile anymore.

Ronan knew it was only 7:45am or so. Not that he was required to punch a timeclock or anything, but this was the "new" Fitzgibbon. Constantly in a pissy mood and spoiling for a fight. "Good morning to you too, princess." Ronan set down the two bakery bags along with the coffee he'd picked up from the expensive place across the street, before digging through the stack of paperwork on the captain's desk to find Fitzgibbon's reading glasses, which he set in front of his boss. Cocking an eyebrow, Ronan grabbed his own coffee and sat down in front of him.

"What did Greeley say last night?" Fitzgibbon wasted no time breaking apart a muffing and tearing into it.

After Ronan's trip to the past last night, he hadn't gotten a lot of sleep. What he had gotten had come in the form of mostly catnaps, leaving him tired and feeling pretty pissy himself this morning. "Look, I get that you're going through a bit of a rough patch here with Greeley acting like a normal teenager for the first time since you've known him and with your love life in the shitter, but Jesus Christ, snap out of it. You've been a bear to deal with since Valentine's Day."

"Oh, have I now?" Kevin's voice was dangerously quiet. His green eyes glittered coldly.

Ronan knew he was treading into dangerous territory. "Yes! Tennyson told me what you needed to do to get Jace back and you haven't done any of it. So far as I can see, you've gone back to all of your old habits here, while Jace on the other hand-" Ronan snapped his mouth shut. He wasn't supposed to tell Kevin anything about Jace Lincoln. According to his marching orders from Tennyson, he wasn't even supposed to bring the other man up in conversation.

Jace Lincoln was the son of the late Matthew Lincoln, who at the time of his death last year, had been one of Boston's biggest real estate developers. He'd also been a raging homophobe who'd been, in essence, paying his son five million dollars a year in hush money to stay in the closet. Jace, in turn, had used that money to fund his homeless shelter, the Tremont Street Mission.

Fitzgibbon's bitch face vanished in a heartbeat. "While Jace, what?" He leaned forward in his seat.

Ronan didn't say a word. He watched the emotions play across Fitzgibbon's face. There was anger, frustration, fear, just like he'd expected to see, but at the core of it all was pain. "According to Ten, and I'm not supposed to tell you any of this, Jace has been working his ass off."

Kevin rolled his eyes. "Jace was *always* working his ass off. That was part of our problem."

Ronan grinned. "That's not what I meant. I mean, yeah, he's still working at the mission, but he's been working his ass off in therapy and going to yoga and reading all these books Ten's been recommending. I think they're the same books he's been recommending to some stubborn bastard I know." Ronan folded his arms over his chest and waited to see how Kevin would react to that news.

"Jace is in therapy?" Kevin's angry tone sobered. "We had problems as a couple but I never thought he had problems like *that*."

"Therapy isn't a punishment." Ronan snorted. "I sound like Tennyson. Shit, don't tell him I said that."

Kevin found a brief smile. "Tennyson suggested therapy to Jace?"

Ronan nodded. "He gave Jace the same advice he gave you at the dildo party. Only Jace took it. He's reading the books, doing the bendy-bendy, and trying to make himself a better man so that if you get your act together, he can be better with you."

"Truman does yoga," Kevin said, seemingly to himself.

Ronan nodded. "And with Cassie being pregnant, he's been going to that Thursday night class alone. I bet he'd like the company."

"Do you have the list of the books? So that I don't have to ask Ten again. I don't want him to think I blew off his advice." Kevin wore a guilty look.

Tennyson knew Kevin had blown him off, but Ronan wasn't about to tell his boss that. He wasn't totally stupid, especially not since he still had the main event yet to come. "I'll email the list to you." Ronan leaned forward over his desk. "Now, are you feeling a bit better?"

"Shit, you've got bad news about the kid, don't you? I fucking *knew* there was something wrong. At least I know I'm not about to be a grandfather."

Ronan burst out laughing.

"What's so funny?" Kevin scrubbed a hand across his face.

"I had to ask the same question, just in case." Ronan shrugged. "It's college. Kids experiment. "Oh, God!" Kevin planted his face into his hands.

"Calm down, Pops! The only bun in the oven is Cassie's." Ronan had to admit he was enjoying this moment of fun at Fitzgibbon's expense.

Kevin's green eyes popped up over his fingertips. "But there is *something* going on, right? Did he tell you what it was? What is it?"

If this was what it was like to be the parent of a teenager, Ronan could sure as shit wait to get there. "Yeah, there *is* something going on. It's not drugs. Not sex. Just a life decision that he is afraid to come to you with, so he's been bottling it up."

Fitzgibbon's brows knit together. "My son thought he couldn't come to me about something? I thought we had an open relationship where he could talk to me about anything."

"You do, Cap, about everything *but* this." Ronan could see the confusion and pain warring in Kevin's eyes. He hated seeing his friend going through this.

"I don't understand." Fitzgibbon scrubbed a hand over his weary face.

Ronan could see that clear as day. "Just listen to what I'm going to tell you. Don't get mad, but if you do, don't interrupt. Deal?"

Kevin sighed. "Okay, fine. Just say it. My mind is spinning with what the hell this could possibly be."

"Greeley had a bit of trouble fitting in with the other kids at school," Ronan began.

Fitzgibbon opened his mouth, but shut it quickly with a snap.

"He said a lot of them were into drugs and sex or were just plain irresponsible with the freedom and money their parents were giving them. It made sense to me since he had to grow up quickly and had already been there and done that with the drugs and the sex." Ronan grimaced. He hated bringing up Greeley's past. "He didn't really make any lasting connections because he was so much older mentally than the kids he was going to classes with. Does that make sense to you?"

Kevin nodded. "I'd ask about making new friends and he'd shrug and run upstairs to study. I guess I didn't pay a lot of attention to it since he was acing his classes and wasn't coming home drunk or high."

"To be honest, Cap, those would have been the signs I would have been looking for too. He said that he enjoyed his classes, but that he doesn't really want to be a drug and alcohol counsellor anymore. There's something else he's found a passion for instead."

"Christ on the cross!" Kevin slammed a hand down on his desk. "I fucking knew it! It's that damn guitar isn't it? Boy wants to join a band or be the next Justin Jonas, doesn't he?"

Ronan burst out laughing. He couldn't help himself. "Uh, Cap, I think you're mixing up Nick Jonas and Justin Bieber and no, he doesn't want to be either one of them or join a band."

"He doesn't?" Kevin started laughing too. "Thank Christ. What *does* he want to do then? So long as he doesn't want to be a musician or the elephant boy in the circus, I don't care."

"I hope you mean that, because he wants to be just like us. He wants to be a cop." Ronan held his breath. Even though Kevin said he didn't care what Greeley wanted to do so long as it didn't involve music or the circus, he didn't believe him. Not when Greeley's career path would involve Kevlar and bullets flying at his head.

Fitzgibbon sat stunned. He didn't move. So far as Ronan could tell, the man wasn't breathing.

Ronan wasn't sure what to do. Kevin looked frozen, like when you hit the pause button on live television. "Cap?"

Kevin shook his head. His glassy eyes refocused on Ronan. "Let me get this straight. Greeley wants to be a cop?"

Ronan nodded. "He said that you've been harping on the dangers of our job and how now, more than ever, members of law enforcement have targets on their backs. He also said you mention how often we've been shot lately."

"Seven bullets, Ronan," Fitzgibbon's voice was just above a whisper. "We've taken seven bullets in a little more than three years between me, you, and Jude. Eight if you count..." Kevin shook his head, unable to say the fourth name.

"I know, Cap. I know. The idea of Greeley willingly signing up for this scares the hell out me. I can't imagine what you must be feeling right now. All I can say is that I sat and listened to what he had to say with an open mind and I saw the look in his eyes. He wants this and he's afraid to talk to you about it."

"Yeah, I can see how I've made it a topic he felt he couldn't approach me about."

"He thought that if I told you about it first that you'd blow up at me and then be calmer when it came to talking about things with him." Ronan grinned.

"That little shit." Kevin laughed. "Smart, like his old man."

"How do you feel that he wants to follow in your footsteps? He blew me away when he included me in that. No one's ever wanted to be like me. I'm hardly a role model."

"It's pretty humbling. I mean I've only been his father for a little less than a year." Kevin shook his head. "I can't remember what my life was like without him in it. Jesus, Ronan, if…"

"You can't play that game. You'll 'what if' your life away. I know Ten thinks like that when I leave the house. I'm sure Jace thought that way too about you."

"It was one of our sticking points." Kevin snorted. "I guess that's Karma. I told him he needed to get the fuck over it since it was my job. Now, here I am about to face the same thing with my boy."

"Does that mean you're gonna let him do it?" Ronan hadn't been expecting this kind of response at all. To be honest, he'd expected a bit more kicking and screaming.

"It means we're going to have a man to man talk about it. No yelling. No bullet-proof vests required. How was the food at Lobster Charlie's?"

"It was good until Ten interrupted us." Ronan frowned, memories of last night flooding his brain.

"That's not like him."

"There's something going on I haven't told you about." Ronan wasn't exactly sure how to tell Kevin about this.

"Work related?" Fitzgibbon instantly switched back into cop-mode.

"Not BPD. There's a situation going on with the Salem Witch community and they came to me for help." Ronan rested back against his chair.

"To you?" Kevin started to laugh.

"I know, right? Some members of their coven have died under what seem like ordinary circumstances, but they think they're being hunted. That's why they came to me. They were hoping I could look into the deaths."

Fitzgibbon raised an eyebrow. He was obviously back in boss-mode now too. "And you did?"

"I did. There was nothing I could see in the reports that indicated there was anything going on but a series of unfortunate accidents within a small community of connected people."

Fitzgibbon shook his head and reached for another muffin. "Be careful, Ronan. If other jurisdictions find out you're looking into their case files again…"

Ronan knew Fitzgibbon was referring to the serial killer he'd uncovered last year. Ronan didn't give a good goddamn about stepping on the toes of other cities. If there was a killer or a conspiracy against the witches, he was going to find it. "There was a development last night, Cap. Another witch died, this time in Salem. It was one of the women who came to my house."

"How did she die?" The muffin paused halfway to his mouth.

Ronan shook his head. "We don't know yet. Waiting on the autopsy."

"I'll say again, be careful. Professional courtesy only extends so far."

Ronan stood up and grabbed his now cold cup of coffee. "I hear you."

"But you're going to do it your way anyway." It wasn't a question.

"Good talk, Cap." Ronan tipped him a salute and walked out the door. He had work to do and witches to protect.

14

Tennyson

When Tennyson arrived at Thai Delight in Swampscott, Jude Byrne was holding court. Standing at the bar, he was surrounded by no less than five handsome young men. As Tennyson got closer, he could hear Jude telling the story about how he'd been shot in the "line of duty," during the Hutchins case. As a visual aid, he kept fingering open his shirt to show the puckered bullet scar on the meaty part of his shoulder. The men were cooing and practically eating out of his hand.

"Hey, snookums! Got room for one more in your harem?" Ten grinned.

"Step off, grandpa!" One of the men shot Tennyson a dirty look and set a possessive hand on Jude's arm. He bent forward to whisper into his ear.

Jude chuckled, all the while snaking an arm around his waist to squeeze the man's ass.

"I'll grab us a table while you finish grabbing Tom, *Dick* and *Hairy*..." Ten made a swirling motion with his index finger toward the gaggle of admirers and headed off to the hostess stand to the sound of outraged gasps. He couldn't help grinning to himself. Most of those guys with Jude couldn't have been more than twenty-two years old at the most. Not that Ten was envious. He had all he could handle with Ronan, and then some.

Ten was busy reading the menu when Jude strutted over to him five minute later. "How many numbers did you get?"

"All of them!" Jude answered, as if that were the only answer possible. "Did you see the bodies on those guys?" Jude fanned himself with his left hand.

"I did. Some of them looked like jailbait." Ten grinned.

"They all had drinks, so they were twenty-one at least." Jude tapped a finger on the menu. "We're not here to talk about my penchant to attract beautiful young men though, are we?"

His penchant to attract men? Christ, Jude was the Pied Piper of sexy young things. Wherever he went there seemed to be a flock of young men waiting to bow down and worship him. Ten didn't think he had as much charisma in his entire body as Jude had in his big toe. "Uh, no. We're not. I haven't really seen much of you since Valentine's Day, so I thought it would be nice to catch up."

"Don't bullshit me, Ten. I know there's something else. Otherwise, Ronan would be here too. It must be something sensitive that you're afraid he's gonna fuck up with his asshole ways, so you're here to smooth things over. So long as you're not here to talk about more witch shit, we're cool." Jude waggled his dark eyebrows.

Fuck... This was already off to a bad start. Thankfully their waiter was approaching. Ten ordered a cocktail and some crunchy spring rolls. He couldn't help laughing when Jude echoed his order, flirting with the waiter the entire time.

Instead of laughing, what Ten should have been doing was figuring out a way to broach the subject of the witches and the psychic block with Jude. Now, he was facing the intense amber glare of the man in question. "Uh, hi."

"Jesus Christ, I knew it. This *is* about witches." Jude's lips curled into a sneer. "How many times do I have to tell you I don't want to talk about what happed out at the Witch Hill house?" His voice held a dangerous edge to it.

"I don't want to talk about that." Ten figured it would be easier to diffuse the situation that way. While he and Ronan had been investigating the house out on Witch Hill Road, Niall Gallagher had been attacked for the second time by a malevolent force of spirit witches who were haunting the property. Jude had used some kind of weapon-word to fend off the attack and free Niall. He'd explained later that the word was Navajo in origin, but had refused to elaborate any further except to say that his father had been killed by a witch.

The suspicious look in Jude's eyes dulled down. "You don't?"

"No," Ten said easily. "Look, I get that you have things in your past that you don't want to talk about. That's fine. I'd never want to push you to talk about things that you aren't ready to share. But, that being said, there is something else going on that I need to talk to you about and I'd really appreciate it if you'd drop the asshole act for a few minutes and hear me out. Can you do that?"

Jude nodded. "Yeah, I can do that. I'm sorry, Ten, I just get a little defensive about things that happened when…" He shook his head. "Tell me what's going on."

Tennyson hated playing hardball like that. He'd wanted this to be an easy conversation to start with because the hard stuff was yet to come. "Ronan and I got some unexpected visitors Sunday night. Seven members of the Salem Witches showed up on our doorstep looking for Ronan."

Jude's eyes widened. "Shit, what he do to annoy them?"

"That's just the thing, they came looking for Ronan's help." Ten was still finding it hard to believe that they'd come to Ronan too.

"His help?" Jude looked stunned.

"This is the part of the story where I'm going to need you to keep your personal feelings to yourself." Ten raised an eyebrow at Jude. "They think they're being hunted."

Jude stared at Ten for a few seconds in silence. "The witches think they are being hunted. Seriously, Ten?"

"Six of them have died in the last two years. According to them, all of them have been seemingly accidental with the exception of one suicide. The women wanted Ronan to look into this for them. He agreed, but then that's where the story takes a turn."

"What kind of a turn?" Jude was all business now, his distaste for the witches, seemingly put away for the moment.

"Did you hear about a jogger being found dead in the woods in Salem yesterday?"

Jude nodded.

"She was one of the women who came to see Ronan Sunday night." Ten's heart pinched in his chest just thinking about Gia Gonzalez.

"I can see why the women are envisioning a conspiracy theory here, Tennyson. I'm sorry that these women are dying. I really am. The question in my head right now is what the hell this has to do with me? I hope to fuck you're not going to ask me to investigate these alleged crimes." Jude sat back against the booth.

Ten took a deep breath. "You know, there are times when I think you are the kindest man on earth, like when you saved my husband's life. Then there are times, like now, when I don't know who you are at all. I don't want you to investigate anything. Like I said earlier, I just want you to listen."

Jude's face pinkened, but he stayed silent.

"All of the witches came into the shop last night. One of them is also a psychic medium like me. The problem that we were facing was that there were no spirits in the shop last night." Ten was trying to hold his own frustration back, but he wanted to slap Jude. He understood that Jude's father had been murdered by a witch, but he couldn't hold them all responsible for that.

Frowning, Jude met Ten's eyes. "How can that be? There are always spirits there."

"Right. That was our first indication that there was something going on. Then we realized that we couldn't reach any of the dead women's spirits. With four mediums in the room working together, we should have been able to reach at least one of the seven souls."

"Seven is an important number in witchcraft," Jude mumbled, as if to himself.

Ten made a mental note to remember that. "Jude, the bigger thing we all noticed is that there seems to be a psychic block around all of this that none of us can penetrate." He let his words hang there, hoping his friend would figure the rest out for himself.

Jude opened his mouth to say something, but was stopped by the waiter arriving with the spring rolls and their drinks. What Tennyson wasn't used to in situations like this was being unable to read Jude. In ordinary circumstances, Ten would have gotten a headful of what his tablemate had been about to say which would have given him a few extra seconds to formulate his response. With Jude, he was on equal footing, as Ronan would say.

"What do you mean there's a psychic block?" Jude's eyes narrowed before he bit into a crunchy roll.

"Cole described it as coming up against a brick wall. To me it's like Superman not being able to use his X-ray vision because a room is lined with lead. I've come across a phenomenon like this only one other time in my life since I got my gift."

"A phenomenon like- Oh..." Jude reached for his drink and took a long sip. "I see what this is now. You didn't want to have lunch to catch up with me because you missed me or we hadn't seen each other in a while. I'm here because I'm the *phenomenon*."

In a way, Jude had him. "That's not true. Ronan and I have been so busy with Emilyn and getting ready for the baby. I've been straight out dividing my time between the Magick shop and the precinct with Ronan. Plus, I've been working with Jace Lincoln. Time just got away from me, Jude." Ten sighed. "Friendship works both ways, you know. You never called us either." Ten didn't want to throw that card down on the table but there hadn't been any funny text messages or inappropriate dick pics from Jude since Valentine's Day either.

"Fine, I'm a shitty friend, but that doesn't mean I get to be your guinea pig either." The look on his face turned sour.

"I didn't say you were a guinea pig. You didn't let me finish."

"Oh, there's more? Are you going to lock me in a laboratory and experiment on me?"

"Jude, please." Ten took a deep breath. He hoped Ronan was having an easier time speaking with Kevin about Greeley's future career plans than he was having now. "Just hear me out."

Jude raised an eyebrow. "Talk."

Ten knew he had a very short window of time. What he needed to do now was lay it all on the table. "When I try to read you, it feels exactly what it felt like the other night. All I wanted to know is if you are actively doing something to make that happen?"

Jude shook his head as if he wasn't expecting Tennyson to say that. "What?"

"Are you actively doing something to keep me and the others from being able to read you? I figured that if you are and there's a way around it, we could use that same thing, whatever it is, to break through what's keeping us from contacting the dead witches." Ten reached across the table to set a hand on Jude's. He was expecting his flighty friend to flinch and was shocked when he didn't. "I know you hate witches and you have a good reason for feeling that way. All I want to do right now is help some women who are innocent. They're mothers and grandmothers and sisters and daughters who've never hurt anyone with their practice of Wicca."

Jude seemed to be silently studying Tennyson. "I'm not actively doing anything to block you."

Ten nodded. "Okay, thank you."

"But," Jude continued, as if Ten hadn't interrupted him. "There is something in place keeping you and anyone else from being able to get to me."

Tennyson would swear Jude had been about to say, "The *real* me." This changed things. "Hypothetically speaking, is there a way to overcome the block? Not the one in place protecting you, but the one keeping us from speaking to the witches or whatever it is that is controlling the situation?"

Jude shook his head. "I don't know. I'm not bullshitting you. I honestly don't know. What is it you think these women can tell you if you managed to get through to them?"

"One of the women committed suicide. Or at least her death was made to look that way. Ronan figures that out of all of the deaths, she would be the one most likely to have seen or heard something out of the ordinary." It didn't matter so much if Ten spoke to the other six, but speaking to Martha could be the key to unravelling this whole mystery.

Jude nodded.

"There's one more thing." Ten wasn't quite so sure that he should tell Jude about this last part, but, in for a penny, in for a pound.

A pained look appeared in Jude's eyes. "What's that?"

"Ronan's started having nightmares. Only I don't think they're nightmares." Ten sighed.

Jude leaned forward. He was wearing his game face now. No one fucked with Ronan when he was around. "What do you think they are if they aren't nightmares?"

This was the kind of reaction he was hoping to get from the mouthy P.I. He'd be more likely to help if Ronan were directly impacted here. "I think they're past lives resurfacing."

"Resurfacing? Why do you think that?" Jude looked like he wanted to help in any way he could now.

"In the first one Ronan had to accuse me of being a witch to save himself and I was burned at the stake in Salem."

Jude shook his head. "Witches weren't burned in Salem."

It was interesting that Jude knew that. He'd file that piece of information away for later as well. "Then in the second dream, it all happened again, but during the time of the Spanish Inquisition. In that life he had to accuse me of being gay."

"Yeah, the church didn't want to burn witches, but it was okay to torch the gays." Jude rolled his eyes. "You think this thing with the Salem Witches is directly connected to Ronan's dreams?"

Ten nodded. "He had the first dream early Sunday morning and then the witches showed up at our house on Sunday afternoon. Doesn't seem like a coincidence to me. I wondered at first if it had to do with what happened out at the Witch Hill House since Preacher Gideon Black was in both dreams."

Jude sank his chin into the cup of his hand and stared out the window for a minute. "Did you research that?"

It had been so long since Jude said anything that Ten figured their conversation about the witches and Ronan's dreams was over. "Research what?"

"If there was a priest named Black during the Inquisition?" Jude's eyes darkened.

It took a minute for Jude's words to sink in. If Ronan had been experiencing past lives, it was possible Gideon Black was too. "Do you think they've been battling each other through the ages? A witch hunter and a defender of the innocent?" Ten couldn't believe those words were coming out of his mouth.

"I don't know, but maybe you need to find out." Jude turned back from the window to make eye contact with Ten.

"I thought there was a reason these dreams were surfacing now and maybe Black is the reason."

"Is there a way to find out for certain?" Jude seemed to be all in now.

Ten frowned. "Yeah, there's a way."

Jude laughed. "It looks uncomfortable for you. Good! I like that."

Ten snorted and rolled his eyes. He guessed he had that coming. "The best past life regressionist that I know of in Salem is Madam Aurora."

"Ah, your old arch-nemesis. Ronan told me all about her on the cruise and how she was the one who was responsible for helping to bring your gift back." Jude chuckled.

Tennyson guessed Jude deserved a laugh or two at his expense. "Why don't you stop by for dinner tonight? I need to tell Ronan that the best thing to do is schedule a session with Madam Aurora and he might react better to that if you're sitting at the table."

"Have you met your husband? If anything, having me there is likely to make him act worse. If you make that pasta thing with the meat and the sauce and your fresh bread, I might be talked into coming. You'll have a better chance of getting me there if Carson and Truman come too." With that, Jude grabbed another spring roll and ate half of it one large bite.

Jude wasn't fooling Tennyson. He knew the reason he wanted Carson and Truman to come to dinner wasn't for their company, but was to see their three toddlers. Ten would never say the words out loud, but Jude was coming along nicely.

15

Ronan

Ten's talk with Jude must have gone better than either of them had anticipated it would go. Around 2pm that afternoon, Ten had texted Ronan to let him know that Jude would be joining them for dinner. Unless of course Ten had chickened out and hadn't spoken to Jude at all about the situation with the witches and the psychic block none of them could get past.

Pulling his Mustang into the empty parking spot in front of his house, Ronan could see Jude's classic Thunderbird was parked two spots up, closer to Carson and Truman's house. He supposed the only way to find out what was going on with Tennyson and Jude was to get out of the car and face the music.

"Ten? I'm home!" Ronan bellowed as he keyed the alarm code.

"In the kitchen!" Tennyson called back.

"I'm in the living room, in case you were wondering!" Jude yelled. "With the love of my life."

Ah, well that explained why Dixie hadn't come running to meet him at the door. Ronan saw the two of them snuggled up on the living room sofa. Jude looked like he'd just woken up from a nap. "Full disclosure, the witches sat on that couch. You've got their scent all over you now." Ronan offered Jude a wicked grin before turning to his dog. "Hello to you too, traitor princess." Turning his nose up, he marched into the kitchen.

"Something smells good." Ronan pressed a kiss to the back of Ten's neck. His husband was stirring a pot of Bolognese sauce. He could see a loaf of Ten's famous freshly baked rosemary bread was sitting on the counter.

"Jude and I had a nice lunch. He came shopping with me and helped me make the bread. Then he napped while it rose and I made the sauce." Ten turned around to kiss his husband.

"Witch City Medium, miracle worker." Ronan rolled his eyes. "Did you cure cancer or ALS too while you were at it?"

"Ronan's just jealous that we had such a nice day together, while he was stuck with Fitzgibbon and his perpetual shitty mood." Jude was still cuddling Dixie who was licking the side of his face, when he walked into the kitchen.

"You know her tongue is her toilet paper, right?" Ronan snickered at the horrified look on Jude's face.

Jude set the tiny dog down and moved to the kitchen sink to scrub his left cheek.

"Hello, Dixie, my little pixie!" Ronan cooed, scooping the dog up. "Daddy's little girl needs a bath. You smell like Uncle Jude."

Dixie picked up where she'd left off with Jude, licking Ronan's face.

"I thought you said her tongue was her toilet paper." Jude raised an eyebrow.

"It is! But she scraped off all of her ass bits onto your face. Isn't that right, princess?" Ronan turned back to the dog.

"It's like living with toddlers." Ten rolled his eyes.

"Speaking of toddlers, where are Carson and Truman's little ones? I've only seen the little monkeys walk on video."

"They'll be here soon. It's always a procedure packing them up to go anywhere, even if it's just three doors down."

"Why are they coming to dinner?" Ronan realized he sounded suspicious, but why was everyone coming over to hear what happened at lunch with Jude?

"It's just easier telling everyone at once." Ten rolled his eyes and grabbed plates out of the cabinet. He held them out to Ronan.

"I'm sorry, Dixie. This is where our love story ends." Ronan set the dog back on the floor. With a frown, he took the plates and started passing them out around the table.

"We're here!" Carson called from the living room.

"WO!" Three tiny voices shouted.

"In here, Cerberus!" Ronan called back. He finished setting the plates on the table and got down on his knees to wait for the babies to find him.

"Cerberus?" Jude snorted. "Do I even want to know why you call them *that*?"

"Cerberus was the three-headed dog that protected the Greek underworld so the dead couldn't leave again. Watch. Learn." Ronan winked at Jude before turning his attention back to the kitchen doorway.

Tiny footsteps pounded the hardwood floor, sounding like a miniature army on the march. "Wo?"

"Kitchen!" Ronan laughed.

Three little humans charged into the room, running on their tiptoes. They all looked like they were on the verge of losing their balance and falling over. "WO!"

The babies slow-motion tackled Ronan. He grabbed all three of them, taking all of the laughing babies down to the floor with him. Dixie pranced around the pig-pile before climbing on top to become queen of the mountain.

"Okay, even I have to admit that's the cutest damn thing I've ever seen." Jude sounded shocked at his own admission.

"I'm glad to see our spawn have grown on you, Uncle Jude!" Truman grinned. "Attack, minions, attack!"

"Wait! What?" Jude watched in growing mock-horror as the babies piled off Ronan and swarmed to him. "Oh no!" Jude howled. "They got me!" He melted to the floor, yelling for help, while the babies screeched in joy.

"Well, that's interesting," Carson gloated.

"It isn't the most interesting news of the day, either." Ten shrugged, moving toward the stove. "Ronan, do you think you and Jude can wrangle the little terrors into their seats so we can get dinner on the table?"

"Help!" Jude cried. "I'm drowning in drool and something else warm I'm not sure I want identified!"

"Oh, I'm sure it's pee!" Truman chirped, plucking baby Bertha off the pile and carrying her toward the living room.

Jude sat up and examined the dark stain on his pants. "Eww, seriously, Bertha?"

The baby waved to Jude over her father's shoulder.

Jude tilted his head to the side and waved back. "Aww, that was too cute."

"See, that's how they get you." Ronan reached for Brian, who had grabbed a hold of Jude's ears. "They follow up something gross with something cute so that you forget your wearing their bodily fluids as accessories."

"Ewww, damn! Now it's cold!" Jude scooped up a now laughing Stephanie. "What's so funny?"

"Oooo!" Stephanie said.

Jude looked up at Carson. "What does that mean?"

"Juuuuuuude!" Carson translated.

The look on Jude's face softened. He held the baby closer and turned away so Ronan couldn't see his face. Ronan knew it was so that no one could see the emotion in his golden eyes.

Twenty minutes later, everyone was settled around the table and the babies were covered in tomato sauce.

"Ronan, what happened when you told Kevin that Greeley wants to be a police officer?" Truman asked. He was cutting up pieces of Tennyson's buttered rosemary bread for the babies.

"I wish I could have been a fly on the wall for that conversation." Jude chuckled.

"I thought he was going to blow a gasket, but he didn't. He was just thrilled that Greeley wasn't back on drugs or having boy trouble." Ronan shook his head as if he were still having a hard time believing that Fitzgibbon had been so calm about this turn of events.

"*That* was his reaction?" Truman's eyes narrowed.

"You saw how he was acting, Tru." Ronan reached for the freshly grated Parmesan. "He was sullen and withdrawn. Kevin's first thought was drugs, then a relationship gone sour. All he wants is for the kid to be happy."

"Yeah but now there's gonna be bullets flying at another one of us." Carson shook his head.

"Are you seeing anything about that?" Ronan was almost afraid to hear the answer.

"No." Carson shook his head. "I see other things, but not that, but remember…"

"The future is fluid," Ronan chimed in. "What other things do you see for him?"

Carson held a hand up. "I'm not saying a word. The last time one of us opened our big mouths about something to come it ended up in a ditch so deep that it might be unrecoverable. No thanks. For once, I'm shutting up. Nope, not saying one more word about Greeley and what's going to happen at the police academy."

"For someone who's shutting up, you're sure saying a lot, *wife*!" Truman grinned.

Carson raised an eyebrow in challenge. "Keep it up and maybe we'll leave the new *thing* that came in today's mail in the box, *husband*."

"What new thing?" Ronan asked.

Tennyson burst out laughing. "Were the batteries included?"

"Shoot, were they?" Truman asked.

"Another satisfied Pure Passion customer." Jude waggled his eyebrows.

"As fascinating as this conversation has become," Ronan rolled his eyes. He really didn't need or want to know that his best friends were about to be satisfied mail-order dildo customers. "I want to know what happened with you and Jude. Obviously, he didn't react too badly to you asking about his ability to block you all from being able to read him or he wouldn't be here willingly."

"Willingly?" Jude asked.

"Yeah, I was afraid we'd need to have this conversation with you tied to a chair and possibly gagged." Ronan chuckled. "I was actually looking forward to that."

Jude leaned forward in his seat. His golden eyes glittered with the challenge. "You and what army?"

"Guess you don't need to find out since you came willingly. We'll save my ninja tactics for the next time you won't bend to our will." Ronan bounced his eyebrows before turning to his husband. "What happened at lunch?"

"You mean after Jude starred in a video for the remake of *It's Raining Men*?" Ten rolled his eyes.

"Jealous?" Jude crowed.

"Christ, no! I have a hard-enough time handling one man. What the hell would I do with five?" Tennyson looked like he was actually trying to puzzle the answer out.

"Ten? What happened at lunch? We can discuss the logistics of a six-way later." Ronan wasn't sure himself how the hell that would work, not that he wanted his husband to be the meat in that man sandwich.

Ten's eyes went glassy for a minute before snapping back into focus. "I told Jude what was going on with the witches and how none us could reach the ones who'd died. Then I mentioned how the psychic block reminded us of what we all felt when we tried to read him."

All eyes at the table swung to the P.I. who was making funny faces at the babies.

"And did Jude agree to help us unlock this thing?" Carson asked.

Tennyson shook his head. "Not exactly."

Ronan felt his temper start to heat up. He watched Jude reach for the bowl of pasta and heap a second helping on his plate. If Jude hadn't agreed to help the witches or Tennyson by revealing the secret to why he couldn't be read, why the hell was he sitting at their dinner table enjoying their food?

"I can feel your heated stare boring into the back of my skull, Ronan." Jude turned to look at him.

"I'm just wondering what kind of agreement you and my husband came to." He tried to hold on to his temper. Ronan might love Jude like a brother, but if he refused to help these women simply because they practiced Wicca and called themselves witches, then things were going to get ugly, fast.

Jude stared at Ronan in silence. He seemed to be carefully measuring his words. "After my father was murdered, there was a spell woven over me. A protection charm. That's really all I know about it. It keeps me safe from witches and from psychic attacks."

The table was silent. Even the babies had stopped babbling and slapping their hands on the trays of their high chairs.

"I don't understand." Tennyson's voice was barely above a whisper.

"I was all my grandfather had left after my father was murdered and this was his way of protecting me." Jude looked up to meet Ronan's eyes. "I called him after lunch, but he hasn't gotten back to me yet. I wouldn't hold your breath, Ronan. He won't be eager to talk about that time in our lives. He's already lost his only son, he's not going to be willing to put his only grandson at risk too. This thing has kept me safe for a long time now and I don't know that…" Jude trailed off, looking surprised that he'd said as much as he had.

Ronan was as shocked as Jude looked. He wasn't expecting that much background information to come spilling out of Jude either.

"I don't mean to pry, Jude, but what kind of protection spell?" Ten asked.

"Navajo," Jude said simply, reaching for his fork. Without another word, he dug in to his pasta.

Ronan exchanged a silent look with Tennyson. It had been a Navajo word that Jude had used to get the witch spirits trying to harm Niall Gallagher out at the Witch Hill House to release him. Things with Jude were getting curiouser by the second. Unfortunately, they were no closer now to helping the Salem Witches than they were before.

16

There was one bit of news Tennyson hadn't shared with his husband and their friends over dinner. He'd sworn Jude to secrecy over the little bit he'd dished over lunch, but Ten had saved the real meat of his news for Ronan.

Ten had sent him off to have a nice shower alone, hoping the hot water would relax him. Ten's excuse for not joining him was that his kundalini needed realigning. Ronan still fell for that line, which was really just Ten's excuse for needing a few minutes for himself.

"Ready or not, here I come!" Ronan walked out of the bathroom still damp from his shower. His skin glistened with the low lights of the bedroom. His hair was still wet and looked darker than its usual shade of dirty blond. Without it styled as usual, Ronan looked much younger, almost boyish, until Ten's eyes moved down his bare chest, to the three puckered bullet scars clustered together. Ronan posed in the doorway with a hand on his hip. "What do you think?"

"About what?" Ten knew damn well about what. Ronan's ego was the size of Texas, there was no way he was going to pump it up without offering a little bit of resistance first.

"The Red Sox pitching rotation!" Ronan rolled his eyes and threw his hands down toward his hips. "Me!"

"Oh," Ten shrugged. "I've seen that before."

"Seen *that* before?" Ronan sounded outraged. "Well, I never!" He was sputtering now. "Maybe I'll just go sleep in the spare room with Dixie!"

"You hate that mattress, drama queen. It hurts your back remember? And your little *precious* snores, which is why *she* sleeps in the spare room! Why don't you have a seat? There's something I need to talk to you about." Ten patted the empty spot on the bed next to him.

"Well this doesn't sound good. My husband thinks I'm a terrifying troll and now he wants to *talk*." Ronan made air quotes over the word talk. He threw himself on the bed like a petulant child. "What? Do you want a divorce or something? Maybe you have a mask for me to wear in public since I'm clearly too ugly to live."

"You could win an Oscar for this performance. Sheesh." Ten patted Ronan's arm patronizingly. "I wanted to talk to you about your dreams and then get me some, but if you'd rather pout for the rest of the night, I can go jerk off in the bathroom and go to bed."

"So, I'm *not* too ugly to live or to get *me* some?" Ronan asked, sounding hopeful.

Ten raised an eyebrow. "If Michelangelo were alive today, he would have chosen you as his model for David. Happy? Can we talk now?" Ten was starting to think he should have just brought Ronan to Madam Aurora instead of trying to talk to him like this. He was sure there would have been pushback, but nothing on this scale. Ronan tended to behave in public and saved the dinner theater performances for at home.

"Now that you've stroked my ego and given me your word that you'll stroke my dick next, yes! You may continue." Ronan's smile was back in full force.

"Oh, brother." If Ten kept rolling his eyes like this he was afraid they were going to stick. "I didn't want to talk about this in front of Truman and Carson just in case you didn't want them to know what was going on with your nightmares."

"Okay, you have my undivided attention now." Ronan reached out to link hands with Tennyson. "Did you learn something new about what's going on with me?"

"Not new exactly." Ten shrugged. "Since lunch with Jude was going so well, I mentioned to him what was going on with you."

"Wait! You didn't think I'd want Truman, my *actual* best friend, to know what was going on, but you told Jude? I hate that asshole!" Ronan grumped.

"Be quiet and listen." Ten was reaching the end of his patience with Ronan and his attitude toward the P.I. "You and Jude are cut from the same cloth. You're practically the same person. He cares about you in his own quiet way and you feel the same about him. He saved your life at the Hutchins' house, Ronan. He carries the scars from that day. He gave me my husband back and I swear to God if you say one more time that you hate him, I'm divorcing you! Are we understood?"

Ronan sulked. "Fine, understood. Can I still call him an asshole?"

"No!" Ten shot back with no real heat in his voice. "Well, maybe on special occasions, hmm?"

"Fine." Ronan took his hand back from Ten. "This little chat helped me figure something out though."

"Oh, and what's that?" Ten couldn't wait to hear this one. He loved it when Ronan got riled up over absolutely nothing.

"You're going to be the mean parent. You can use that voice when little miss throws a tantrum or misbehaves. Then I'll be the good parent who swoops in and wipes away her tiny tears and sneaks her candy on the down low."

"Yes, Ronan. I'll be bad cop. You be good cop. We'll switch it up from when we're at work." Ten shot him a glare.

"Ohh! Those tiny claws prick, Ten!" Ronan hissed in mock outrage.

Tennyson burst out laughing. "You are such a ridiculous child sometimes."

"Admit it though, you love me." Ronan looked like an eager puppy.

"God, help me. I do." Ten brushed a gentle kiss against Ronan's hot lips. "Now, can we talk about what happened today or do you want to continue this verbal skirmish."

"I don't know." Ronan folded his arms over his chest. "I'm kind of enjoying skirmishing with you, although it would be a lot more enjoyable if we were dueling with our *swords* instead of our words."

Ten's dark eyes skimmed down Ronan's half naked body. There was a large bulge where moments before there hadn't been one. There would be time to deal with *that* later. For right now, Ten needed to tell Ronan about Madam Aurora. "Jude and I both think you need to have a past life regression to get to the bottom of your nightmares."

"Adios, boner!" Ronan said to the bulge in his briefs. "It was nice stroking you." Ronan shook his head and turned back to Tennyson. "Why is Jude involved in this? You just said you didn't bring this up in front of Tru and Carson because you didn't know if I wanted this kept secret, but it's okay if Jude knows?"

Ronan had a point. "Jude took a bullet for you. Two of them in fact. I think that means we can trust him to have your best interests at heart. Besides, we both know he has a heightened intuition. He knew there was something up with you. Aren't you the least bit curious about what he had to say?"

"Now that my dick is wilted like week-old lettuce, yes, I'm interested. It's not like I've got anything better to do." Ronan sighed heavily.

Ten patted his shoulder. "Since I've only been interested in you and your well-being in all of this, I didn't stop to consider anything else in these dreams. Jude agreed that the dreams were past lives trying to resurface but he offered a reason as to why now."

Ronan's mood sobered. Gone was the pouty look on his face. "Jude thinks he knows why these past lives chose now to come back and haunt me?"

"Yes. We both assumed it had something to do with the situation with the Salem Witches coming to you for help. Jude agreed with that, but took it a step further."

"A step further? I don't understand." Ronan's confusion was written, clear as day, on his face.

"What were the common elements of those dreams?" Ten hated walking Ronan back through the trauma of those dreams, but this was the only way to get to the bottom of things.

"You and me," Ronan answered quickly. "Me betraying you. You being burned at the stake. Twice. Shit, Ten, I'm the Judas Iscariot of this little plot."

Ten reached out to take both of Ronan's hands in his own. "Let's not lose focus here, okay? What else was a common factor in both dreams?" Ten was trying to steer Ronan away from remembering how he'd met his own fate in his past lives.

Ronan's brow knit together in obvious concentration. "Oh. Gideon Black. He was in both dreams. Jude thinks this is about *him*?" Ronan shook his head as if he couldn't believe the words that were coming out of his mouth.

"You both seem to be moving through time together." Ten left his thought there, wanting to see if Ronan could take it the rest of the way.

"What? Like we're battling each other? Like good versus evil?"

"I'm not sure. That's why we need to get more information, to help you put the pieces back to together in the right order."

"What do you mean in the right order?" Ronan looked more confused now that ever.

"Keep one thing in mind, Ronan. You were only seeing a piece of those lives. A snapshot."

"What do you mean?" Ronan rubbed a hand over his face.

"If you only watch the end of *Titanic* you miss the love story, right? You'd just think the entire movie was a tragedy."

"I'll never let go, Ten!" Ronan grinned cheekily.

Ten slapped his shoulder. "You're missing my point."

"No, I got your point. I was only seeing a tiny bit of this past life. Probably the most important part. The part my subconscious needed me to see the most. Aside from having to watch you die twice, which I refuse to believe is the point of these memories resurfacing, I have to think Gideon Black is what my mind needs mc to see."

"That's what Jude thought too. He suggested that we research his family tree. We know Gideon was in Salem during the Witch Trials because Mariah Goode told us he was. I'm sure we'll find his name in the public record, but Jude thinks we're going to find an antecedent of Gideon involved in the Inquisition too."

The look on Ronan's face darkened. "He thinks we're chasing each other through time, doesn't he?"

"Something like that, but there's only one way to know for sure."

"What is that? Ambien? Or something over the counter so I'll sleep longer and dream more?" Ronan cringed.

"No, I think you need to see someone who's trained in past life regression." Ten held his breath. He wasn't sure how Ronan was going to react to the idea of this suggestion.

"What, you mean a shrink? No fucking thank you! I had enough of that touchy-feely shit in rehab, thanks."

"Not a shrink. A trained psychic who knows how to hypnotize and relax you enough so that these memories will come to the surface without you being asleep and with you having the ability to drive."

"What do you mean, drive?" Ronan's voice still had a suspicious tone to it.

"In a dream you only get to see what your mind is showing you. In a directed hypnotism, you can be asked to see what we need you to see."

"You mean my interaction with Gideon Black?"

Ten nodded. "We have the best past life specialist in the country here in Salem."

"Thank, Christ. I'll be fine with anyone else then. Who is it?" Ronan's spirits actually lifted a bit.

"Madam Aurora."

"Ah, shit! I spoke too soon." Ronan's chin rested against his bare chest. Obviously, he still hadn't forgiven the psychic for denying Tennyson a job when he came to Salem fresh off the bus from Union Chapel, Kansas twelve years ago.

"It will be okay, Ronan. I trust Aurora to help you." It was true. Ten did trust her.

Ronan nodded. "Since you died in the two lives I've seen snapshots of, it means Gideon's beaten me." Ronan's blue eyes snapped up to meet Tennyson's dark ones. "Jesus, Ten, do you think he's here now? Back in Salem again?" Fear burned in his eyes.

"I don't know, babe." Ten pulled Ronan into his arms. The problem was, Ten was afraid he did know.

17

Ronan

While Tennyson had very clearly stated last night that Madam Aurora was the best past life resurrectionist, or whatever the fuck she was, in the country, what he'd failed to mention was that he'd made Ronan an appointment with her for *this* morning.

Ten claimed that what with all the licking, sucking, and fucking that had followed their very serious discussion, it had slipped his clever mind. Ronan had thrown the bullshit flag on that one. Not that he hadn't been completely satisfied by all of the said licking, sucking and fucking, but Jesus Christ, warn a guy when you were bringing him to a place like this.

The "place like this" was Madam Aurora's shop on Essex Street in downtown Salem. It was a trendy boutique in the front of the shop, offering clothes, shoes, and accessories for the modern witch on the go. The second section of the store was where things got more serious, offering tools of the trade, at least that's how Ronan would describe it.

There were actual cauldrons, essential oils, spell candles, roots, poppets, crystals, and so much more that Ronan's head was literally spinning with everything the store had to offer. Ten had to drag him to the back of the shop where Aurora held her private readings.

Madam Aurora's reading room wasn't all that different from the ones at West Side Magick. There was a table and four chairs for her psychic readings. Sitting in front of the seat at the head of the table was the largest crystal ball Ronan had ever seen. It looked to be nearly the size of a volleyball. Bertha's globe, which Carson kept in her reading room, was about the size of a softball. Ronan itched to touch this one, but was afraid that one of his past lives would surge to the front of his consciousness, showing him something he wasn't prepared to see.

"It won't bite you, Ronan. Touch it and see what happens," Madam Aurora urged from her seat in front of the clear ball.

Ronan looked back at Tennyson and after a quick nod from his husband, reached out to touch the crystal ball. It was smooth and cool to the touch. He felt his eyes slipping shut and decided to just go with the flow, which was a completely new experience for him. In his mind's eye, he saw a picture of himself and Tennyson smiling down into a white crib. A tiny infant swaddled in a pink blanket lay sleeping on her back. One tiny fist was clutched to her cheek. Feeling a rogue tear slipping down his face, he pulled his hand back from the warming ball.

"See, it didn't bite." Aurora smiled knowingly at him.

"Did you send me that image of our daughter so I'd forgive you?" Ronan swiped at the tear.

"I don't control what people see in the crystal's depths, Ronan." Aurora turned her attention to Tennyson. "We both know you've already forgiven me for my foolishness where your husband is concerned. You just like to play the role of badass in front of him."

Ronan snorted. Maybe Aurora had a small point. She'd been the one who'd given Tennyson his gift back after he'd locked himself out of being able to access it last year. He'd always be eternally grateful for everything she'd done for Ten. He did tend to be a world-class grudge-holder, on the outside anyway. "Fine, you're forgiven."

Ten rolled his eyes. "You've been making me feel bad about bringing you here for two hours when you'd forgiven her already?"

"I was making you feel bad for bringing me here with almost no advanced warning." Ronan winked at Aurora.

"How exactly would you have prepared for today if you'd known you were coming, Ronan?" Aurora asked.

Okay, that was a fair question. One that had a really bad answer. "I probably would have gotten mad at Ten and then tossed and turned all night and kept Ten from his sleep too. So, it was probably good that Ten didn't tell me what was going on."

"Why don't we begin so that you don't have any more time to worry about what's going to happen, now, okay?" Aurora took Ronan by the left elbow and guided him to a purple velvet chaise that was against the back wall of the room.

Ronan took a seat and allowed Aurora to settle him back against the plush fabric. She even put a soft throw over him and set about lighting candles and then dimmed the ceiling lights. He watched while Tennyson took a seat at the table and pulled out his camera and tripod. He assumed his husband was going to record what was about to happen. Knowing Ten was going to be in the room with him was going to be a big comfort.

"Are you ready to begin, Ronan?" Aurora asked.

"What do I need to do?" Ronan could feel his nerves starting to crackle.

"Stop trying to control the situation for a start." She raised an elegant brow at him. "You're safe here. We're going to go through a relaxation exercise and then I'm going to take you back to your life during the Witch Trials. Ten said you're interested in seeing the relationship with Gideon Black, so I'll ask you to key in on that."

"What if I see it happen again?" Ronan felt his heart speed up. If he had to watch Tennyson die again, he didn't think his heart could take it. The way his husband screamed when the flames reached him. Then the way he went silent when his body couldn't take the pain any longer.

"We aren't going back to watch that, Ronan. All we're interested in is Black, right. If you end up in that place again, turn around and don't look. Do you understand?"

Ronan nodded. He had a feeling it was like watching a train wreck in that he would be unable to look away.

"You will look away!" Aurora angry-whispered. "This is not meant to make you suffer. I need you to learn as much as you can so you can help save my girls. Now close your eyes so that we can begin."

"Why did they choose me, Aurora?" Ronan whispered back. His eyes locked on to hers.

"I told them you could be trusted, that you fought for people who weren't always strong enough to fight for themselves." Aurora leaned in closer to Ronan. "I never got married, Ronan. I never had children of my own. These witches are my family. You need to do everything in your power to save them. To save us. Starting with this regression. Now stop pouting like a little boy and be the man I know can do the job." Aurora sat back.

Ronan nodded. He could see the fear mixed with determination in her eyes. "I'm ready to get to work."

"Close your eyes and focus on your breathing. Feel everything around you slowing down. Focus only on the sound of my voice."

Doing as Madam Aurora asked, Ronan focused on his breathing. He remembered doing belly-breathing exercises during his time in rehab. He felt his entire body start to relax as Aurora yammered on about feeling his body melt into the sofa as if he were part of it. If he were a more whimsical man he would say the feeling was almost like floating.

"Are you relaxed now, Ronan?" Aurora asked, sounding as if she were under water.

"Yes." His own voice sounded oddly far away. Oh well, no matter. He was enjoying this otherworldly floaty feeling.

"I want you to go back to Salem at the time of the Witch Trials. What can you tell me about your life back then?" Aurora still sounded like she was underwater. Ronan would have to tell her about that later.

He could feel another presence there with him. Another man. A good man. When he opened his eyes, he was looking at himself, only dressed differently. The man carried a crude version of a nightstick. "Who are you?" Ronan whispered.

The doppelgänger smiled. "You know who I am. I am a police officer in Salem Towne. Only we were not called that in my day. You know more about me than you think, Ronan."

"I was a Watchman. Keeping the peace and law and order. I was the one who arrested Tennyson. Only he wasn't Tennyson." Ronan felt his face pull into a frown, as if the words he was saying didn't make sense to himself.

"What was his name?" Aurora asked gently.

"Why can't I remember?" Ronan asked.

"He wasn't yours to love back then. He was mine." The look-alike reached out, setting his fingers against Ronan's left temple."

Ronan jerked, not at the contact, but at the easy flow of information coming into his mind. He smiled when Tennyson's name came to him. It suited him so well. "Wolfgang Grimme. That's spelled with an "E" on the end. I called him Wolf. He called me…" Ronan stopped in his tracks. His eyes slipped shut again.

"What did Wolf call you?" Aurora's voice has softened. It no longer sounded like it was coming from underwater. She sounded closer now, as if she were standing right next to him.

Ronan opened his eyes, but he wasn't looking at Madam Aurora's reading room back in modern-day Salem, Massachusetts. He was standing in front of the cabin he'd walked out of that dark night when Fitzgibbon had knocked on his door.

The structure looked different in the light of day. It was a simple clapboard cabin with two drafty, ill-fitting windows. To the left of it, Ronan could see a tiny vegetable garden and could swear he could hear the lowing of a cow. He must have been doing okay for himself if he owned a home and had a cow.

"Ronan, what did Wolf call you?" Aurora asked again. He turned to his side to see her standing beside him.

"How is this possible? Did you live during this time too?" Ronan could feel his double standing to his other side and wondered if Aurora could see him too.

"I'm not really here Ronan. You brought me along on this journey with you." Aurora set her hand on the crook of his arm.

The reason for her being here made sense, but that didn't make Aurora's presence or her hand on his arm any less real. He didn't want to be back in this strange place alone, especially if he had to witness what happened to Tennyson, Wolf, rather, all over again.

Ronan turned from her, back to his twin, he guessed. "I've seen all of the information you sent me, but I don't know your name. Who are you? Or who was I in this life?"

"I will share all I know, Ronan, but you must have a care. You cannot change anything that occurred during my life, but that does not mean that others cannot see your journey here. Do you understand me?"

Instinctively, Ronan had some idea that this warning had to do with Preacher Gideon Black. He nodded.

"I shall step back and allow you to see my life from my eyes. You will only have to say my name and I shall be there with you." The look-alike smiled and reached for Ronan's hand. When they made contact, he vanished, but Ronan somehow knew everything about him and his life, starting with his name.

 "My name is Samuel Goodman. I'm descended from John Goodman who sailed on the Mayflower."

"Standing here in front of your home isn't really helping us though, is it, Samuel?" Aurora's voice was gentle, but meant to prod him along at the same time.

Nodding sharply, Ronan closed his eyes. He knew instantly where they were. The heat on his face was intense. A feeling of pure evil permeated the very air surrounding him. He knew when he opened his eyes, he would see Tennyson's pyre aflame. Steeling himself against the inevitable, he opened his eyes. Standing to his left was preacher Gideon Black. Out of the corner of his eye, he could see Aurora to his right, but knew no one else there could see her.

Looking around, it was the same scene as it had been in his dream, but for the people standing around him. Gone were his friends who'd shown up in the nightmare to stand in for the good people of Salem Towne come to witness the execution of a witch. He didn't recognize any of the people standing around him, but Samuel did.

Samuel Goodman was ticking off the names and occupations of all of the townspeople inside Ronan's head as his eyes moved from person to person. "John Bradford, town doctor, William Carver, constable, Moses Rogers, dairy farmer," Samuel's voice echoed in his head.

"This is all fascinating history, Samuel, but what is it I need to see? Please don't let it be Wolf dying again. My heart can't take that for a second time."

"Were you reunited with him?" Samuel's voice asked.

Ronan could see Samuel in his mind's eye nibbling on his lower lip the same way he did when he was unsure of the answer he was about to get. He held up his left hand and using his thumb spun the titanium band around the third finger. "Not only were we reunited, I married him."

"Married? I am not going to ask how such a thing is possible. I will rejoice in the fact that Wolf's promise was kept. As for what it is that you need to see here, I am afraid it comes just after… I am sorry, Ronan. For both of us."

Ronan felt a comforting presence surrounding him as Wolf's screams filled the night air. He somehow managed to keep his composure as he stared past the flames. In his mind's eye, he focused on the vision he saw in Madam Aurora's crystal ball of himself and Tennyson watching their little miss sleep peacefully. He wasn't seeing the flames, nor the forest, nor the wretched townspeople, who'd come to see the spectacle. He was looking at his daughter's sleeping face.

"Carver tells me you were reluctant to turn this one over." The putrid stench of Gideon Black washed over Ronan, forcefully pulling him from the vision of his family.

Samuel's voice whispered in Ronan's ear. He merely repeated the words, "Grimme was a good healer. With winter coming on, it will be a shame to be without his skills. Wasn't your sister saved by his herbs last year?"

Black waved a hand in the air. "Any fool with a mortar and pestle could have done the same. There are some who claim you carried feelings for this man that go beyond the bonds of friendship."

"Is that where this witch hunt turns next, Black? To rumor and innuendo?" Ronan felt his blood start to boil. "I've also heard what went on at Mariah Goode's cottage after the sun set. Her child carried eyes that looked like yours. Should you be accused next, *preacher*? Should a scarlet letter accompany *you* to the scaffold?"

Black laughed. It was a dark and malevolent sound. "Do you think talk like that scares me, Goodman? I may be guilty of the sin of fornication, by a least my sin is *natural*." The last word was hissed.

"I don't know what you are talking about." Ronan knew exactly what Black was talking about.

"You may not cast spells and speak with the dead, but burying your *rod* within another man is just as vile. It may not be today, *sinner*, but I will catch you at it, and when I do, you will burn just as your lover did." Evil glee danced in the man's dark eyes.

"You will not win, Black," Ronan said simply.

"Oh no?" The reverend hooked a thumb back at the pyre. "All that remains of your precious Wolf are ashes upon the wind."

Ronan resisted the urge to look at the bonfire. It was bad enough he could smell it. "You think you have defeated Wolf, when in fact all you have done is make him stronger. We will be reunited. Mark my words, Black."

"Yes, you will be reunited. Just as you were in Castile, where it all began. Just as you were in Paris. Just as you were in Tipperary. Just as you were here in Salem. Just as you will be in places to come." Black started to laugh. "Just as I will be reunited with you both again and again until the final battle."

Ronan's own eyes slipped shut. He felt Aurora's hand tighten on his arm. This was the reason the past lives had resurfaced. This was what he'd come back to hear. Castile was the beginning, was it? His blue eyes popped back open. "Let me guess, a raven-haired beauty stole, then broke your heart. This is your way of paying her back. Of paying them all back. Right? One woman defied you, now they all must pay *her* price."

Gideon's eyes darkened. His left hand snaked out to grab Ronan's wrist. "You think you're clever, don't you, *Ronan*?"

Gasping, Ronan tried to pull his arm back, but Gideon's hold tightened. Could a man in a vision of a past life hurt him? Up until a few seconds ago, he wouldn't have thought a man living in 1692 could have recognized a present-day version of himself either. This moment was proving anything was possible.

"Oh yes, I know exactly who you are and where you've come from. I also know what you've done to the others." Gideon's nails dug deeper into Ronan's flesh.

"What others?" Ronan ground out from behind his gritted teeth. "What are you talking about?" He tried again to wrench his wrist away from the crazed preacher.

"Mariah Goode and the other witches. I know what you and your precious Tennyson did to them," Black snarled.

Ronan started to laugh. Oddly enough, none of the other townspeople turned to stare at them. It was as if he and Gideon Black were in their own bubble of suspended animation. "Oh, you mean how we sent their long-suffering spirits into the light at last. It must have really frosted your ass when Grace Goode was reunited with her mother's soul too, huh, Papa?" Ronan yanked his arm again, this time managing to free himself from Black's iron grip.

"That little bitch was not my child. She was the child of the beast!" Black roared.

Ronan could feel Black's sour breath wash across his face. The truth was written in his eyes though. "Mariah was another woman who cast you out, wasn't she, Gideon? There she was, alone in this world, having to sell the most precious thing she had in order to survive and even under those circumstances, the only way she'd allow you to take her was by leaving her coins on the table." Ronan laughed. "Even when it was obvious that Grace was your child, Mariah still wouldn't marry you."

"Shut your vile sodomite mouth!" Black hissed.

"Did you start the witch hysteria here in Salem, Gideon?" Ronan accused. "Did you? Or were the wheels already in motion and you just joined in the fray? A man of God protecting his vulnerable flock against the insidious evil of witchcraft." Ronan shook his head.

Black laughed, baring his sharp teeth. "There is evil in this town, Ronan. Can't you feel it? It's down deep in the roots. It's in the soil. Every so often, more of it bubbles to the surface to infect the next generation."

"You're insane." It wasn't a flip observation, Ronan could see the roots of his insanity sunk deep within his soul. The way he'd spoken of the evil being deep within Salem, Black had been speaking about himself. "You couldn't take the rejection of a woman, so, you used the only weapon left in your arsenal and you accused her of witchcraft. You let Mariah rot in prison for months in order to get her to bend to your will and when she wouldn't, you used her child, *your* child, against her. That sweet, precious baby that the two of you created together, you used as a weapon and when Mariah did as you asked, you killed her anyway." Ronan could feel his emotions rising to the surface, but he'd be damned if he let Black see them overtake him.

"I gave her one last chance!" Black bellowed. "That morning, I went to see Mariah in the jail. I begged her to marry me. I had her confession all planned out. What she'd say. The way she would beg for my forgiveness. How I would preach against the sins of witchcraft and fornication. How I would use her as an example. How Mariah's confession and repentance would bring the Witch Trials to a close. She said no. NO!" Black screamed.

Ronan could see how truly crazy Black was in this moment. It also occurred to him that these memories were still fresh to him. Mariah Goode would have only died within a few months of this moment. "Why Grace?" Ronan's voice was barely above a whisper. He wasn't even sure Gideon had heard the question, until the preacher's emotions calmed. The fire and fury drained from his countenance.

A malignant smile curled his lips. "I wanted the bitch's last moments on God's earth to be filled with as much pain as I was feeling in that moment."

Nodding, Ronan took in the words of the man of God. "You're still feeling that pain now. According to Mariah, she died moments after Grace."

"It took three hundred and twenty-six years for them to be reunited though, didn't it? I'm looking forward to witnessing every second of those years to come." Gideon laughed. "I believe I won that little skirmish. Didn't I?"

Feeling sick to his stomach, Ronan turned to Aurora, who was looking a bit green herself. "How the hell do I get out of here? Click my heels three times?"

Gideon Black laughed. "I'll see you soon, Ronan. You too, bitch." He locked eyes with Aurora. "Unless of course you meet with a tragic accident before my arrival." Black made air quotes over "tragic accident." He laughed again, the sound of it turning Ronan's insides. "You tell Tennyson, I've got my torch waiting for him."

"Over my dead fucking body! You won't touch one hair on his head." Cold fury lit in the pit of Ronan's stomach. Black wouldn't touch Tennyson if it was the last thing he did.

"That's fine with me. You'll burn just as well. This time he can stand by helplessly and watch *you* die!" Black started to laugh again.

Ronan's vision started to fade out at the sides. He was afraid he was going to pass out and get stuck in seventeenth century Salem and not be able to get home in time to warn Tennyson about Black.

"Ronan?" Tennyson was shaking his shoulders.

"Ten?" Ronan rasped. His throat felt parched, like he'd been wandering in the desert. He tried to sit up but found he didn't have the strength.

"Just rest for a minute. I'll be right back." Ten got up from the side of the chaise.

Ronan reached for him, only catching the hem of his shirt before his husband slipped through his grasp. He could only hope that wasn't a precursor of what was to come.

18

Tennyson

It had been hell on earth listening to Ronan face off again Black in 1692. Thankfully, he'd had the forethought to bring their camera and mount it on the tripod, because there was no way he would have been able to hold it steady enough to film what he'd witnessed.

Ten had been able to hear all of Ronan's words as clear as day, but try as he might, he'd been unable to hear or see what had gone on with Ronan and Gideon Black.

Last August when Ronan had been shot and was in a medically induced coma, Tennyson had somehow been able to join Ronan in that netherworld state of consciousness. While Ronan had been regressed into his past life, Ten had been trying that same technique to join Ronan in the seventeenth century. For whatever reason though, it hadn't worked for him, while it had for Madam Aurora.

While Ronan had been under hypnosis, he'd noticed Aurora hadn't seemed as solid as she should have been. He knew he sounded crazy for even thinking it, but he'd known Aurora was somehow with Ronan on his journey. A touch of jealousy had singed his frayed emotions, but at least Ronan wasn't alone or defenseless against Black.

Fumbling through his bag, Ten grabbed a bottle of room temperature apple juice and a box of animal crackers. They were Laurel's favorite and he'd caught her feeding them to Ronan a time or two. His husband would often finish off the box when the toddler wasn't looking or had finally fallen asleep. "Okay, here you go." Ten twisted the cap off the juice and handed the bottle to Ronan

Ronan downed the juice in one pull while Tennyson wrestled with the plastic bag holding the crackers.

"I'll get you some more. How are you feeling?" Ten didn't want to take his eyes off Ronan. His husband looked like death warmed over. While he'd been under, he'd sweat like he'd been running a marathon, now, he had dark circles under his eyes and looked like he could sleep for a week.

Ten had done some research about past life regressions before Ronan's session with Madam Aurora and he'd read that people, on the whole, had found these sessions cathartic. Most used them as a means of working through some kind of life issue, like trust or trauma. If Ten had to make a guess, he'd say that thanks to what he'd witnessed, Ronan had a whole heap of additional trauma added to what he was already dealing with.

"Like ten gallons of shit in a five gallon pail," Ronan muttered, his mouth stuffed full of animal crackers.

When Ten turned around, he could see what he thought was an elephant dangling out of Ronan's mouth. He grabbed another bottle of juice and a second box of crackers, just in case and set them down next to his husband.

"Aurora, what the hell happened?" Ronan's tired eyes were popped wide open. "How did Black know it was me?"

"Know it was you?" Ten asked. His stomach flopped around like a fish on a dock. "He recognized you as Ronan and *not* Samuel?"

Aurora nodded. "Tell Tennyson what happened to you and then I'll explain what I think occurred." Her look was grim.

Ronan drew a shaky breath. He reached out for Ten's hand.

Ten grabbed on with both of his. Ronan's skin was on fire. He was sure that if he took Ronan's temperature the thermometer would say he had a fever. He'd read that sometimes regression patients ran warm, but this was something else. Ronan felt like he was burning up.

"I was relaxing and breathing, just like Aurora said and when I opened my eyes, I was standing in front of the cabin that I saw in my nightmare of Salem."

"The house you were living in when Fitzgibbon came to take you to my trial?" Ten asked gently.

"Yeah." Ronan nodded. "But, I wasn't there alone. Samuel Goodman was there too."

Ten found a smile. "How is that possible? You *are* Samuel Goodman."

"He was there, Ten. He told me all about Wolf. All about you." Unshed tears glittered in Ronan's eyes. "I could see the love he had for you reflecting back at me. He asked if we'd been reunited like you'd promised we would be. I told him that not only were we reunited but that we were also married…" Ronan ducked his head. He took a deep breath, obviously trying to get himself back under some semblance of control. "You should have seen the look in his eyes. It was triumphant. Like he'd won too."

"We did win, Ronan. Love always wins." Ten felt his own emotions starting to wobble out of control.

"Maybe not." Ronan shook his head. "Aurora interrupted and said that being at the cabin wasn't helping us get to the bottom of my nightmares. Samuel jumped me back to the night you died. It was still going on. I could hear you screaming." Ronan gripped Ten's hands tighter. "Other townspeople were standing around watching you burn. Black came up to Samuel and started giving him shit about how reluctant he was to turn you over and how the preacher knew the reason why."

"Ah, he accused Samuel of being a pillow biter." Ten rolled his eyes.

Ronan grinned. "Not in those exact words. I turned it around on him and threw Mariah Goode in his face. He didn't like that very much. Turns out he was in love with her, as his own past life was with another woman back in Castile."

"Castile?" Ten shook his head. "Wait a minute. Black was aware of his past lives too?" That shouldn't have been possible. It also shouldn't have been possible for Ronan to have been able to hold a conversation with his "past self" or for Aurora to be able to join him in this past life, but all of those things had happened.

"Samuel had warned me that others could see me during this trip back to the past. This must have been what he meant. All of a sudden when I was talking about Mariah, Black knew who I was. He knew I was Ronan and not Samuel." Ronan took another shaky breath. "Ten, he knew about other lives. Black mentioned Paris and Tipperary in Ireland. I never even visited those lives. He said there were other lives to come after Salem. He knew your name in *this* life."

It made sense to Tennyson from the standpoint of time that there would have been other lives they'd lived together from the time of the Spanish Inquisition, which began in 1478 until the Salem Witch Trials in 1692. "What else did he say, Ronan. I could sense the fear in you. It's still coming off of you now."

"He said there's a final battle to come. He admitted he was the driving force behind the deaths of the Salem Witches and he said he's coming for us. *Both* of us." Ronan shivered, despite the heat radiating off of him. "You too, Aurora," Ronan added.

"Yes," she muttered. "I heard that quite clearly."

Fear, unlike anything Tennyson had ever known in his life soaked into his bones. "Explain what happened to him, Aurora."

"It's like Ronan said. He met Samuel Goodman as if Samuel were a separate person. I could see them speaking to each other as if they were twins. They were dead ringers for each other but for the clothes they were wearing. Samuel told Ronan all about himself and then sort of merged into Ronan."

"What, like a possession?" Ten had an instant flashback to Rod Jacobson and all of the havoc that man and his evil spirt had wreaked upon all of their lives.

"No. I wouldn't say that." Aurora shook her head. "It was more like a merging of consciousness, if I had to pick a way to describe it. What happened with Gideon though was different."

That's what Tennyson was afraid of. "What do you mean different?"

"We were dealing with Gideon Black in his own time. He had a knowledge of his prior lives that Samuel and Ronan didn't have. Ronan knew about his life in the time of the Inquisition because of his nightmare, but had no knowledge beyond what he saw in the dream. Black had full command of all of his lives, it seemed. Then there was the moment when Black knew it was Ronan speaking to him and not Samuel Goodman."

"He's omniscient too?" Tennyson asked.

"What's that?" Ronan looked back and forth between Aurora and Tennyson.

Tennyson squeezed Ronan's hand. "It means you're all-knowing and all-seeing, like God, but in this case, Gideon Black has this ability in connection with his own lives, while you only know what's going on with your present life, and even that has its limits."

"Limits?" Ronan frowned. "What do you mean?"

"Do you remember taking your first steps? Or your first day of school? Do you remember every minute of your time with Tennyson?" Aurora asked gently.

"No, I don't." Ronan looked up at Tennyson. "I wish I did, babe."

Tennyson understood where he was coming from. Their time together was so finite. One day it would end. They'd come close to it ending twice already and Ronan was lamenting the fact that he didn't remember every single second.

"Be sappy on your own time, boys. Not only is Gideon omniscient when it comes to his past, it seems he has the same powers with his future. He didn't give any details away, cagey bastard, but he knows about the lives you all have led after Salem and that the final showdown is coming."

"It shouldn't be a problem then." Ronan grinned at Tennyson. "I know what the S.O.B. looks like. All I need to do is find him and stop him. Piece of cake."

"Not so fast there, Ronan." Madam Aurora held a hand up. "It was pure coincidence that you and Samuel were dead ringers. Just because you and one of your past life ancestors looked alike doesn't mean that Black and his present-day incarnation will too."

"Seriously, Aurora?" Ronan tried to stand up, but his legs refused to hold him. He landed hard on his ass back on the chaise. "I figured it would be a matter of doing an online search of Salem residents and looking for his picture. Or, barring that, getting our sketch artist to do a mug shot of Black based on my description, but you're saying that's out now?"

Aurora nodded. "Yes. So, as a plan B, you're going to need to figure out a way to lure this bastard out of hiding and into the open."

Tennyson shivered. He had a feeling the only way to do that was with human bait. Himself.

19

Ronan

Ronan was sitting on the back deck looking out over the yard when Dixie started to bark. It wasn't like the dog to yip at Tennyson, so he knew it wasn't his husband approaching him from behind.

"Hey, Uncle Ronan," Greeley's voice called out from the screen door. "Mind if I join you?"

Greeley was just the breath of fresh air he needed right now. "You bet, kid. Grab me a soda, would you?"

"Already done." Greeley stepped outside, closing the screen behind him. He handed Ronan one of the two cans of Coke he was carrying. "Thought you could use a little company this afternoon."

"Did you now?" Ronan raised an eyebrow at the teenager before cracking open his soda.

Greeley frowned. "I kept feeling this weird vibe from you, so I decided to come over and investigate like any good cop would do."

Ronan snorted. "Like any good *cop* would do?"

"Well…" Greeley laughed. "Thanks to your little chat with my father, I'm all systems go to apply to the police academy and changed my major to Criminal Justice."

"What?" Ronan couldn't believe his ears. He knew his talk with Fitzgibbon had gone well, but he knew how much the idea of Greeley carrying a gun and a badge terrified his boss.

"I know, right!" Greeley's smile stretched from ear to ear. "Since I'm only eighteen, I need to take classes and attend the academy part time. It turns out Salem State offers an academy and their Criminal Justice major counts as the classes I need to enroll in. I can't be a full-time officer in Massachusetts until I'm twenty-one years old, so that gives me time to finish my degree and complete the academy."

Ronan shook his head. "Christ, kid. I don't know what to say. I remember how proud of you I was when you agreed to go to rehab and then when you graduated. I didn't think it was possible to be prouder of you than I was in that moment. Then you got your GED and you got into Salem State and all of a sudden I was proud of you all over again." He took a deep breath, knowing if he kept rambling on, his emotions were going to get the best of him. "You keep doing that. Keep making me proud, okay?"

"You do the same thing you know? All of these cases you and Uncle Ten solve together. All the people you help. I feel the same way about you. I'm super proud of you every day."

"Yeah?" Ronan couldn't believe his ears.

Greeley nodded his head. "That's why these last few days have been weird. Off." Greeley's look turned confused. "There's something going on with you that I can't put my finger on. So, instead of spinning my wheels, I figured I'd come over and just ask you what in hell is up?"

"Nosy bastard." Ronan rolled his eyes. "Promise me you'll always use that intuition on the job, got it?"

"Always, Uncle Ronan. Now, stop deflecting and start talking." Greeley waggled his eyebrows.

Ronan had to hand it to the kid. He was good. "I started having nightmares a few nights ago. I was seeing Tennyson being burned at the stake during the Salem Witch Trials. I thought it had to do with the work we did out at the Black Cat Inn with Tobin Woods and Niall Gallagher, but then I had a second dream."

"What was the second dream about?" Greeley leaned closer. The look in his eyes showed his investment in Ronan's story.

"The Spanish Inquisition. Ten was being burned again, but this time not only for being a witch, but for being gay too. The common thread in the dreams was Preacher Gideon Black."

"That's bizarre. So, you were thinking that he's the key here?"

"I wasn't really thinking anything until the witches showed up on our doorstep." Ronan shook his head.

"Witches? As in real witches?"

Ronan nodded. "The Salem Witches are one of the oldest organizations in town. They're practicing Wiccans, but they're also business owners, mothers, wives, sisters…" Ronan trailed off. He could see Gia Gonzalez's face in his mind's eye. Knowing she was lying on a mortuary slab now broke his heart.

"What did they want?" The twinkle in Greeley's eyes indicated he already knew the answer to that question.

"My help. They think they're being hunted." Ronan knew now that they were.

"Again." It wasn't a question.

"Right. I agreed to do whatever I could to help them. I looked into all of the police reports of the six women who have died over the last two years and they all looked accidental. Whoever is doing it is a pro. Then another woman died."

"Gia Gonzalez? I saw that on the news. They found her on one of the jogging trails here in town. The autopsy still isn't back yet."

"She was here in my house, Greeley. Asking for my help and I failed her. I failed them all." Raw pain sliced through Ronan like a knife.

"But that's not what's wrong with you now." Again, not a question.

"Right. Ten spoke to Jude about what was going on with me and they both agreed what I was experiencing wasn't nightmares but flashbacks to past lives."

"Holy shit!" Greeley bounced in his seat before tempering his emotions. "I mean I've heard of that kind of thing before where people swear they were Cleopatra or Abraham Lincoln. They think you lived during the Witch Trials and the Inquisition? That blows my mind." Greeley was quiet. His fingers steepled together in front of his face while he seemed to be pondering the situation. "Obviously these lives have some kind of connection to what's going on with the witches. Have you figured out what that is yet?"

This kid was going to be one hell of a detective someday. "It seems Gideon Black has been after Tennyson throughout the ages."

"Uncle Ten? Why?" Greeley looked confounded.

"I haven't figured that out yet. His original obsession with witches started because a woman spurned his advances, so he accused her of being a witch. Traditionally, witches weren't executed during the time of the Inquisition. The Catholics didn't like to get their hands dirty with the occult, but they didn't mind roasting your ass for other crimes such as sodomy or fornication or other crimes against the Good Book." Ronan rolled his eyes.

"So, Uncle Tennyson was burned ostensibly for being gay, but in actuality for being a witch?"

Ronan nodded. "I didn't get to go back into that life to see how that all came about. Actually, I didn't get to find out how Ten got caught up in things this time around either."

"It sounds like Ten did something in Spain that Black has been making him, and you by extension, pay for going on past six centuries now. You need to find the Black descendant alive now, and fast."

"I don't think it's going to be that simple, kid. This guy is smart. I highly doubt there's some asshole named Gideon Black the tenth running around Salem preaching about fire and brimstone." Wouldn't life be so much easier though if that was actually the case. Ronan would be one step ahead of the fucker for a change instead of running to catch up.

"If I were you, my first stop in the morning would be to the Salem Public Library. They have those genealogy computers there. You never know what you might find that could help you out in the end."

Ronan nodded. "Good idea." Greeley had given him a lot to think about. Things he would never have let his mind wander to if not for Greeley's different perspective. The most important thing here was keeping Tennyson and the Salem Witches safe. Come hell or a return appearance from Gideon Black, that was exactly what he was going to do.

20

Tennyson

Tennyson couldn't help notice how much calmer and centered Ronan had been after Greeley had visited. He'd been wracking his brains for a way to get Ronan to calm down and maybe try to take a nap after they'd gotten back from the reading with Madam Aurora. The only thing he'd come up with was sex and that was the last thing on his mind after what Ronan had revealed about Gideon Black showing up in the reading like a possession of sorts.

Ronan had come back in from the deck with Greeley to tell him about Fitzgibbon's change of heart about letting him change his major and attend the police academy. After walking Greeley to the door, Ronan had kissed Ten and announced he was going to take a nap. Ten had felt like he was in *The Twilight Zone*. Never in the year plus that he'd known his husband had Ronan ever voluntarily taken a nap.

Now, two hours later, Ten was starting to wonder if Ronan was okay. Dixie had stayed down here with him, so he didn't have that extra alarm if there was something wrong with his slumbering man upstairs.

The thought had struck him that if Gideon Black had been able to get to Ronan in his past life regression, would he be able to get to him in his dreams? His mind made up, Ten was off the couch and halfway up the stairs without a plan in mind. When he peeked around the bedroom door, Ronan was curled up in a ball on Ten's side of the bed.

In his sleep, Ronan looked so much younger. His dirty blond hair was sticking up all over the place, as if Laurel had a go at him with too much gel. His inky lashes lay against his cheekbones, but instead of his usual intense look, Ronan's face was completely relaxed. If you didn't know Ronan O'Mara, you'd think the man was an angel in his slumber.

Ten was about to turn and head back downstairs when something caused Ronan to frown in his sleep. Stepping into the room, Ten sat on the end of the bed and smoothed out the wrinkles in his husband's forehead with the pads of his thumbs.

Ronan sighed, his lips curved into the beginnings of a smile. "I was frowning because you wouldn't take off your pants in my dream."

Ten barked out a surprised laugh. That was the last thing he was expecting Ronan to say, but at least he wasn't dreaming about Gideon Black. "Would taking them off in real life make up for disappointing you in your dream?"

His electric blue eyes popping open, Ronan nodded.

Easing off the bed, Ten went for the button fly of his jeans and then the zipper.

"Ohh, fancy!" Ronan leered obscenely at the aqua and navy striped briefs Ten was wearing.

Turning around, Ten slapped his ass before pushing his jeans down the rest of the way.

"Mmm, baby, get those sweet cheeks over here." Ronan was tossing his shirt over his head and lying back so he could tackle his own pants.

"Are you okay, Ronan? I mean that session was pretty intense today. I don't want to push you into doing something you're not ready for."

"I'm the one who does the pushing, remember?" Ronan winked at his husband before shimmying out of his pants. His erection straining at his briefs was proof that Ten wasn't about to make Ronan do anything he wasn't ready for, but to be honest, a good stiff breeze got Ronan in the mood.

"Speaking of fancy!" Ten let out a low whistle. Ronan was wearing his Bermuda briefs. They were brick-colored like the Bermuda shorts worn on the island. Ronan had loved them so much, he'd grabbed a week's worth the last day they'd been on vacation. He wore them on what he called special occasions. Although Tennyson had no idea what was so special about today.

"Needed a little extra courage for the past life session," Ronan said as if he'd read Tennyson's mind. He shrugged before throwing the briefs in Tennyson's direction.

Ten wouldn't disagree with that statement, but now was not the time to discuss it either. He walked past his stunningly naked husband who was stroking his equally stunning erection.

"Hey! I'm right here!" Ronan squawked.

"I can see that," Ten rolled his eyes. "but the lube is in your drawer." Plucking it out, he showed it off like Vanna White revealing a puzzle on *Wheel of Fortune*.

Seeing Ronan splayed out on the bed like he was an all-you-can-eat buffet changed Ten's trajectory. His original plan was to ride his husband like a jockey on Derby day, but standing near his messy blond head gave him a different idea. "You know, you're a mouthy bastard." Ten climbed up on the king-sized bed, half straddling Ronan's head.

"Me? Half the time your so damn chatty I can't get a word in edge-" Ronan's mini-rant was stopped mid-sentence by Tennyson's dick being stuck in his mouth. While he'd been ranting, Ten had climbed up on the bed and lowered his dick into Ronan's open mouth.

"Ahh, the sound of silence," Ten half-laughed. His mouth was now hovering over Ronan's leaking cock. The question was, did Ronan deserve reciprocation?

"Mmppff?" Ronan challenged.

Ten started to laugh. He assumed, "Mmppff" was dick-in-the-mouth for, "Well?" Hmm, his husband was being a good sport, sucking Ten's dick, when his own was still dry, but for the pre-come leaking from its tip. Ten supposed Ronan deserved his due, maybe not all at once though.

Shooting his husband a sexy, upside-down wink, Ten licked the free-flowing nectar gathering at the tip of his erection.

Ronan moaned his appreciation, sending vibrations down Ten's shaft. God, he loved his husband's mouth on him like this. He had no idea why they didn't do this more often. Probably because Ronan was always in charge, bossing him around, barking out orders. Ten liked this much better.

Enveloping the head of Ronan's cock in his mouth, Ten swirled his tongue around the slit, his hand pushing against Ronan's thighs, urging him to part them. When Ronan obeyed, Ten fondled his balls, weighing each hot sac in his hand before moving down to his husband's dark hole.

Ronan stiffened up momentarily, as if he were unwilling to allow his husband to breach his most private place.

Tennyson was having none of that. Reaching for the discarded bottle of lube, he coated his index finger in the warming liquid, smearing it against Ronan's puckered skin. When he wiggled his finger against the tight muscle there was give in it this time. Ronan was letting him in. When his finger scraped past his husband's prostate, Ronan growled, opening himself up more to Ten's invasion. *Gotcha now, you horny bastard,* Ten couldn't help thinking to himself.

While Ten was reveling in his small victory, Ronan had gotten to work, swallowing around his dick and working him deeper into his mouth. Jesus Christ, Ronan deepthroated like a porn star. Not that Ten had ever been with one but, shit, if he slid any further down his throat, his husband wouldn't be able to breathe. Or talk…

Ten moaned his appreciation for Ronan's talents, and his silence, using his finger against his sweet spot. He could hear Ronan's sharp intake of breath.

For his part, Ten wasn't going to last much longer either. The combination of Ronan's mouth on his dick while servicing his husband at the same time was driving him wild. The vibrations caused by the desperate little moans Ronan was making ended up being what tipped him over the edge. He didn't even have time to warn Ronan. Before he knew it, his dick was jerking and he was spewing down Ronan's throat.

Ronan didn't seem to mind. He moaned obscenely and started to swallow.

The feel of Ronan swallowing around him made it that much more intense for Tennyson. His eyes slid shut and he stayed there, in the moment, while his release roared through his entire body.

When he was finally able to think again, he increased his efforts to do the same for Ronan. He knew he was going to get more than his regular mouthful, what with the way he was giving Ronan's prostate a workout. Ten felt Ronan's fingers dig deeper into his ass cheeks and knew it was only a matter of seconds.

Ronan's entire body tensed beneath Tennyson. His cock jerked and started to spill into Ten's mouth.

Ten started to swallow as the bursts came, but couldn't keep up with the flow coming from Ronan. He relaxed and let the salty release build before swallowing for a third time. He could hear Ronan whimpering and felt his hands start to slip from his ass.

When that weak trickle flowed over his tongue, Tennyson released Ronan.

"Sweet Jesus," Ronan panted. "Why don't we do that more often?"

"Because you're bossy." Ten let a rogue giggle slip past his sore lips.

Ronan snorted. "Really? Is that why?"

Ten nodded, shifting onto his back. "You're always like, 'Suck my dick. Get on your knees.' You never think about this because you're too busy trying to fuck me."

Ronan lifted his head up and gave Ten a pointed look before he burst out laughing. "You're right. I'm a bossy bastard. How do we fix that?"

"*We* don't fix that. *You* do. It's a simple fix." Tennyson crawled toward his sweat-slicked husband, resting his head on Ronan's chest. "Stop being so damn bossy. See? Simple."

"I'll work on it as soon as I save the witches, Ten." Ronan pressed a kiss to Ten's sweaty forehead.

Tennyson was afraid Ronan was going to say that. It all came back to the witches and Gideon Black.

21

Ronan

It had been years since Ronan O'Mara had stepped foot inside a library. If he had to hazard a guess, he'd say the last time had been during his days at the academy when he'd met a cute recruit who'd loved to read. Their only date had been to the Boston Public Library. Ronan had carried his enormous stack of books and he hadn't even been rewarded with a good night hand job for his trouble. He'd been a first-class dick back then. Not much had really changed in the intervening years.

The old Salem Public Library was a three-story red brick structure with Corinthian columns. The building really had that old-world look of Salem. There was a newer, flashier library building across town, but this one housed all the Witch Trial documents and for whatever reason had the computers set aside for people researching their genealogy.

He felt a little bit bad about being here, after all he'd lied to Fitzgibbon about needing the day off. Hell, Ronan had vacation days stacked up like cordwood. All he needed to do was let Kevin know he was taking one, which he'd done, but Ronan had taken it a step further by telling his boss that he wasn't feeling well.

It wasn't a lie, to tell the truth. Ronan was still feeling off after his past life regression with Madam Aurora. It had been an interesting experience meeting Samuel Goodman and having a few minutes to speak with him and literally having the experience of walking around in his shoes. The shit got real very quickly when Samuel had brought him to the night of Tennyson's murder. There was no other way to describe it. Sure, historians would call it an execution, but Wolfgang Grimme was murdered in the commission of a hate crime.

It wasn't even having to relive Ten's past-life death that had Ronan feeling off his game. It was the way that Gideon Black had recognized him and seemed to have known what he was doing in 1692.

How could Ronan possibly have any hope of defeating Black if the man knew what he was up to and was already a step ahead?

Ronan shook his head. He couldn't think about that now. He had work to do. He had one mission to accomplish at the library today. To research the Black family. He had a bad feeling it wasn't going to be as easy as typing the name into a search box, but he wasn't going to put the cart before the horse. At least not yet.

He waited patiently at the circulation desk until a librarian was free to help him. She gave him a quick tutorial on how the genealogical software worked and left him alone to work in silence.

Staring at the blinking cursor, Ronan was hesitant to type the name in to the computer. It was just a name after all. It couldn't really hurt him, could it? He knew there was power in names, but he didn't think Gideon Black had the ability to reach through the spirit world and hurt him now. He'd been vulnerable in the past life regression, but sitting here in 2018, Gideon Black would have to step into Ronan's world. He didn't think the bully was brave enough to do that. Not in such a public place and not in the light of day anyway. Ronan had a feeling Black did his business in the dead of night.

Stretching out his fingers as if he were about to play the piano, Ronan set them down on the keyboard. He typed Gideon Black's name into the ancestry database and hit the Enter key. Within seconds, he had thousands of hits.

Remembering what the librarian had told him about using the search filters, Ronan was able to use Massachusetts as a parameter and that knocked the results down to a more manageable thirty names. Scrolling quickly through them, he was able to find *the* Gideon Black he'd been looking for.

Born in 1662 in nearby Salisbury, Massachusetts, Gideon Black was born the youngest of thirteen surviving children to William and Anne Black. Ronan shivered. Shit, the *thirteenth* child? It seemed his birth order had his life planned out for him long before Black had even taken his first breath.

As Ronan kept reading, it also turned out that Gideon's first breath was also his mother's last. Anne Black was listed as having died in childbirth. There was your original sin right there. With his first breath, Gideon Black was a murderer.

Although, truth be told, that scarlet "M" could just as easily be slapped on William Black for continually getting his wife pregnant. Skimming quickly through the rest of the records Ronan saw that Gideon should have been the youngest of fifteen children. Two of his siblings had been stillborn. Doing the math quickly in his head, William Black's long-suffering wife had fifteen children in only seventeen years.

Not an expert by any stretch of the imagination, Ronan could well guess the female body wasn't built to stand up to that kind of abuse. He made a mental note to spoil Emilyn extra rotten before her insemination procedure next week and then after it and then all through her pregnancy. Before reading about Anne Black, he'd wanted a houseful of kids with Tennyson. Now, he was thinking two would do. After that, they'd adopt. He'd be damned if he put Emilyn at risk.

Shaking his head, Ronan turned back to the computer screen. He punched the Print button and watched as page after page of the Black family tree started to spit out.

He could see that Gideon settled down and got married in 1694, the year after the conclusion of the Salem Witch Trials. His wife's name was Lucinda Alden of Amesbury, Massachusetts. It seemed Gideon had gone back to his roots, as Amesbury bordered Salisbury. Or, perhaps a more realistic scenario was that after the hysteria of the Witch Trials had subsided, Gideon Black had been told he was no longer welcome in Salem.

Whatever the reason for Black's change of geography, he had seven children with Lucinda, four of whom survived to adulthood. Ronan hit the Print button again, watching as the papers arranged themselves neatly in the tray.

Ronan spent the next two hours hitting the Print button on the various generations of the Black family. They were here through the

Revolutionary War, with sons dying for liberty. Blacks had died for the North in the American Civil War. Same went for Blacks fighting in the trenches in France during World War I, and then dying in the Pacific in World War II, then there were the conflicts in Korea and Vietnam. A funny thing happened around the 1970s. The Black family disappeared from the ancestry database.

Shaking his head, Ronan went back to the 1940s generation. There were thirteen descendants in that generation. There was that number again. Thirteen.

Ronan shivered in the too-hot circulation room. The database listed all thirteen members of the family getting married. It also listed dates of death for some of them. Two members had been killed in action in Vietnam, but that's where the data stopped. None of them, according to this database anyway, had children.

Grabbing all of his printouts, Ronan headed back to the circulation desk, where the same librarian who'd shown him how to use the computer earlier was checking out books for another patron. "Hello, Detective O'Mara. Did you find everything you were looking for?"

"Almost. The last few generations of the family I was researching are missing. The family records stop with people born in the 1940s. Is that right or am I doing something wrong here?"

The librarian, whose nametag read, "Lydia," nodded. "I'm afraid that's correct. The Baby Boomers are a huge generation and we're working as hard and as fast as we can to get all of that information uploaded.

There were so many post-war marriages and babies and so on that we just can't keep up with the small staff that we have here."

Ronan figured as much. "I appreciate your help today, Lydia."

"Don't mention it." She patted his hand. "If you want to make a difference, vote for the candidates who think raising taxes for the fireman and libraries is a good thing!"

"You bet!" Ronan agreed as he strode for the door with his stack of research under his arm. Not that his voting record was going to do him any good today. He was walking away without the crucial pieces of information that were going to help him find and nail Gideon Black's descendant before he could hurt any other witches.

22

Tennyson

Ten was pacing back and forth in front of their large picture window facing the street, waiting for Ronan to get home from the library. He'd texted fifteen minutes ago to say he was on his way, but still hadn't made it home yet. It was only a two-mile drive from where he was coming from and he should have been home ten minutes ago.

It wasn't like Tennyson to pace in front of a window waiting for his man like this, but he had some news he knew Ronan would be interested in hearing. Gia Gonzalez's autopsy report was in. Not only was it in, but it had been hand delivered by an old friend.

"Tennyson, sit down," Suffolk County Medical Examiner Vann Hoffman urged. "He's not going to get here any faster with you wearing a hole in the floor."

Tennyson stopped short, so short that Dixie crashed into the backs of his calves. She let out a pitiful whine and walked toward the kitchen.

"See? Your own dog has had enough of your shit." Vann rolled his eyes. "Poor little girl."

His shoulders slumping, Ten sighed. "Thank you for doing this for us Vann."

"Yeah, sure. I know exactly what you're thinking." The handsome M.E. grinned at Ten and sat further back into his armchair.

"Oh, so you've gotten a touch of the sight now? Is that from banging Broughan? He fuck the gift of sight into you?" That sounded bitchy even to Tennyson's ears.

"Broughan's an energy healer, not a psychic. Osmosis doesn't work that way." Vann rolled his eyes, sounding every bit the scientist he was.

"This case scares me, Vann. If there was no foul play that means Ronan is still in the thick of this alone." Ten started to pace again. "If Gia's autopsy proves there was foul play involved in her death then the Salem Police can step in and investigate. This will lead to the police in the towns where the other witches were killed opening investigations into their deaths too."

"That's what you hope will happen, right? And if that happens that would mean that Ronan would be out of investigating them all, right?" Vann surmised.

Ten nodded. He could feel his heart jackhammering against his rib cage.

"That's an awful lot of dominoes having to fall the right way, Tennyson. Even if Gia was murdered, it doesn't mean the deaths of the other six women will be reinvestigated. Getting six other jurisdictions to agree on anything would take a friggen miracle." The look on Vann's face was grim.

"We did it with the serial killer case. All of the other towns cooperated then." If all of those other town cooperated once, they could do it again.

"You just said the magic words, Tennyson." Vann raised an eyebrow. "Serial killer. No town wants to be branded on the nightly news or on *Dateline* as the one who refused to join in the hunt for a madman. This is one possible murder."

"Wait, what?" Vann's words stopped Tennyson's pacing in its tracks. "What do you mean *possible* murder? Haven't you read the file?"

Vann shook his head no. "I wanted to open it with Ronan. I didn't want him to think I'd had time to gloss things over or had thought of ways to cool his fiery Irish temper down."

"Jesus Christ, Vann!" Ten felt like he was losing his mind. "Please tell me you thought of those things anyway, just in case this whole thing goes belly up." Ten's mind started scrambling for ways to calm Ronan down. Shit, that also meant he needed to think of ways to get Ronan to drop this whole thing in case that file said Gia wasn't murdered.

"Calm your hemorrhoids, Tennyson. I'll handle Ronan."

"Oh, you'll *handle* me, will you, Doctor Hoffman?" Ronan sneered from the door. "Is that after you *handled* my husband while I was gone?"

"Jesus fucking Christ, Ronan! Eat a bag of dicks, will you?" Ten screeched, his nerves stretched to the breaking point. "This is serious here!"

Ronan burst out laughing. "I can see that, Ten. Vann was so scared his skin actually turned white. He looked like Michael Jackson for a second. You okay?"

Vann laughed along with him. "Shit, man! You scared ten years off my life. I thought you actually believed Ten and I had been doing the nasty." Vann pulled Ronan in for a man-hug.

"Nah, Ten's knows he's got it way too good with all of the magic in my wand." Ronan waggled his eyebrows.

"Fucking seriously?" Ten muttered.

Ronan grinned over Vann's shoulder at his husband. "To what do we owe the pleasure, Doc? Man troubles with Broughan and you came to the happiest couple you know for relationship advice?" He stepped away from Vann to pull Ten in for a kiss.

Ten pushed Ronan's pursed lips away.

"How have you not killed him in his sleep yet?" Vann asked.

"I don't think I could pull off playing the grieving widow." Ten waggled his eyebrows. "I'd be like the kid in the Christmas Story movie when he gets away with lying to his mom about how he broke his glasses after he shot his eye out."

Ronan's mouth hung open. "You've actually thought this through?"

"Do you actually listen to yourself?" Ten threw his hands out. "You really think Vann drove all the way up here from Southie for relationship advice?"

"Your chicken parm?" Ronan asked.

Ten's shoulders sagged. He shook his head no.

"Tickets to the Witch Museum?" Ronan tried, looking back and forth between Vann and his husband.

Ten's eyes bugged out. He wore a fucking-seriously look on his face.

"Time with the babies and they weren't home?" Ronan fisted his hands on his hips, the frustration clearly showing on his face.

Ten rolled his eyes.

"Vann? Help me out! I'm drowning here!"

"I have Gia Gonzalez's autopsy report." He held up the manila envelope.

"You have what?" Ronan shook his head and blinked a few times. "You've had that the whole time and you both let me play the fucking fool?" Ronan walked into the breezeway. When he came back into the living room, he was carrying his notebook. "Jesus fucking Christ," he muttered to himself. "What does it say?"

"I haven't opened it yet. I was waiting for you." Vann's voice was gentle, but all business now.

Tennyson turned toward his husband as he sat next to him. He could see Ronan's entire focus was on Vann.

Vann broke the seal on the envelope and pulled out a stapled packet of papers, he skimmed through them quickly, his trained medical examiner's eyes knowing exactly what pieces of information they were looking for. When he reached the last page, his neutral look soured. "Shit."

"Shit, good? Shit, bad? What kind of shit, Vann?" Ronan asked, leaning forward in his seat.

"It says Miss Gonzalez's cause of death was blunt force trauma to the head. Manner of death, though, Jesus." Vann shook his head. "It was ruled inconclusive."

"Inconclusive? What the hell does that mean?" Ten asked. He was looking back and forth between Ronan and Vann.

"Inconclusive means the medical examiner who conducted the autopsy couldn't tell if the injuries were caused by another person, in which case it would have been a homicide, or if the injuries were an accident like if she tripped and fell and hit her head." Ronan sank his head into his hands. "Motherfucker."

"I wish I could have been more help." Vann set a hand on Ronan's shoulder.

Lifting his face, Tennyson looked up at Vann. "How did you get this report anyway? Gia died here in Salem and this is Essex County. You're a Suffolk County M.E."

"I got a phone call from a concerned *citizen* of this great town who asked if I could get my hands on this report. Since he was the one who introduced me to my forever love, I owed him a favor. I was able to pull some strings. Turns out the Essex County M.E. is a former satisfied customer."

Ronan's face crumpled. "Jesus, *former* lover you mean?"

Tennyson started to laugh. "Well, he hardly means the type of customer who ended up on his autopsy table."

"Ronan, sometimes it actually is who you *blow*, rather than who you know!" Vann dropped Ten a wink. "Speaking of which, I have a sexy as hell redhead who's waiting at home for me! Later gators." Vann headed toward the front door humming the chorus of *Ebony and Ivory*.

"What are you going to do now?" Ten asked when Vann shut the front door behind him.

"I need to call Madam Aurora and have her get the witches together so I can tell them about this." Ronan got up and paced toward the kitchen. Dixie zipped toward him. "Hello, my princess." Ronan scooped up the little dog and held her close. "It's not like this autopsy report is going to be the top headline on the six o'clock news. They all deserve to hear it first-hand from me."

Ten watched his husband head into the kitchen. He knew what Ronan was saying was right on, but he couldn't help wishing the witches had picked a different man to champion their cause.

23

Ronan

Ronan was exhausted. Even though he'd only spent a few hours at the library and then spent half an hour listening to Vann Hoffman go over Gia Gonzalez's autopsy, he felt like he could sleep for a week.

As he drove across town toward Essex Street and Madam Aurora's shop for the second time in the last two days, Ronan couldn't believe how far he'd come in a mere sixteen months. When he'd first met Tennyson, he didn't believe in psychics and witches and their familiars were Halloween nonsense used to bring tourists to Salem.

Now, here he was, married to one of the most well-renowned psychics in Witch City, USA, and speaking of witches, he'd somehow become the man they'd turned to when a madman started murdering them one by one. Ronan was more convinced now than ever that there was in fact a modern-day witch hunt afoot in Salem. Even though Gia Gonzalez's autopsy officially said otherwise.

He easily found a place to park right in front of Aurora's store. Noticing the Closed sign was flipped over, Ronan turned the door knob anyway and wasn't surprised when it opened for him. He walked back to the reading room where he'd had his past life regression session yesterday.

Christ, it didn't feel like it was only yesterday. To Ronan, it felt like years had passed. "What's up, witches?" Ronan called out to them as he strolled through the door.

"Ronan!" Corazon rushed to him, wrapping her thin arms around him and hugging him tight.

Lyric Vaughn laughed musically, proving once again that she'd been aptly named.

"In the name of the Goddess, he isn't Clint Eastwood come to save our town from coarse ruffians." Callum Churchill rolled his eyes dramatically.

"It's good to see you, Ronan." Aurora greeted, pulling Corazon off of him. "You have news on two fronts I see."

"Would you like to share with the class, Aurora? Or can I tell my own news?" Ronan grinned at the witch-psychic. Or was she a psychic witch?

Aurora raised an eyebrow at Ronan. "You can tell all of your news, Ronan." She turned away for a brief second before pinning him again with her laser-sharp stare. "And by the way, Ronan, I'm a legacy seer and a Wiccan, not a *psychic witch*." She glared at him before turning her attention to the others.

Ronan could feel his ears burning. Well, she'd shown him, but that's what she got for listening in on his thoughts when she hadn't been invited to the party. "Like Aurora said, I do have news, but none of it's good."

Callum Churchill sighed heavily. "What the hell are you doing here then?"

Ronan hadn't wanted to go here, but since Callum seemed to be all queen, there didn't appear to be any other choice. "Since you don't seem to be strong enough to keep this coven safe, Churchill," Ronan started, his voice cold as ice, "they came to *me* for my protection. If you don't like it, then figure out a way to keep these women safe yourself, but until that time, shut up and listen." Ronan took a shaky breath. "Gia Gonzalez was my friend too. She came to my house and begged for my help and I failed her. That's on me. I won't stand idly by while someone tries to hurt another one of you."

Callum Churchill grimaced at Ronan's harsh words, but stayed silent and remained in his seat.

"What do you know about Gia?" Andromeda asked.

"I work closely with the Suffolk County Medical Examiner and he was able to pull some strings for me and get a copy of Gia's autopsy report. It was released today." Ronan felt his hands twisting together under the table with all of his built-up anxiety.

"Tell us what it said." Aurora reached for his hands, gently pulling them apart and keeping the left one in her own.

Ronan felt a sense of instant calm come over him just like when he used to hold the fluorite crystals Tennyson was forever handing him when they first met. He felt the knot of tension that had taken up permanent residence between his shoulder blades start to loosen. "Her cause of death was blunt force trauma to the head."

"What does that mean?" Corazon asked. "I hear it on those true crime shows my husband likes to watch but I don't know what that means."

"It means something with a blunt end hit Gia in the head. Blunt meaning not sharp. So maybe a flat rock or a baseball bat, maybe even a fist, if there was enough force behind it." Ronan looked around the table at the women.

"So that means she was murdered?" Callum Churchill wore a self-satisfied smirk.

Ronan shook his head. "That's only cause of death. There are two pieces of the puzzle in an autopsy, there's cause of death and manner of death. Her manner of death is listed as inconclusive. The medical examiner couldn't tell if the blow to the head was accidental or caused with intent."

Callum's smooth brow wrinkled at Ronan's statement. "I don't understand. You told us Gia's cause of death was a blow to the head. How can that *not* be murder?"

"It wouldn't be murder if she tripped and hit her head or if she crashed her car or someone crashed into her causing something to impact her head."

"She was on a jogging path in the middle of the woods, Ronan. I hardly think she was hit by a car." Callum raised an elegant eyebrow.

Ronan pushed the manila envelope over to the smug warlock. "The crime scene pics are inside, along with the autopsy report and the autopsy photos. A piece of friendly advice though, don't look at them. If you loved Gia, remember her the way she was. These pictures have a way of sticking with you."

Callum didn't move a muscle, he sat staring at Ronan. His icy eyes burning with rage and something else Ronan couldn't quite place. "Why are you here. Why did you bring these things to us?"

Ronan had a feeling if looks could kill he would have been dead now twice over. "Whoever is orchestrating these murders is a pro. They're so good at what they're doing that its tricking local law enforcement into ruling these deaths as accidental."

Callum's face broke into a smile. Ronan would almost call it beatific if not for the cruel smile twisting his lips. "You realize that you sound as if you've gone off the rails, right? *You* are a member of the law enforcement community, yet you sit here and tell us that you think some criminal mastermind is killing us off so well that whoever this shadow killer is they're doing it so well that he's fooling everyone?"

Ronan shook his head, turning to look at Madam Aurora. He had no doubt now that she was the one who insisted the witches turn to him for help.

"What would the next step be, Ronan? You've read the autopsy report. You've also read the accompanying police report. There was were no foreign fibers found on Gia's body, nor was there foreign DNA. This case is dead in the water."

"Ordinarily, I would agree with you, Aurora, but not now." Ronan had an idea that could possibly resurrect this case from Davy Jones' locker.

"Oh, and why is that, Ronan? Are you going to put on your red cape with the giant 'S' on it and fly off to save the day?" Sarcasm, dripped from Callum's words.

Ronan found his first authentic smile of the day. "No, Callum, I don't need to wear a cape because one of the best legacy seers in Salem is sitting next to me. Come on, Aurora. We have work to do." Ronan stood up not realizing he was still holding Aurora's hand. Shit, he really had come a long way. "Ladies? Are the rest of you coming too?"

"Where are we going?" Lyric Vaughn asked sounding more curious than anything else.

"To the crime scene." Ronan shrugged. He turned to Callum who actually looked impressed for the first time all night. "What? Did you think we were going out for scones and lattes?"

"You're not a member of the Salem Police Department. This is out of your jurisdiction. Or have you forgotten that?" Callum asked as he stood up.

"How did he end up in this group?" Ronan muttered to Aurora as he headed for the door.

"He's a legacy seer as well," Aurora whispered.

"Of course he is, thanks to Abigail." Ronan shook his head. "Does anyone like him?"

"Everyone but you," Aurora sighed. "And it seems the feeling is mutual."

Ronan snorted. As if that news was a fucking surprise.

24

Tennyson

"Wo?" Baby Bertha cried, her tiny feet stomping on the tiled kitchen floor. It was the tenth time in as many seconds that the baby had cried out for him.

"I don't know where he is, honey." Tennyson was beside himself. Ronan should have been back an hour ago. His husband knew Carson's family was coming for dinner and Ten had been trying to hold everyone off for as long as possible. It was obvious now they were going to need to eat without Ronan.

"What the hell is going on, Ten?" Fitzgibbon asked. He'd been a late addition to the dinner party after Greeley had announced he'd had other plans and wouldn't be home for supper. "First Ronan calls out sick today with the lamest ass excuse I've ever heard in thirty years of law enforcement, now he's a no-show for your famous chicken parm? What the fuck gives?"

Ten was torn. Kevin wasn't just Ronan's boss. He was also their friend. Should he just tell him what was going on or keep it for Ronan to tell when he finally got here? *If* he ever got here.

"Just spill it, Tennyson. We can sort out who betrayed who later. If he's in trouble and needs someone to save his stupid ass, you know it's going to be me." Fitzgibbon shot him a knowing look.

"Whose stupid ass needs saving? If it's Ronan, you know I'm in," Truman said with a grin.

"WO!" Bertha bellowed. Tiny tears tracked down her cheeks.

"There's another country heard from," Carson snickered. "Who would have thought Ronan would have been her hero?"

"She was always the one he'd cuddle when he brought me lunch. Bertha was always the fussiest out of all of them and for some reason, he always scooped her up first, making funny faces and blowing raspberries against her neck. He was always up for a challenge." Truman laughed.

"Jesus Christ, could you all please stop talking about my husband in the past tense like he's fucking dead!" Tennyson knew he was about to go over the deep end.

"Ten, he's fine." Carson soothed. "He's just tromping around the Salem Towne Forest with a bunch of witches and some hunky, but bitchy, warlock. No worries."

Ten's mouth hung open. "He's what?" Ten screeched. His voice was so shrill that it stopped Bertha's tantrum dead in its tracks. She whimpered and ran to Truman, wrapping her arms around his legs.

"Can someone clue me in here?" Fitzgibbon sat down at the table. "As a friend, not as Ronan's boss. I promise, whatever you all tell me won't be held against him tomorrow morning, if the dumb bastard decides to come back to work."

Carson grabbed Tennyson's shoulders and guided him toward the table. "I'll get you something to drink."

Tennyson obeyed and took his seat at the table. "Vann Hoffman was here earlier. He had Gia Gonzalez's autopsy report."

"Why does that name ring a bell?" Truman sat next to Tennyson. "Carson, why do I know that name?"

"I know why you know that name," Fitzgibbon's voice was pitched low and dangerous. It was the kind of voice you *didn't* want to hear from a cop, especially if he was speaking to you.

"Now Kevin," Carson sat down next to him and patted the clenched fist next to his drink. "We all heard you promise that you were here as Ronan's friend, not his boss, right?"

Kevin growled, but didn't answer one way or the other.

"Gia Gonzalez was the woman who was found dead on the jogging trail last week." Tennyson found his own hands balling into fists, but he kept them under the table.

"You mean the *witch* who was found dead in the Salem Towne Forest!" Fitzgibbon boomed. "The same forest Ronan is tromping around through right now!"

Tennyson and Carson exchanged uneasy looks with each other, but didn't say a word.

"I don't need the two psychics at the table to confirm for me what I already know!" Fitzgibbon shouted.

Brian and Stephanie started to cry and came running in from the living room where they'd been watching *Toy Story*.

"Uncle Kevin's sorry for being such a blowhard, isn't he?" Truman cooed, scooping up the babies. "Yes, he is and he's going to use his indoor voice from now on, right?" Truman dropped Brian into his lap without waiting for an affirmative answer.

"Uncle Kevin is sorry, little man." He gave the baby a brief cuddle before shooting Tennyson the stink eye. "Talk. What does Vann Hoffman have to do with Gia Gonzalez?" His voice was softer, but still held a dangerous edge.

Ten took a deep breath. He hadn't realized how dangerous the waters were until he heard the tone in Fitzgibbon's voice. "Vann Hoffman showed up, completely unannounced, with Gia Gonzalez's autopsy report."

Fitzgibbon raised a sardonic eyebrow. "Completely unannounced?"

"It might not have been unannounced to Ronan, but it was to me, Cap. I had no idea he was coming. Vann hadn't read the autopsy report. He was waiting for Ronan to get back before he opened it." Ten winced, he realized his mistake just after the words left his mouth.

"Jesus, Ten, I know Ronan wasn't really sick today. Just what in the name of hell was he off doing anyway?"

Ten looked around the table. These were their friends and as of this moment, only Jude knew what was really going on with Ronan. They deserved to know what was really going on. "The night before the Salem Witches came to visit him, Ronan had a nightmare."

Carson's blue eyes narrowed. "No, he didn't. Jesus, Ten. Why are you just telling us about this now? Mom didn't even know about this, because if she did, she would have told me."

Fitzgibbon raised a hand, as if he needed to ask a question in a fifth-grade math class. "Uh, for the rest of us who *aren't* psychic. What the hell was this dream that *wasn't* a dream?"

"It was a past life trying to resurface. Ronan went back to the time of the Salem Witch Trials. He was brought to my execution by the Salem Towne Constable to watch me die, which he did. Preacher Gideon Black was there gloating over what was happening."

Everyone at the table looked thunderstruck. Fitzgibbon most of all.

Tennyson decided to push on, there would be time for questions at the end. "He had a second dream a few nights later, but this time it was during the time of the Spanish Inquisition. I was burned at the stake then too and Black was there again. It was after that dream that I started to suspect that Ronan wasn't having dreams, but past lives resurfacing."

"How can he be helped?" Truman asked.

"I figured the dreams were resurfacing now for a reason. Jude agreed with me." Ten took a deep breath and prepared for the shit-storm that was about to explode around him.

"Jude? Jude knew about this, but not us? Are you fucking kidding me?" Fitzgibbon put his hands over Brian's little ears when he let the f-bomb fly. The baby batted at his big hands.

"Kevin, we needed Jude's help here. You know how sensitive Ronan is about letting his personal stuff out in the open here. Jude had information I thought we needed so I had to let him in on what was going on."

"You mean the information about how Jude blocks us out? Carson asked. "He get back to you about that yet?"

Tennyson shook his head. "Nothing. He said his grandfather wouldn't be willing to let anyone in on how he's protected from witches or psychic attacks. I don't blame him for wanting to keep Jude safe."

"Explain again why this is important to Ronan?" Fitzgibbon sounded weary now.

"Carson, Cole, and I can't contact the spirits of any of the dead witches. If we could, we'd be able to ask if there was foul play involved in their deaths. There's some kind of psychic block around them all, as if they're being held prisoner. Not even Bertha or Erin can get through it from the other side. This leads me to believe whatever is going on is being done intentionally to keep us out." Ten looked around the table. Carson was nodding along with him. Truman looked like he understood where Ten was going, but Fitzgibbon's look was impassive.

"I'm guessing there's more to tell with Ronan and his past lives?" Fitzgibbon asked.

Ten nodded. "Madam Aurora is the best past life regressionist in the country. Ronan had an appointment with her the other day."

A look of pain flashed across Kevin's face at the mention of Aurora's name. Ten knew he was thinking about her prophecy involving himself and billionaire philanthropist Jace Lincoln. Aurora had said the two of them were destined to be forever loves, which so far, had not come to pass. "What happened?"

"She was able to take him back to his past life here in Salem during the Witch Trials. He actually met himself."

Carson snickered. "God help us, two Ronans."

"His name in that life was Samuel Goodman. He was a descendant from one of the Mayflower passengers. Samuel agreed that the reason this life resurfaced was that there was something Ronan needed to see. It was a conversation with Gideon Black after my execution, but then something else happened."

"Black showed up live, didn't he?" Carson asked.

"How'd you know?" Tennyson turned to his best friend. He shouldn't have been surprised that Carson knew this bit of information, him being psychic and all. The funny thing was that Tennyson didn't think Carson came by this information by using his gift.

"Mom told me about something like this happening to her. She didn't like to do past life regressions. She said they freaked her out. She had a couple of clients who wanted to do them when this stuff was all the rage back in the 1980s. People wanted to hear that they'd been

Napoleon or George Washington or Nefertiti in their past life, when in fact they were usually peasants at best or whores at worst." Carson shrugged.

"What happened to freak Bertha out?" Truman asked.

"She had this client who'd escaped a bad marriage. Her husband had been one of those stalking mothereffers. He'd been relentless with her and their kids and it had gotten him killed. The bastard had tracked her down in Salem and was running across the street to grab her but hadn't looked both ways. Dead on impact." Carson shook his head. "Two weeks later, she came in to see Mom for a reading and everything was looking bright for her future now that he was dead, so she decided to book a past life reading. All her friends were doing it and she wanted to join in on the fun. Well, it turned out she and the dead husband had been linked through time. He'd been after her since their souls had met in Ancient Egypt. Somehow or other, his spirit had found a way to come into the regression and he was able to get to her again during the session. His malevolent spirit scared Mom so badly that she never did another reading like that again."

Tennyson was quiet for a moment, sitting with what Carson had just told him. "Do you think it's the strength of the spirit that gave it the power to come through like that?"

Carson chewed his upper lip. "Maybe. I'm not sure. It's something to ask Mom about for sure the next time you talk to her."

"What happened with Black, Tennyson? What did he say to Ronan?" Fitzgibbon sounded more concerned now than angry.

"He said there was a final battle to come and that he was the one responsible for what was happening to the Salem Witches."

Fitzgibbon started to laugh. He was laughing so hard tears were flowing from his eyes. "A ghost told Ronan he was killing *living* people?" Fitzgibbon managed between fits of the giggles. "Then he said there was a final battle to come?" Kevin kept laughing. "Jesus, Ten, if this were a movie plot we would have walked out and asked for our money back."

"Kevin, I don't understand." Ten didn't see anything funny in this at all.

"Look, Ten, I remember when you ended up bruised when you'd lost the use of your gift and spirits roughed you up a bit because you couldn't do your job, but the idea of a ghost murdering seven people from beyond the grave? Come on, even you have to admit that's a little far-fetched."

"All I know is this, these women came to Ronan. They asked for his help and he's giving it to them. They knew he was the right man to turn to, not only for his reputation in this life, but because of his reputation in past lives."

Kevin's attitude sobered. "I get that, Ten. I really do, but the problem I'm having here is in *this* life. Ronan is lying to me. He's calling out of work. He's asking Suffolk County employees to access autopsy reports he shouldn't have access to. He's crossing the line. I'm telling you this as his friend. If this keeps going on, I'm going to have to get involved as his boss. It won't be pretty, Ten. None of the good things he's done for the BPD in the past will weigh in his favor, but all of the other shit, the

Garcia shooting, his trip to rehab, all of it will float back up to the surface. Mark my words. Find a way to stop this now, before any of *that* happens."

Ten opened his mouth to respond, but was stopped by Ronan's ringtone chiming on his phone. Ten walked to the kitchen island to answer it. "Ronan, where are you?" Ten felt all of the color drain out of his face at his husband's answer. The fact that Ronan was safe paled in comparison to where he actually was. "You're *where*?" Ten took a deep breath. "Are you there officially or as a courtesy?" Ten nodded. He was starting to see black spots in front of his eyes. "Okay, we'll be right there." He hit the end button on his phone and looked over at Fitzgibbon, "It might already be too late. He's at the Salem Police Station. Chief Jackson is *this* close to throwing his ass in a cell for the night."

25

Ronan

The hard, wooden bench at the Salem Police Department was killing Ronan's ass. He supposed he deserved it. If he hadn't been such a fucking dick to Chief Jackson and Officers Graff and Dixon, he'd be home right now with Tennyson and their friends instead of waiting for Ten to pick him up at the station like a common criminal.

Every time the main station door opened, Ronan looked to his right, hoping to see a friendly face, but every single time, it was a stranger.

Sitting here like this reminded Ronan of the one time he'd gotten into trouble back during his time in parochial school. He'd sat on a bench very much like this one, only he was so short at the time that if he sat back all the way, his feet didn't touch the floor. His mother had to leave her job early to come in and meet with Father O'Brien. With money as tight as it was in the O'Mara household, Erin had laid into him later for costing her valuable hours at work in order to deal with his behavioral problem. Needless to say, Ronan had never ended up on Father O'Brien's bench ever again. He only hoped he could say the same about the Salem Police Department's bench.

When the main door opened again, Ronan turned to look at it and didn't see his husband striding through it hellbent for leather, but his boss who happened to be wearing his BPD badge on a chain around his neck like he did when they were working undercover. "Oh, fuck," Ronan muttered to himself. His boss looked pissed. Not the kind of pissed Kevin got when the barista at Starbucks put fake sugar in his coffee. Oh, no, this was three seconds from going full-out global nuclear war on his ass, pissed. By the time this shit show was over he was going to be dead or fired or possibly both.

"I'm looking for Chief Cisco Jackson," Fitzgibbon said, completely ignoring Ronan. "I'm Kevin Fitzgibbon from the BPD. I'm here about *him*." Kevin hooked his thumb over his shoulder at Ronan. He still wasn't making eye contact.

"Oh, he's free to go as soon as someone comes to pick him up," The young officer behind the counter explained.

"I appreciate that, but I'd still rather speak to the chief, if he's available?" Kevin's tone was quiet, but all business.

Ronan knew that tone. It was the one that said you'd better do what I'm asking before I have to get rough with you. In other words, do it before I go Hulk SMASH on your stupid ass. He almost hoped the young officer didn't get Fitzgibbon's subtle message.

"I'll go check." The young officer hurried off.

Ronan was a bit disappointed. Why should he be the only one in for an ass chewing? Because he most certainly was in for one. Two in fact. Possibly three. He had no doubt in his mind that Fitzgibbon and Jackson were about to double team him and not in a good way, then Fitzgibbon was going to ride his ass the entire way home and then Tennyson was going to have his shot. Shit, he might have been better off sleeping in the forest.

"The chief will see you now." The young officer buzzed the door open for them.

Fitzgibbon turned and looked at Ronan for the first time. He didn't say a word, he just pointed to the door.

Ronan didn't hesitate. He just obeyed. This wasn't looking good at all. He could feel Kevin behind him breathing down his neck.

"I had a feeling you weren't going to be that easy to get rid of." The chief of police rolled his dark eyes at Ronan and stood up to meet Fitzgibbon. "Cisco Jackson."

"Kevin Fitzgibbon." He shook with chief. "I'm Detective O'Mara's boss." *For now*, seemed to be left hanging in the air like an exhaled plume of cigarette smoke.

"Please sit." Jackson indicated the two chairs in front of his desk. He ran a hand through his wavy dark hair and pinned Ronan with a no-nonsense glare.

All of those old parochial school memories of that day with his mother and Father O'Brien came flooding back to him. He was even sitting in the same seat as he'd been that day. His mother to his left and the father in front of him, only this time it was Fitzgibbon to his left and the chief in front of him. No matter how he sliced it, he was in the shit now.

"So, Ronan, you want to tell me how we all ended up here tonight?" Fitzgibbon shot him a pointed look. "The short version. I don't want to be here all night."

Out of the corner of his eye, he saw Chief Jackson bite his lower lip. Ronan knew the chief had his number already. "Vann Hoffman brought me Gia Gonzalez's autopsy report. I brought it to the witches. We went to visit the crime scene to see if there were any psychic impressions the regularly-abled police didn't find. There were. Here we are." Ronan folded his hands in his lap and smiled angelically at Fitzgibbon.

Fitzgibbon's left eyebrow shot into his hairline. "I don't mean to encourage long stories, Ronan, but you seem to have left out the fucking story. Now stop being cute and tell me how the fuck my best Cold Case Detective ended up inches away from being arrested for fucking disorderly conduct in the middle of the fucking Salem Police Station!" Fitzgibbon's voice got louder with every word. By the end, he looked seconds away from having a stroke.

Ronan sighed. Here's where things were going to get messy. "Fine. I asked Vann Hoffman to see if he could get a copy of Gia's autopsy. He did. He brought it to the house today, only I didn't know he was coming. The report said she died from blunt force trauma, but that the manner of death was inconclusive. Cap, all of the witches who've died in the last year died in the same manner, no foul play, but we have something on our side that the regular cops don't."

"Psychic powers," Fitzgibbon muttered, turning to Jackson. "In case you weren't aware, Ronan is married to Tennyson Grimm who works with Carson and Cole Craig at West Side Magick. All three of them are psychic mediums who talk to the dead, among other things."

Jackson nodded, the beginnings of a smile curved his thick lips. "I believe those names were bellowed in the ruckus."

"Jesus fucking Christ, you caused a *ruckus*? In a police station? I should arrest you myself." Fitzgibbon shook his head. "Continue with the story."

It was on the tip of Ronan's tongue to remind his boss that he was out of his jurisdiction here and he couldn't arrest Ronan for so much as jaywalking, but he figured he was in enough hot water and decided to just shut his ever-loving pie-hole for once in his life. "We went out to the Salem Towne Forest where Gia's body was found. Callum Churchill and Madam Aurora got a sense of the scene."

"Callum who?" Fitzgibbon interrupted, looking more frazzled than ever.

"I think I can help you there," Cisco grinned at the captain. "Callum Churchill is our resident wordsmith. He wrote a book called *Nobody's Witch* about the life and times of his ancestor Abigail Churchill who was one of the victims of the Salem Witch Trials. It's made him a local celebrity. He's also a psychic and member of the Salem Witches."

"You're telling me this man is a witch? Doesn't that make him a wizard?" Fitzgibbon shook his head and rapidly blinked his eyes.

"Warlock actually, but yes, he's a practitioner of Wicca." Cisco's grin set off twin dimples which Ronan was dead sure made *him* a local celebrity as well.

"Okaaaay." Kevin shrugged. "I'm familiar with Madam Aurora's particular skillset."

Cisco snorted and quickly tried to cover it up with a cough. He wasn't fooling Ronan.

"What did the witches figure out from the crime scene, Ronan?" Fitzgibbon sighed. He turned to Captain Jackson. "Do you see what I have to deal with here?"

"Oh, I saw it all right. Up close and personal. Right about here." Cisco held the palm of his right hand about a half an inch away from his nose.

"Fuck. My. Life." Fitzgibbon turned back to Ronan. "Talk, asshole! I'm fucking starving and thanks to you, I'm *not* enjoying your husband's kick ass chicken parm."

At the rate Fitzgibbon was going, Ronan might not make it home. Some member of the Salem Police Department was going to find his body in a ditch along Route 114. "Aurora found signs of a struggle. Callum confirmed her findings. That was all they got though, just some psychic residue. The best way to describe it is like soap scum left in the tub after you take a shower. Callum dropped me off here and they all went home. I figured I could get someone to listen to me and reopen Gia's case."

"Because you're such a calm, logical, law abiding, police officer?" Fitzgibbon's voice had gone quiet.

Ronan knew he'd passed the point of no return. Fitzgibbon's nuclear reactor had just gone red and he was minutes from melting down completely. The next words out of his mouth were crucial not only to his career, but to his friendship with Kevin and possibly for his marriage. "These women came to me because they saw me as their last hope. Someone is hunting and killing them one at a time. They've tried going the traditional route and seeking out law enforcement in the towns where their friends died and nothing happened. They tried to used their gifts to get answers and something is blocking them. I'm their last hope, Cap. I failed them too. Gia Gonzalez is dead because I couldn't help these women. I won't be able to live with myself if another member of this community dies. What if they'd gone after Gia's five-year-old daughter? What if Lyric Vaughn, her wife, and infant are next? What if this crazy fucker doesn't stop with the witch community? What if the psychics are next and he comes after Carson or Cole or Ten?" Ronan stood up and paced a few steps around the small office. "I know I fucked up today, Cap. All I can do is apologize to both of you."

"Let me guess," Cisco sighed. "Those blue eyes get him anything he wants?"

"Most of the time," Fitzgibbon grumbled. "He is a damn good detective, when he isn't being an asshole!" Fitzgibbon looked back over at his detective. "This is your last freebie, Ronan. I swear to God, one more incident like this and I'm suspending your ass. You can't go around causing scenes in other police departments. Am I understood?"

"Yes, thank you, Cap. I won't do anything this stupid again." Ronan knew he'd won, but it would be best if he tried to look humble. "I don't know how to thank you, Chief Jackson."

"Try staying out of trouble." The chief raised an eyebrow. "And if you can't manage that, stay out of my fucking police station the next time you want to raise some Cain. Think you can manage that?"

Ronan nodded. He didn't trust himself to speak. There was a rogue giggle sitting on the tip of his tongue, the kind that always wanted to fly free in church or when his mother was lecturing him about something important.

"Do we owe you anything for his trouble?" Kevin asked wearily.

"Nope!" Cisco laughed. "I think you pay enough dues dealing with his shit every day."

"Hey!" Ronan squeaked, before thinking better of his reaction. He was getting off easy here. He could have been arrested on a whole slew of charges and been spending the night in jail as a guest of Chief Francisco Jackson. Instead, he was going to get to go home and sleep on the awful mattress in the spare bedroom with his snoring dog, if Tennyson let him in the front door, that was.

26

Tennyson

It was déjà vu all over again. Tennyson was back to pacing in front of the living room window while Dixie scampered around behind him. It was just the two of them now, with Carson and his crew having gone home after dinner. He'd wanted to face his jailbird husband alone and Truman had been all too happy to let him.

Carson, on the other hand, had wanted to stay for the fireworks. Before they'd left, Truman had pulled him aside to let Ten know that the spare bedroom would be made up and ready to go should Ronan need a place to crash tonight.

With the mood Tennyson was in, Ronan just might need that bed. He'd gauge himself on the anger meter at somewhere between an erupting Vesuvius and melting down Bridezilla. Either way, Ronan wouldn't test him if he knew what was good for him.

He'd done a lot of stupid shit in the time they'd known each other but throwing a toddler-sized tantrum in the middle of the Salem Police Department had to rank at the top of the list.

"Come on, Tenny, you know Ronan's just looking out for those poor women." Bertha Craig was standing in the middle of Tennyson's circuit around the living room. "You saw how devastated he was after Gia died."

"Of course, you're on his side." Ten rolled his eyes.

"Are there really sides here, Tennyson? Ronan's looking out for women who are being hunted. Are you actually going to give him shit for that?" Frustration bled through into Bertha's voice.

Ten sighed. He did sound like a world-class asshole. "Bertha, he was almost arrested. He could have spent the night in jail. This little stunt could have gotten him suspended from his job. It could get him fired! If he lost his job, we'd lose our health insurance and then who would cover Emilyn for her insemination and little miss when she's born?" Ten could feel himself getting hysterical.

"I get that, Tenny. I really do, but that young lady will never hug her daughter again. She won't be there for her first day of school, or when she walks down the aisle, or when she becomes a mother. Ronan's trying to make sure none of the other witches suffer a similar fate."

Instead of being soothed by Bertha's words and realizing that he and Ronan were so much more blessed than the Gonzalez family, he only felt angrier. Ronan fucking up like he'd done affected their family. He was supposed to give his donation to the fertility clinic next week for Emilyn's insemination. What if he was in jail and couldn't make the appointment?"

"Don't worry, he's not going to miss that appointment." Bertha set a hand on Tennyson's face.

"Aren't you the one who's always saying that the future is fluid?" Ten accused. "This is my baby we're talking about!" Ten could feel his emotions threatening to break free. He and Ronan were so close to having it all and now Ronan and his bullheaded ways were about to blow it up.

"Actually, little miss belongs to both of you." Bertha had her mom-voice on in full-effect. "You listen and you listen good, Tennyson Grimm. I know your mother was never one to sit down and have this kind of talk with you, but things don't always go your way. Ronan's not always going to behave like a perfect little lap-dog obeying your every command. These women came to him for help. What kind of man would he be if he'd turned his back on them? Would he be the kind of man you'd want to father your child? Would he be the kind of man you'd want to raise a daughter with in this crazy world? Learning his values and his code of conduct?"

Ten knew Bertha was making a lot of sense, but right now he was just so mad he couldn't see it. "He'd be the kind of man who'd be alive and employed to see her grow up. The kind of man not relying on unemployment checks to put food on the table and keep the lights on."

"Bullshit!" Bertha barked back. "You know goddamned well that if push came to shove, Ronan would be working every job he could get, janitor, supermarket checkout clerk, shoeshine boy, whatever it took to take care of you and that baby."

"I'm just so angry right now, Bertha. You're making good points. I'll have time to think about them later, after I've spoken to my husband."

"Fine, but I'll leave you with this," Bertha stepped around Tennyson so he could see her. "Next week is one of those special moments in your family's history that you'll never get a chance to do over. Do you want your daughter to be conceived in love or in festering anger? Think about that." With those words, Bertha was gone.

Damn, Ten hated when Bertha had the last word like that, especially when it was such a good point. He was mulling over his two choices when Dixie yipped and barreled off toward the front door signaling that Ronan was home. He wasn't going to have a chance to think about anything now.

"Hey, Ten? I'm home." Ronan called out. His greeting was quickly followed by the beeps of the key pad indicating he was setting the alarm.

"In the living room." Ten's plan was to play it cool and see what Ronan had to say to him. He would save both blazing barrels for later.

When Ronan walked into the living room he wore an exhausted look on his face. "I'm sorry I ruined dinner, babe." He stopped in front of Ten.

Tennyson could see Ronan was truly sorry. That wasn't really cutting it for him right now. "What the fuck happened tonight, Ronan? What did Fitzgibbon say? Are you fired? Suspended? Were you fucking arrested? Do you have to go to court? Jesus fucking Christ, Ronan!" Tennyson screeched. His hands were balled into fists at his sides and it's a damn good thing they were because Ten was just pissed off enough to swing at his husband.

Ronan took two giant steps backward, as if he could see the intent in Tennyson's eyes. "Why don't we sit down and I'll answer all of your questions one at a time."

"I don't want to sit down, Ronan. I want to know what the hell possessed you to go into the Salem Police Department and start ranting and raving like a five-year-old when you didn't get your way!"

Slipping his hands into the front pockets of his jeans, Ronan rocked back on his heels. Disappointment shone in his blue eyes. "You need to calm the hell down and stop using your gift to peer into my head. You're not seeing a full picture of what happened tonight. Why don't we talk about this later when you've had a chance to calm down?" Ronan turned and headed toward the stairs.

"When I've had a chance to calm down? I wasn't the one making a scene downtown!" Ten roared.

"No, you're the one making a scene now. Without all of the facts." Ronan turned back toward Tennyson. "When I went into that police station tonight, I had all of my facts in order. I was perfectly calm. I knew what I needed to do to get my point across. I spoke to the right people. Asked all of the right questions and gave them all of the right information and in return, they dismissed me and my evidence. They didn't even use the guise of professional courtesy to lie to me and say they'd look into Gia's case. So, I asked to speak to their supervisor, who on this shift, happened to be the chief of police. He wasn't listening to me either. Just like you're not." Ronan shrugged. "Maybe if I'd used this tone of voice instead of the one I'd used, things would have turned out differently. I wasn't arrested. I'm not fired or suspended. And I'm sure as hell not sleeping in the same bed with you after the way you came at me tonight. Find some other place to sleep. Our bed is off limits to you." Without a backward glance, Ronan turned and walked up the stairs.

Well shit. Maybe Tennyson should have listened to Bertha after all.

27

Ronan

For only the second time in his married life, Ronan O'Mara had slept alone. Tennyson hadn't even come into the bedroom to change or to brush his teeth last night and Ronan had been too pissed and too worn out to find out where his husband had lain his head or washed up.

When he'd stumbled downstairs in the morning, Tennyson was gone. Not surprisingly, he hadn't left a note telling Ronan where he was or telling him to go to hell. Ronan took that as a win.

One of the things he hadn't had a chance to tell his harpy of a husband last night was that Fitzgibbon had told him to take today off to get his head straight. He'd be expected back at work first thing tomorrow morning with his head back in the cold case game. Ronan couldn't promise anything, but he'd sure in hell make it look good.

He was glad for the day off, there was someone he needed to speak to about Gideon Black. Someone who might have more information than a damn computer printout. Parking the Mustang on Witch Hill Road, Ronan looked up at The Black Cat Inn.

Climbing out of the car, Ronan let out a low whistle. So much work had been done to the dilapidated Victorian mansion since the last time he'd seen it six weeks ago. Gone was the peeling decades of paint and pieces of warped gingerbread molding. In their place was a fresh coat of paint and molding that made the house shine like the diamond she was. The wrought-iron fence surrounding the property had been sandblasted to remove the rust and it had been repainted as well. The cracked concrete walkway leading up to the front steps had been replaced and said steps no longer listed to the right.

"What do you think of my old girl?" Tobin Woods, The Black Cat Inn's General Contractor, asked from behind Ronan.

"Damn, you've got her shining like a new penny." Ronan turned around to greet his friend.

Tobin Woods was six and a half feet tall and made of pure muscle. Looking at him now, Ronan would swear the man had added another twenty pounds in mass since the last time they'd seen each other. His toned build in combination with his blue eyes and blond hair made him an instant candidate for the glossy cover of fitness magazines.

"Not only that, she's ahead of schedule! Niall's over the moon." Tobin's grin lit up Ronan's sour morning.

Niall Gallagher was the owner of the bed and breakfast and was Tobin's fiancé. The two had met each other back in April when Tobin had applied, hungover and with the previous night's rum leaching from his pores, for the renovation job and had somehow gotten it.

"That's great news. You'll have to sign Ten and I up for a night here when you're open for business." *If we're still married,* Ronan added silently to himself.

"Are you kidding me? After what you and your friends did to help Niall and me out, I'm sure it will be on the house!" Tobin slapped a meaty hand against Ronan's shoulder. "But, I'm guessing the reason you're here has nothing to do with getting a comped night stay. Am I right?"

Ronan nodded sharply. He could feel his emotions bubbling to the surface and wasn't really in the mood to cry in the middle of Witch Hill Road.

"Why don't we go inside. I know Niall had some muffins that were about to come out of the oven. He's been testing his recipes out on my work crew to see if they're good enough for his guests once we're open for business."

"Let's see if they stand up to Cassie Craig's muffins over at West Side Sweets." Ronan found a weak smile.

"She actually gave one of her recipes to Niall to use at the Inn as a cross-promotion, so that people will go to West Side Sweets after having breakfast with us." Tobin tugged Ronan toward the porch and into the renovated house.

"Amazing!" Ronan sucked in a breath. The last time he was here, the house was drafty, loaded with cobwebs and there was a giant pentagram drawn in the middle of the living room floor. The room looked nothing like it had back in April.

"Oh, honey bun!" Tobin called out in an exaggerated voice. "Could you come out here for a minute?"

"For the love of all that's holy, Tobin! You know I'm busy working on this new recipe and I can't be disturbed, so unless we're being haunted by the ghost of Sam Adams this time, can you fuck off and leave me in…" Niall trailed off when he caught a glimpse of Ronan standing next to his man.

"Pull back the claws, Miss Frisky." Tobin smirked at his lover. "I just wanted to tell you that Ronan was here for a visit."

"Ronan!" Niall's face brightened. "I'm so glad to see you! I wasn't really telling Tobin to fuck off, it's just that he bugs me a million times a day and I was just looking for a little peace today. I can't seem to get these rum raisin muffins right."

"You should call Cassie," Ronan suggested.

"You don't think she'd mind?" Niall was so red with embarrassment Ronan was afraid he was going to spontaneously combust.

"Not at all."

"Okay, I will. Thanks, Ronan." Niall ran back toward the kitchen. "Oh, wait!" He ran back to Tobin. Standing on tiptoe, he pressed a kiss to Tobin's cheek. "I wasn't really telling you to fuck off." Niall kissed him again. "I love you."

Tobin's stern face cracked into a smile. "I love you too, but that doesn't mean I'm not going to warm your ass later." Tobin winked.

Ronan watched as Niall's face turned even redder than before. He suddenly wished he'd called Tobin instead of driving across town to talk to his friend.

"Let's sit." Tobin led him to the ornate dining room table that looked like it could seat twenty people comfortably. "You look like you've seen a ghost. What happened?"

Tobin was always a bottom line kind of a guy. It was the reason he'd been the one to suggest the contractor to Tennyson and the Craig brothers as the right man to remodel West Side Magick for them earlier this year. "I need to talk to you about Gideon Black."

"Shit, that's a heavy topic for this early in the morning." Tobin shook his head. "What is it you need to know?" Tobin was about to continue speaking when Niall came into the dining room carrying a tray with a basket of muffins and a steaming carafe of coffee. He set it down wordlessly and headed back into the kitchen.

"I've been having past lives resurfacing. One of them was during the time of the Witch Trials. Black had Tennyson's past life burned at the stake."

Tobin sat blinking at him. He didn't move and didn't appear to be breathing. "You and Ten are Samuel Goodman and Wolfgang Grimme, aren't you? Are you kidding me, Ronan?" Tobin got up and paced around the large table. "Are you actually telling me that you were Samuel Goodman in a past life?" Tobin looked pale as the ghost he'd just accused Ronan of seeing.

Ronan nodded. "Tennyson took me to see Madam Aurora for a past life regression therapy session. I met Samuel during the regression and we had a chance to talk for a few minutes. I wish I had the words to properly explain to you the love he felt for Wolf."

"So, they *were* a couple." Tobin slapped his hand down on the table as he resumed his seat. "There was rumor and innuendo about it, but I was never able to prove anything through the historical records."

"They were definitely a couple, but I have nothing to offer you for the record." How magnificent that would have been though, to offer evidence of a gay couple from the seventeenth century.

Tobin's eyes were lit up like a child's on Christmas morning. "Where does Black come into things?"

"Did you hear anything on the news last week about the death of Gia Gonzalez?" Ronan wasn't sure how much of the story to tell Tobin.

"You mean the member of the Salem Witches?" Tobin raised an eyebrow at Ronan to indicate he was completely up to speed.

It seemed he didn't have as much to catch Tobin up on as he thought. "Right. A few days before Gia died, she and other members of the coven came to see me. They think someone is hunting them and killing them one by one in ways that are made to look like accidents."

Tobin nodded as if this wasn't the first time he was hearing the story. "I've heard rumblings of this story. Just rumors really. Are you thinking Black has something to do with the deaths of the witches?"

Ronan nodded. "During the past life regression, Black recognized me as Ronan. He told me there was a final battle coming and that he was responsible for what was happening to the witches."

"Jesus Christ," Tobin muttered under his breath.

"I went to the Salem Public Library to research Black's family tree to see if I could figure out which of his modern-day descendants were still alive or living in the area, but the ancestry database was a dead end."

Tobin frowned. "What do you mean a dead end? Is everyone actually dead?"

"I don't know. That's just the thing. The database ends with the 1940s generation. It lists members of that generation who were married or KIA in Vietnam, but nothing after that. No children."

"You're shitting me? How is that possible?" Tobin reached into the pocket of his tee-shirt to pull out his iPhone. Unlocking it, he started pounding notes into it with the meaty index finger of his right hand.

"I spoke to the librarian on duty. A woman named Lucinda, or Lydia or something with an 'L.' Anyway, she said that since the Baby Boomers are such a large generation and with budget cuts, it's taking their reduced staff a long time to get all of the records into the computer." Ronan shrugged and reached for a muffin.

"You were hoping I might have some information about Black's descendants?" Tobin asked.

Ronan, his mouth stuffed full of Niall's amazing pineapple muffin, could only nod. That was exactly the reason he'd come here today. He was hoping Tobin would know the information off the top of his head, but his friend was only the historian for the Woods family. It was ridiculous to think he'd know everything about the Blacks too simply because one of that family's members lived during the time of the Witch Trials.

Tobin tapped his finger on the table. "You know, another good resource for modern genealogy is Callum Churchill. He did a lot of research for *Nobody's Witch* that took the book into this century."

Ronan swallowed hard. "I was afraid you were going to say that."

"Do you remember what I said about the Witch Trials when you and Tennyson first came out to the house to try to figure out what was haunting it?"

Ronan nibbled on his bottom lip trying to remember what Tobin was talking about. "You said that if we didn't understand history that we were doomed to repeat it."

"That's right. We're part of a special group of people, Ronan. You, me, Tennyson, Callum. We're descendants of the Witch Trials in one form or another. It's more important now than ever that we stop this modern-day witch hunt in its tracks. Back in 1692, the hunt was out in the open. It was a public spectacle, with neighbor accusing neighbor, but what's going on now is unfathomable. Actual witches are being murdered this time around with insidious plots being hatched in the dead of night where no one can witness the evil. How could we ever hope to stop something that's skulking around in the shadows?"

"Tennyson doesn't understand why I have to do this." Ronan's voice was barely above a whisper. He had no idea how to explain this to his husband and didn't understand why Tennyson hadn't yet figured it out for himself.

"Explain it to me," Tobin urged.

"In my dreams I've watched him burn twice, Tobin. The way the flames danced toward his clothes and then raced up them. I could hear the crackle of the fire followed by his cries of agony. The sound of silence though, that was the worst." Tears dripped down Ronan's face to splash against the wooden table. "Even though they were dreams, I could smell his burning flesh. It sticks in your nose like no other odor I've ever smelled in my life. Days after the dream, I could still smell it. Then there were the looks of twisted joy on the faces in the crowd. They were happy to see him burn. Maybe they were just relieved it wasn't themselves lashed to the stake, but in my mind, there was more to it. There was almost a childlike glee in their eyes." Ronan looked up at Tobin and saw the bigger man was also swiping away tears of his own. "I had to see it a third time during my session with Aurora. He looked me in the eyes each time, Tobin. My husband knew before he died that I failed him, but his final words to me were always that we'd be reunited. Can you imagine that? Going to your own death knowing that the man you loved failed to save you, but being happy in the knowledge that you'd see him again someday?"

"We always say that we love our husband or wife enough to die for them, but in reality, do we? Would we make that ultimate sacrifice?"

Ronan nodded. Thank Christ someone finally understood why he had to help the witches. "Gideon Black told me that Ten and I lived all of these lives together. According to him, I failed Tennyson in all of them. I won't fail him in this one. I've already failed Gia. She has to be the last one." Setting a hand on Tobin's broad shoulder, Ronan got up from the table and headed for the door.

28

Tennyson

Nothing was going right for Tennyson. Dixie had refused to go out this morning and then had done her business right in the middle of the kitchen while she looked at Tennyson. After he'd cleaned that mess up, he'd spilled coffee on his pants and had been running so late, there hadn't been time to change. Then, to make matters worse, his first two clients of the day had cancelled on him which meant he had the time to go home and change his stained pants, but he hadn't wanted to risk running into Ronan.

"Let me guess, you didn't take my earlier advice to call your husband, right?" Carson asked from behind a sulking Tennyson.

"Carson, he told me he didn't want me sleeping next him in our bed." The message to leave Ronan alone had been pretty obvious.

"Yes, I remember that part of the conversation. What I don't remember is you telling me why he said that."

Tennyson had specifically left that part of the fight out of his retelling of it. "I jumped on Ronan with rapid-fire questions without giving him time to answer any of them and then I accused him of having a meltdown in the middle of the Salem Police Department like a toddler."

Raising an eyebrow at his friend, Carson took a step back from him. "Ronan didn't tell us about melting down in the police department, just that someone needed to go pick him up there. So, that begs the question how did you know that's what happened?"

Sighing, Ten shook his head. "I picked that detail out of his head and used it against him."

"Ah, so that's what had Ronan angry at you and saying he didn't want you sleeping in the same room with him." It wasn't a question. "I don't mean to pry, but didn't you promise him on the cruise that you'd stop doing that very thing?"

Tennyson frowned at his best friend. He had told Carson all about his behind-the-eight-ball New Year's Resolution that had to do with staying out of Ronan's head. That resolution was busted for sure now. "Yes, I did say that I was going to try to be better at staying out of Ronan's head, but I was just so angry at him last night for putting our family in jeopardy like that."

Carson shook his head. "I don't understand how he put your family in jeopardy. You said earlier that he wasn't arrested and wasn't even issued a fine, right?"

"Right, but he could have been arrested. We have Emilyn's insemination coming up next week, Carson. What if he missed his donation appointment?" Tennyson had gotten so used to the idea of his daughter being in their lives that the thought of missing out on her was devastating.

"I see where you're coming from, Ten. I really do, but you need to chill out over this. Has it occurred to you that there's something bigger going on here?"

"What do you mean something bigger? Ronan's just off on another one of his fly-by-the-seat-of-his-pants, leap-before-he-looks adventures."

"Is that what you think this is, Nostradamus?" Ronan asked from behind him.

"Shit." Ten spun around to see Ronan standing behind him. He was holding a coffee in one hand and a bakery bag in the other. He'd bet a year's salary the coffee was for him and the bag held one of Cassie's peach muffins which happened to be his favorite thing on her menu. Ronan knew Ten didn't eat when they were fighting. "What are you doing here? I thought you didn't want me around."

"Jesus Christ," Carson muttered. "Watch this, dumbass." He rolled his eyes at his best friend before turning to Ronan. "Good morning, Ronan. It sure was nice of you to surprise me like this after I was a big stupid-head last night! And look! You brought me my favorite breakfast. I'm so sorry I said dumb things to you. Why don't you follow me into the reading room where I can tell you, in detail, all of the incredibly wrongheaded things I did and when I'm finished, I'll suck your dick."

Ronan snorted, cracking half a smile. "That's not half bad, Carson. I'd give it an eight."

"Yeah, well after that shit went down on the cruise, I got real good at apologizing to Truman. I realized my pride wasn't worth losing my marriage. Hear that, Tennyson?"

"Loud and clear." Ten shook his head. He knew Carson was talking sense. "Come on, Ronan." Ten led the way toward the reading room. He hoped Ronan had something to say since he was at a bit of a loss himself. After all, Ronan was the one who told Tennyson he didn't want to sleep with him.

Ten held the door open for his husband and shut it behind him. When he turned around, Ronan was standing in front of him.

He took a step forward, pushing Tennyson back until there was nowhere to go.

"Ronan?" Ten asked breathlessly.

"Time's too short to waste fighting with you." Ronan kissed Ten hard, pinning his smaller body against the door.

Ten moaned, wrapping his arms around Ronan's hips and pulling his husband closer to him.

"I'm sorry I was such a dick telling you to sleep in another room last night," Ronan panted, before nibbling down the column of Tennyson's throat.

"I'm sorry I yelled at you the minute you walked through the door and read your mind to see what happened at the police station." Ten went for the button on Ronan's jeans and quickly slipped his hand inside, once the zipper was down. "I'll do better, I promise."

"Christ, you're doing fine right now!" Ronan grinned.

Ten didn't need to use his gift to see that. Ronan's flesh was rock hard in his right hand and his breathing was coming in sexy little pants. Using his left, he pushed down at the ass of Ronan's jeans to give himself more room to operate. "That's it babe, I've got you. Let go and come for me."

Resting his forehead against, Tennyson's, Ronan obeyed. He whispered Tennyson's name as his cock jerked in his husband's hand.

Ten held Ronan close through the storm. He knew Ronan needed that closeness more than he needed the physical release. When Ronan was finished, Ten left him where he was to grab the box of Kleenex from the table and cleaned them both up the best he could. "Feeling better now?"

"A little bit." Ronan took a seat at the table after he put himself away. "Come sit." Ronan tapped the spot at the table where Tennyson sat for readings.

"Ronan, I don't understand." Why the hell did Ronan want him to sit in the chair he used when he was working? This fight was precipitated by him using his gifts to peer into Ronan's head. Why would Ronan want him to do that now? Willingly?

"Part of the reason we're fighting is because I don't have the words to explain to you why helping the witches is so important to me. I need you to see it for yourself. I'm inviting you in, Ten. For the sake of our relationship and our about-to-be-conceived daughter, please, do it."

It was hard for Tennyson to refuse Ronan anything on a good day, but sitting here now and seeing the earnest look on his husband's face, it was impossible to refuse this request.

Nodding, Ten took a deep breath. He cleared his mind of all outside influences and opened his gift wide. He found himself standing inside the cottage Ronan had described during the Salem Witch Trial dream.

"You must save yourself when they come to arrest me," a man who was Tennyson's twin said.

"Wolf, no!" Ronan's twin, Samuel Goodman, answered fervently.

"Yes, my love. I could not bear it if I were the cause of your death."

"Like I am the cause of yours." A rogue tear spilled from Samuel Goodman's eye.

"It matters not. We will be reunited. You have my word." Wolf reached up to cup the side of Samuel's face.

Tennyson realized what he was witnessing. This was the last time Wolf and Sam saw each other before Samuel was forced to arrest him on witchcraft charges. Ten could feel the anguish in Samuel. The man knew this was all his fault; that if he'd just kept his hands and his feelings to himself, none of this would be happening now. He wanted to shout to Samuel that love was always a risk worth taking, but just as he was about to open his mouth, the scene changed again and Tennyson found himself standing in a dark forest lit only by a raging bonfire.

He could see himself, Wolf rather, lashed to a wooden pole. The look in his eyes was one of acceptance, but he could feel the fear rolling off him. It was almost as powerful as the wave of heat generated by the fire.

Turning to his left, he could see Gideon Black standing with Samuel and a man he could only assume was Constable Carver.

"Do you accuse Wolfgang Grimme as a witch?" Preacher Black asked over the roar of the flames

"I do," Samuel agreed, looking sick to his stomach.

"I condemn thee to the flames!" Black screamed.

Tennyson watched in horror as a hooded figure walked toward Wolf and set the twigs around him on fire. It didn't take long for the fire to climb toward Wolf and then to ignite his clothing. Ten could see how brave his past-life self was being in light of what was to come. Then the screaming started. A bolt of pain, unlike anything Tennyson had ever felt in his life slashed through his body. It grew steadier and steadier, as his body grew hotter. He began to cough and choke. Then the smell of burning flesh hit him, turning his stomach. Wolf's screams of agony stopped.

Ten wanted out of Ronan's head, but he had to stay here. He had to stay for Ronan. For Samuel. For Wolf. For the Salem Witches. For his little miss, who one day would inherit her mother's gifts.

29

Ronan

Ronan had never seen Tennyson so exhausted or heartbroken after a reading in the entire time they'd known each other. He'd have to give his husband credit though, he'd thought that after Ten witnessed his own death in Salem he would have thrown in the towel and stopped watching the macabre version of his own home videos, but he'd hung in there and watched an almost identical scene repeat itself in Spain.

It had been hard enough for Ronan to watch Tennyson die repeatedly in these past life memories, but it must be something else entirely to watch yourself die. Ronan had known he'd been offering Tennyson a terrible choice by inviting him into his head to see things from his point of view. Yes, by the end of it Ten was going to see why saving the witches was so important to him, but on the other hand, he was going to walk away with Kodak moments no man should have to see, let alone remember.

When they'd gotten home, Ten had curled up on the couch with Dixie, who'd somehow understood that Ten needed to cuddle with her. Ronan had done his part by making his husband his favorite chamomile tea and finding a *Law & Order: SVU* marathon for Tennyson to get lost in.

Afternoon turned to evening as they sat watching Detective Stabler kick ass and show off his spectacular abs. Ronan called out to Greek Life for their favorite Mediterranean pizza with extra feta and got an order of baklava, knowing the honey in the sweet dessert would help Tennyson get his strength back.

Ronan had spent the time when Stabler was fully clothed and obeying the law trying to figure out a way to get the police to reopen one of the witch cases. If he could find evidence in just one of the cases that would prove the death wasn't an accident, that would give him the solid footing he needed to prove that one death was part of a larger conspiracy at work.

He went back over all of the cases in his mind. Jessa McIntyre died in a house fire. Athena Mathieu was killed in a car accident. Kendra Watts died in a slip and fall accident at home. Michelle Kingston drowned at Walden Pond. Martha Patterson took her own life and Kim Patricia died from an accidental drug interaction. Lastly there was Gia Gonzalez and her fatal blow to the head while running.

Ronan tried to walk through each of the deaths as if he were the responding officer on duty. How would he have looked for evidence or clues the killer left behind at each scene? That was the big question. Since each of the deaths had been ruled accidental or suicide in the case of Martha Patterson, evidence wasn't collected in the same manner. For example, since Michelle Kingston was swimming alone and had no known enemies, there was no reason to cast footprints on the beach of the pond, or to write down the other license plate numbers in the parking lot, or canvas witnesses for what they might have seen the day she died.

The house fire was interesting though. Maybe Ronan could hire an independent firm to go over the arson investigation report to see if anything was missed. He remembered seeing an episode of *Forensic Files* where a woman had been convicted and sentenced to die in one of the Carolinas for setting fire to her son's bedroom and on appeal this arson investigator was able to prove that faulty wiring and a leak in the roof were the real cause of the deadly fire.

That kind of investigation could take time though, time Ronan and the witches didn't have. "Holy fuck! The car!" Ronan shouted, startling Tennyson.

"Wha?" Ten asked sounding like he had no idea what century he'd just woken up in.

"Shit, did I wake you up, babe?" Ronan was a dick, no two ways about it. He should have known that Tennyson had fallen asleep.

Ten blinked up at Ronan like it was taking him a minute to place his face. "Um, I think so." He wore a goofy grin. "That session with you this morning really sapped all of my energy. Eating helped, but damn, I feel like I could sleep for a week." Ten sat up and stretched. His left shoulder popped. "What were you shouting about a car? Did something happen to the Mustang?"

"No." Ronan shook his head. "I was sitting here trying to figure out a way to prove that one of the witches was murdered," Ronan started. He couldn't help noticing the almost imperceptible tensing of Ten's entire body over the topic of conversation. Ten might have gotten a first-hand glimpse of why Ronan felt like he had to help the witches, but apparently, he still wasn't on board entirely with the cause. "It occurred to me that one of the women died in a car accident. Since the wreck was considered an accident, the police didn't send the vehicle to an impound lot."

"I don't understand what that has to do with anything." Ten yawned before scrubbing a hand over his face.

"If the police had impounded Athena's car, we wouldn't be able to get to it and look it over for clues."

"*We?*" Ten asked. The edge was back in his voice.

"Well, not you, babe. You don't seem the grease monkey sort. I've been working on cars since I was in high school and Jude with that old Thunderbird of his, and I bet Tobin knows his way around an engine block too, even though he drives a brand-new Ford pickup."

"I didn't mean *we* as in you and me, Ronan, I meant we as in you and whoever are still going to investigate this thing even though you've been warned to stay away from it. I understand your need to protect these women, but your career is on the line here, Ronan."

"And that's more important than saving lives?"

Tennyson sighed. He bowed his head toward his chest.

Ronan could tell his husband was looking for the right words to say. Most likely he was choosing his words carefully so that he wouldn't reignite their earlier fight. He opened his mouth looking like he was about to answer Ronan's question when his phone started to jingle. "Hold that thought." Ronan pressed a kiss to Ten's lips.

Picking up his phone he saw Aurora's name on the caller ID and knew in his heart this wasn't a social call. "O'Mara." Ronan held his breath.

"You need to get to North Shore Medical Center now." Aurora was crying.

Ronan felt his stomach clench. He looked up at Tennyson who wore a look in his eyes as if he already knew. "Who is it, Aurora?"

"Lyric, Ronan. It's Lyric, and…" Aurora started crying too hard to finish her sentence.

"Aurora, it's Lyric and who? Is it Katie? Was Katie in the car with her?" Katie was Lyric's wife and a former Boston Police Officer. The two of them had met several years ago when Katie had brought some evidence down to Lyric in the DNA lab.

Tennyson shook his head no.

"Jesus, Ten, if it wasn't Katie…" Ronan sucked in a harsh breath. If the other person in the car wasn't Lyric's wife, that only left one option. Katie and Lyric had a year-old daughter. "Astrid? Aurora, was it Astrid?"

"Yes," Aurora cried. "Get here now!" The line beeped three times and went dead.

Ronan couldn't move. He felt like he was paralyzed. What the hell did he do now? He'd been sitting here on his ass all night long cuddling his husband while Lyric and Astrid had been in an accident. "Tennyson, what…?"

"I'm calling Truman." Ten already had the phone in his hand.

Truman. His best friend. That was a good place to start. If the worst happened tonight to either Lyric or that precious baby Ronan was going to need Truman. Truman would keep him from doing something disastrous and if that failed, his best friend would hold him tight if the worst happened as a result.

30

Tennyson

It was the longest ten-minute drive of Tennyson's life. He sat in the backseat of Truman's SUV holding Ronan's hand. He'd been reaching out with his gift and trying to contact Bertha and Erin O'Mara, but so far, he wasn't getting any information about Lyric or Astrid Vaughn.

What he was getting was a mountain of guilt, regret, and blame blasting off his husband like heat from a bonfire. It was on the tip of his tongue to ask Ronan just what in hell he thought he could have done to prevent this from happening, but decided at the moment to keep that question to himself. Catholic guilt was a powerful thing and there was no way a three-minute conversation in the backseat of an SUV was going to undo thirty years of indoctrination.

"I'm dropping you off at the door and then I'll park the car," Truman said.

"Thanks, Tru," Ronan muttered. Those were the first words he'd spoken since Ten had called Truman.

Truman looked up to lock eyes with Tennyson in the rear-view mirror. His green eyes were grim. Ten could feel the worry radiating off him. Truman was worried for everyone, Ronan, Astrid, Lyric, the rest of the witches, himself.

When Truman parked the car in front of the ER doors, Ronan straightened his shoulders and took a deep breath. It was as if he was hiding his true emotions and going into cop-mode. He was going to be strong for everyone, so they could feel free to fall apart on his strong shoulder. "You ready?" he asked Tennyson.

"I'll meet you in the waiting room," Truman flashed a brief smile.

"Did we call everyone?" Ronan asked.

Truman nodded. "Carson was doing that when I left."

"Thank him for me. Thanks to you too, Tru, for doing this and for whatever happens later." Ronan hopped out of the car without waiting for his best friend's response.

"What the hell do you mean for whatever happens later?" Tennyson asked as he ran to catch up with Ronan who was practically sprinting toward the emergency room doors.

Ronan didn't stop to answer the question.

"Damn it, Ronan!" Tennyson grabbed his elbow and managed to swing his larger husband around, throwing off his balance.

"Ten, not now!" Ronan growled. The look in his eyes was determined. His nostrils were flared.

"Yes, now!" Ten gave his husband the once over. "You look like you're about to go in there and start a fight. Dial it back a bit. We don't know what's happened yet. Aurora is an emotional woman and Lyric is like a daughter to her. It could be that she and Astrid have cuts and scrapes."

Ten took a deep breath. "But if they don't, if it's more serious than that, the last thing the people in there that love them need is for you to come bursting through the door like *Rambo* all 'roided up and ready for blood."

Ronan sighed. His shoulders dropped and he tilted his head all the way back. "I'm terrified of what we're going to hear when we walk in there."

"I know you are. I am too. But this leather jacket badass attitude isn't going to win you any points. They don't need cop-mode Detective O'Mara. They just need *you*, Ronan."

Nodding, Ronan reached for Tennyson's hand and led him toward the doors which whooshed open for them.

Glancing quickly over the people in the waiting room, Ten didn't see any familiar faces. Ronan must not have either, since he was striding toward the intake desk.

"We're looking for Lyric Vaughn and her daughter Astrid. They were brought in after a motor vehicle accident."

Ten had to admit he was proud of Ronan. He didn't name drop that he was from BPD and didn't whip out his detective's shield. Maybe a tiger could change his stripes.

"Are you family, sir?" the attendant, whose nametag read, "Brenda," asked.

Ronan reached into his back pocket and pulled out his wallet where his spare detective shield sat. "Detective Ronan O'Mara from the Boston Police Department. Ms. Vaughn is a member of our DNA Lab."

Well, so much for a tiger changing his stripes. In this case though, Tennyson wasn't going to hold that against him.

"I'm not asking for the condition of Lyric or her infant daughter. I want to know where her friends and family are. We're here to support them." Ronan offered the woman a gentle smile.

The smile looked more like a grimace to Tennyson, but the big guy was trying. He hadn't cursed or issued one demand. Yet.

"Family waiting room. Down the hall to the right." Brenda waved a hand in the general direction.

"See, I can be nice." Ronan took off in the direction she pointed.

"I'll wait for Truman," Ten called after him. He needed these few minutes to try to calm himself down. One way or the other, this incident had just reopened the floodgates. Even if this really was just an accident, Ronan was going to be like a dog with a bone, hounding the Salem Police until every possible lead had been exhausted. He needed to call Fitzgibbon and maybe try to head this thing off at the pass. It wasn't the most honest approach here, but maybe it could save Ronan's job, his pension, and their health insurance.

He was about to pull his phone out of his back pocket when Truman and Fitzgibbon came running into the ER together. Trailing along closely behind them were Niall Gallagher and Tobin Woods.

"Tennyson? How are they? How are Lyric and Astrid?" Fitzgibbon was panting. He bent double trying to catch his breath.

"We don't know yet. Ronan went ahead to the waiting room and I stayed back here to wait for Truman. I was just about to call you, Cap." Tennyson stared down at the floor.

"Oh, is there something I should be aware of, Ten?" Kevin's green eyes lit with curiosity.

"It's just that, I had finally managed to get Ronan calmed back down with this whole conspiracy theory thing." Ten shook his head. "And now with this, he's going to go full steam ahead again. You threatened to suspend him over what happened at the police station with Chief Jackson and I'm afraid that this is going to push him over the edge."

"Did I hear my name?" a handsome Hispanic man asked from behind Fitzgibbon. "Cisco Jackson. You must be the famous Tennyson Grimm I've heard so much about."

Ten nodded. He sent the chief a quick wave with the index finger of his right hand. "I'd say it's nice to meet you Chief, but I have a feeling I'm going to hate you in the near future for beating up or locking up my husband."

Cisco burst out laughing. "Duly noted, Tennyson. I won't hold your husband's antics against you."

Fitzgibbon shook his head. "First of all, we both know Ronan only made you *think* he'd calmed down over this whole *conspiracy theory thing*, Tennyson. He's still convinced there's someone out there picking off these women one by one."

"I'm afraid I'm going to be the bearer of bad news then." Cisco crossed his arms over his broad chest.

Tennyson sighed. His chin hit his chest. Of course, the chief had bad news. "Lay it on us, chief."

"I've just come from the scene. We've had our accident reconstruction team out there and they've determined it was a single car accident. There one set of skid marks, no signs of damage to Lyric's car that would indicate another vehicle hit, rammed, or bumped hers. We're thinking one scenario is that she may have swerved to avoid an animal in the road. It was late. Fort Avenue is dark and desolate this time of night. Accidents happen." Cisco set a hand on Tennyson's shoulder. "Let's go see if Lyric and her daughter are okay."

Tennyson felt rooted to the floor. Ronan wasn't going to take the "accidents happen" theory very well. "Tru?" Ten's voice trembled.

"I'm on it, Ten." Truman jogged ahead to catch up with the police chief, Niall and Tobin. Thank God for Truman's intuitive understanding of the situation.

"Are you okay?" Kevin asked as they turned to follow behind.

"No, Kevin. I'm not. I've never seen Ronan like this before. I know why he's acting like this. I get now why he's so hellbent on protecting these women, but when push comes to shove and he loses his shit in there. That reason isn't going to save his badge or our health insurance."

Fitzgibbon's eyes narrowed on Tennyson. "You want to try explaining it to me?"

"In these past life flashbacks, Ronan keeps losing me, or rather the past life version of me. According to Gideon Black we've lived all these lifetimes together and he's bested us in all of them. Ronan's had to watch me die every single time. Earlier today, Ronan invited me into his mind so I could see these things."

"Wait, you watched yourself be burned at the stake in a past life?" Fitzgibbon looked skeptical at best. "Look, I'm trying my hardest here to follow along with things. I could believe that spirits attacked you when you lost your gift because I could see the bruises on you and I knew damn well that Ronan would never hurt you like that, but I just can't *see* this past life stuff."

"I know you can't, Kevin, and that's what scares me the most. You always have our backs on the cold cases we work because you believe in my gift. You're in free fall here. So, when Ronan loses his shit in there, like we both know he will, he's lost his greatest ally." Ten shook his head. "Jesus, Kevin, Emilyn's procedure is next week. Ronan has an appointment at the clinic on Tuesday to make his donation. One of his swimmers will create our little miss. That embryo will grow into our daughter." Ten could feel tears pricking at the backs of his eyes. "Do you see where I'm heading here? Our family needs you on Ronan's side tonight more than ever. I would never presume on our personal friendship here, Kevin, but Jesus Christ, our baby..."

The hard look in Kevin's eyes softened. "Let's go see what the situation is in that room before we go jumping to any conclusions, okay?"

Nodding, Ten walked down the hallway with Kevin. Truman was waiting outside the door. "Shit, are they…"

Truman shook his head no. "They're waiting for you so they don't have to tell the story twice."

Of course, they were waiting for Tennyson so that he'd be there to help control Ronan when all of the different shits hit the fan. Lyric and Astrid. What actually happened out on Fort Avenue. The fact that Fitzgibbon thought this past life stuff was bullshit. Steeling himself for what was to come, Ten pushed the door open.

All of the witches were there. Callum Churchill had his arm wrapped around Hazel, while Aurora and Corazon were crying quietly in the back row of chairs. Andromeda was standing alone in the far corner, while Niall and Tobin were sitting together with Jude, of all people, holding Katie's hand. It was a world gone mad if Jude Byrne was sitting in the waiting room to support a witch's wife.

"Katie? How are Astrid and Lyric?" Tennyson sat in the empty chair to her left.

"Lyric's in surgery." Tears flowed freely from Katie's dark eyes. The doctor said she slammed into the steering wheel pretty hard. I didn't understand everything he was saying, but something about her spleen and liver?" She started crying again and rested her face against Jude's shoulder.

He wrapped an arm around her shoulder and looked over at Tennyson.

"It might be a ruptured spleen," Callum Churchill supplied. "They also suspect internal bleeding from some kind of damage to her liver."

Ten nodded. "And Astrid? What about the baby?" His sixth sense was wide open, but he wasn't getting anything and he still hadn't seen hide nor hare of Bertha or Erin and he'd been throwing out his own personal Bat Signal since they'd gotten the phone call from Aurora.

"They have her in X-ray," Katie wept. "My little angel in that big, awful machine by herself. They wouldn't let me go with her. She was in the rear-facing car seat, but still…"

Remembering meeting Lyric's grandmother who was also named Astrid, Ten reached out to her, but wasn't getting a response either. Ten had a feeling all of the nanas were with the people who needed them most at the moment. He knew that's where he would be.

Out of the corner of his eye, Ten saw the police chief approaching them. Ronan was with him. His stomach did a slow roll. This was where the rubber met the road. He cringed internally at the unfortunate use of metaphor, but it was apt in this situation.

"Mrs. Vaughn, I'm Salem Police Chief Francisco Jackson. I'm very sorry for what happened to your wife and daughter tonight."

Katie nodded. "Thank you. I appreciate you being here for us."

"Ronan was telling me you were a member of the Boston Police Department before baby Astrid was born."

"Right. I gave up the flashy world of walking a beat in Roslindale to stay home and work diaper patrol." Katie gave a little laugh. It sounded hollow.

Cisco offered her a genuinely warm smile. "I was out at the accident scene before I came here and I wanted to let you know that Lyric's car was the only one involved. There were skid marks from only one car and we didn't find any evidence on the car of it being hit or bumped."

Tennyson's eyes were on Ronan as the chief delivered the details of the accident scene. He watched for signs of Ronan getting angry and unbelievably, saw none. Ronan's hands weren't curling into fists, his breathing hadn't sped up, his eyes didn't have that wild, almost feral look to them. He was simply nodding along with Cisco as he delivered the facts to Katie.

Ah, that was it, Ten thought to himself. Ronan was keeping the volcanic rage inside because the cop was speaking to Katie. Once he was done speaking with her, Ten would bet the house that Ronan was going to ask to speak with him outside. That's where the shit was going to hit the fan. He looked over at Fitzgibbon who looked like he was trying hard to hide his own shock at Ronan's unlikely behavior.

"Ronan, may I have a word with you outside?" Cisco took his arm, not waiting for an answer.

Ten watched in disbelief as the police chief practically dragged Ronan out the door. He was too shocked to follow and didn't think he was invited anyway. He wasn't surprised a moment later when Fitzgibbon and Truman followed them out the door. Ten couldn't help thinking for the second and probably not the last time tonight, thank God for Truman Wesley.

31

Ronan

This couldn't be good. Cisco had Ronan's arm in vise-grip hold. He had a feeling there were going to be bruises there tomorrow from where the cop's thumb and forefinger were digging into his flesh. Not wanting to make a scene in front of Katie and the witches, he allowed the chief lead him out of the room, but make no mistake, he was going to want some answers for being manhandled like a common fucking criminal in front of his friends like this.

"Calm the hell down, Ronan," Cisco muttered as if he were reading Ronan's thoughts.

"You practically perp-walked me out of the room, chief. You want to take your meat hook off of me?" He yanked his arm away from the cop just as Fitzgibbon and Truman walked out of the waiting room behind them. *Great, a fucking audience.*

"I just wanted you to hear the rest of the evidence from me." Cisco fisted his hands on his hips.

"There's more evidence?" Fitzgibbon asked. He sounded as if he were in cop-mode.

"Two pieces I didn't want to mention in front of Ms. Vaughn's wife. The first was there wasn't an animal corpse at the scene and the second being that one of my officers found Lyric's phone on the floor of the passenger side of the car," Cisco said with a finality that indicated that was the crucial piece of evidence.

Ronan shook his head. "What?"

"Lyric's phone ended up on the passenger side of the cabin. This is usually what we see happen when a driver has the phone in their hand at the time of impact." Cisco's voice was soft, as if he were trying to soothe Ronan's temper as he was speaking.

Oh. That's what the chief was trying to drive toward here. Single car accident. One set of skid marks. No sign of paint transfer from another vehicle. No dead animal. Cell phone that was bounced around during the impact. Cause of the accident: distracted driving.

Ronan nodded along with what the police chief was telling him. If this man was too fucking stupid to see what was going on in his own city with not one, but now two women who happened to be members of the same organization that had a long, storied history of violence in this particular New England town, then Ronan was just going to have to prove it to him. He wasn't so far gone that he couldn't see that here was neither the time nor the place to begin the chief's education. "Where's the car now, Cisco?"

"We had it picked up by Witch City Towing. Thing looked totaled though. Why?" Cisco narrowed his eyes as if he were trying to figure out what possible reason Ronan could have for asking that question.

"Well, first of all Lyric and Astrid's personal items are still going to be in that car. Astrid has this stuffed monkey I gave her when she was born that she doesn't go anywhere without. She's going to want that for bedtime. Plus, the Vaughns are a one income family now that Katie stays home with Astrid. Lyric's injuries sound pretty serious which is going to make money even tighter. Maybe there's something we can do to get the car fixed and back on the road. You know, start a Give Me Money page online or something." Ronan shrugged.

"You mean a Go Fund Me page?" Cisco grinned at Ronan.

"Yeah, that." Ronan loved playing stupid. People fell for it all the time and the two biggest dupes were criminals and cops. God, he wanted to roll his eyes, but he was so close to winning.

"I know the guy who owns the tow shop, Hunter Conroy. I'll shoot him a text and let him know you'll be stopping by to pick stuff up and that you'll be arranging to take the car off his hands tomorrow."

Ronan found his first real smile of the night. "Thank you, chief. I appreciate that. I'm sure Lyric and Astrid will too."

"You let me know if there's anything else I can do to help. I gotta get back out on patrol." Cisco inclined his head toward the emergency room door.

"Patrol?" Ronan half-squawked. "You're the chief of police. What the hell are you doing out on patrol?"

"This is my city, Ronan. I'm a Salem boy, born and bred. Just because there was nothing I could do about Gia Gonzalez's death, it doesn't mean I was happy about it." His dark eyes shifted to Fitzgibbon. "Captain." Cisco nodded at Ronan's boss before he headed toward the emergency room door.

Ronan saw Truman sigh and his entire body visibly relax.

Fitzgibbon turned and got into Ronan's face. "I don't know what kind of bullshit performance that was, Ronan, but I swear to fucking Christ, if you do anything to fuck up your appointment at the clinic next week, I'll suspend you so fast that you'll choke on my dust, you got it?"

"Cap, I don't-"

Fitzgibbon held a hand up. "Don't play stupid with me, Ronan. We both know you were gaming that man with every trick in the book. What I don't know is why he was letting you get away with it."

"We're all on the same side here, Kevin." Ronan shook his head. He should have known Kevin would have seen right through his little performance, but it still hurt being called out on it.

"What side is that?"

"Justice!" Ronan bellowed, before remembering he was in a hospital. He took a deep breath. "You heard what the chief said, that they think Lyric was texting and driving or was somehow distracted by her phone. That's bullshit and you know it! We've worked with her for five years, Cap. I knew her from my time in Homicide long before I ever came to your unit. She's precise and meticulous. More than that, she loves her baby. That little girl is her entire world and she would never do something as foolish as texting and driving or fucking with something on her phone when she was only two miles from home."

"That's why you want into the car!" Fitzgibbon pointed a finger in Ronan's face. "I fucking knew you were up to something!"

"The Salem P.D. ruled the crash an accident, so no evidence was collected. Everything that was in the car at the time of the impact is still in the car now. That includes Lyric's phone and that stuffed monkey I gave the baby."

"That part of your bullshit story was true?" Fitzgibbon sounded shocked.

"Always go with the truth when you can, Cap! Katie will know the code to Lyric's phone and we'll know what she was or *wasn't* up to at the time of the accident." Ronan was about to ask Kevin what he thought of his brilliant plan when he spotted a dark-skinned doctor in surgeon's scrubs heading toward the waiting room.

"Are you all here for Lyric Vaughn?" the doctor asked.

"We are." Ronan nodded. "Are you her doctor?"

"I am. Why don't we all head inside and we'll talk." The doctor had a rather grim affect about him.

Ronan didn't like the looks of this at all. He reached out for Truman as Fitzgibbon grabbed the door.

There were gasps as the surgeon walked into the room. Ronan and the others were a step behind.

"I'm Doctor Walker Harmon. Where is Katie Vaughn?"

Katie raised her hand. Jude wrapped an arm more tightly around her.

Ronan watched as the surgeon walked to her, removing his skull cap as he went, revealing a bald head, which showed off more of his mocha skin and vibrant hazel eyes. The doctor had broad shoulders that tapered down to a slim waist and an ass that looked like it was carved from marble. Ronan knew exactly why he was sizing the man up as if he were a cut of grade-A Angus beef at a butcher shop. Any second now, this man was going to deliver either the best or worst news of their lives. Ronan was just trying to stave off the inevitable for a few more seconds.

He watched as Dr. Harmon knelt in front of Katie, taking both of her hands in his much larger ones. His heart clenched in his chest when Katie cried out, reaching for the surgeon, wrapping her arms around his neck.

"Sweet Jesus, no," Ronan whispered. He felt as if his legs weren't going to support him any longer. Watching two of Tennyson's past lives burn at the stake because he'd been unable to save them had been devastating to watch. Learning that Gia Gonzalez was dead had ripped his heart out, but this, losing Lyric, a woman who'd been a friend to him through his awful marriage and subsequent divorce from Josh Gatlin, the shooting of Manuel Garcia and everything that had happened since he'd been assigned to the Cold Case Unit, that would kill him for sure.

"No, Ronan, look!" Ten slipped his hand into Ronan's and pointed to Katie and Jude who were now laughing.

"Erin and Bertha are giving us the thumbs up too," Tennyson whispered.

"What?" Ronan couldn't believe his ears.

"Come sit, pal." Truman was wrapping an arm around his chest from behind and leading him over to a nearby chair. "You looked like you were about to hit the deck there."

"Katie screamed and grabbed the doctor. Jude was crying too. I thought Lyric was…" Ronan shook his head again.

"Everyone, Katie has given me permission to tell you all that Lyric made it through the surgery. I was able to save her liver and her spleen, but the next few hours will be critical. She won't be performing Swan Lake any time soon, but Katie tells me that wasn't her strong suit to begin with."

Katie snorted and started to giggle.

"Astrid?" Aurora called out. "What about our little one?"

"Astrid is just fine. She has some cuts from the flying glass which the nurses have been tending to. We've kept her away from the waiting room since we didn't know how things would go. Is there someone who can take her away from the hospital so she can have sweet dreams tonight?"

"Ronan!" Katie called out. "You and Ten can take her for the night, can't you?"

It's a good thing Ronan was sitting down otherwise he would have ended up on the floor. Katie trusted him to take their most precious gift. It was an overwhelming show of trust.

"We can, Katie," Tennyson said. "There are pack and play cribs at our house from when Truman's babies visit."

Ronan nodded. "Chief Jackson gave me permission to get Lyric and Astrid's personal effects out of her car. I'm going to have it brought to a garage in the morning and we'll see about getting an estimate on repairs."

"Oh, Ronan, you don't have to do that." Happy tears spilled from Katie's eyes.

Jude's eyes narrowed on Ronan. "Yes, he does. I'm going to help with the repairs too, Katie. The last thing you and Lyric need to think about right now is that car. You let us handle everything. Ronan, why don't we head over there now, so that you can grab the baby's bag and that monkey toy."

Katie nodded. "Astrid will want to have Ronan with her."

"I'm right here, Katie." Ronan pointed to himself. He'd heard before that trauma could induce confusion, but he'd never seen anything like this before. He was sitting only a few feet away from her.

Katie snorted. "No honey, *Ronan* is the name of the monkey."

Jude started to laugh. "Of course, it is! Maybe we'll stop by the cafeteria on our way out and get you a banana!" He stood and pressed a kiss to Katie's head. "You have my number if you need anything."

Katie nodded, giving Jude's hand a squeeze.

"Come on, Uncle Monkey. We've got a job to do!" Jude wrapped an arm around Ronan's shoulder.

Just for that last crack, Ronan wasn't going to tell Jude about the way Doctor Walker Harmon was staring at Jude's ass as if it were prime rib and the doc was starving.

32

Tennyson

Astrid didn't want to be put down. No matter what Tennyson tried to do to soothe the one-year-old, she didn't want to leave his arms. To be honest, Tennyson didn't want to let her go either. He dressed her in a pair of Baby Bertha's pjs and settled her against Ronan's pillow while he changed.

Katie had sent him home with her car seat, since Ronan said he and Jude were going to be a while at the tow yard. It seemed Katie knew exactly why Ronan was so gung-ho to get to Lyric's car without having to be told. It dawned on Ten that she and Lyric must have had a conversation about what to do if something like this were to happen to her.

Settling back against the pillows, Astrid crawled into Tennyson's arms. He'd turned the television on before getting into bed and he tried to relax with the solid weight of the baby in his arms.

"That was a close call," Bertha said from his left. She pressed a kiss against Astrid's downy head.

"It sure was, Bertha. In more ways than one. When I saw Cisco grab Ronan by the elbow and haul him out of the waiting room..." Ten shook his head and cuddled the baby a little closer.

"You're a natural with her, you know." Bertha sounded wistful.

"You're a natural at changing the subject. Do you know something about this thing with Ronan and the witches that I don't know or am too close to see?" It wouldn't be the first time in his life that Tennyson was too close to a situation. He'd never been one of those psychics who was able to get a good read on himself. He'd always needed to go to other people for help with his own questions.

Bertha sighed. "Tenny, I don't know what else I can say in this situation. It's not like you to be such a stubborn son-of-a-bitch."

Ten's eyes bugged open. It wasn't like Bertha to talk to him like that. He supposed he had it coming. He was being uncharacteristically stubborn about this whole situation, but there was more on the line here than Bertha knew.

"Don't give me that shit, Tennyson. You watched yourself die twice today in the most horrible fashion possible." Bertha shook her head. "I can't imagine a worse way to die. Can you?"

Ten shut his eyes and thought about it for a second. Being mauled by a bear like Leonardo DiCaprio in *The Revenant* would be pretty awful, as would being shark bait like Quint in *Jaws*, but all in all, Ten would have to admit that burning was probably the worst way to die. "I agree, Bertha."

"What you've done over the course of your past lives is downright courageous. Sacrificing yourself for Ronan is the ultimate act of love and you've done it time and time again. Why are you having such a hard time with the role reversal?"

Is that what this was? Ronan flipping the script? "In all of our other lives what I did only affected the two of us. Now, there's so much more at stake. Shit, no pun intended."

Bertha raised an eyebrow at him, shooting him a look that said that under any other set of circumstances that last line would have cracked her up. "Tennyson, that little soul belongs to you and Ronan. She is destined to be your daughter. I don't know why you are so hung up on the swimmer that does the deed. If Ronan does screw the pooch, no pun intended…" Bertha cackled. "And messes up the clinic appointment next week, you won't lose that little soul. She is already your child."

Was that the reason Tennyson was so pissed off at Ronan for jumping in feet first to save the witches, possibly at the cost of his own career?

"Are you angry that he's risking everything for their family instead of your own?" Bertha asked gently?

Ten's mouth dropped open. "What?"

"Well, it's kind of like your own family back in Kansas, isn't it? Kaye and David were all about the church and the congregation, meanwhile you were at home suffering. Are you upset that Ronan is putting the needs of the coven before the needs of your family?"

"I don't know." Ten pressed a kiss to Astrid's head. It was true. He had no idea if he was coming or going right now. "This is so unlike any other case we've investigated before. Usually we have the backing of Fitzgibbon and the whole BPD behind us and now…"

"And now, Ronan doesn't even have *you* in his corner. Fitzgibbon doesn't believe that Gideon Black is on the warpath. You don't believe that Ronan should be risking his career or his neck for the witches. It's a world gone mad when all Ronan has on his side in a witch fight is the witch-hater..." Bertha trailed off.

Ten nodded.

"It's just a job, Tenny. It's just money. Do you really want to lose your husband or this life you're building together over this? On any other day you'd be the first one to jump into a fight to protect someone weaker than yourself. On those days you witnessed with Ronan today, you were the one literally throwing yourself into the flames to protect him. Let him do the same. He has so much guilt over failing you and now Gia and Lyric. Let him help, Tennyson." With that, Bertha was gone.

Tennyson laid back against the pillows. He could tell Astrid had fallen asleep. She was dead weight in his arms now. He looked down at her angelic face, her delicate lashes against her cheeks, the way her Cupid's bow mouth was slightly parted. He couldn't help noticing the way the tiny fingers of her left hand clutched his tee shirt as if to anchor herself to him. All that mattered to him in this moment was protecting her from harm.

Ten knew where Ronan was coming from in all of this. He knew the guilt that was driving him to figure this thing out. Hell, one of the things that had drawn him to Ronan was the man's need to protect the innocent. He just couldn't see past the way this investigation could affect their family.

He and Ronan were obviously destined to be together. There were times when Ten wanted to kill Ronan and then minutes later he loved the man so much his heart was near to bursting. Ten was so close to having everything he'd ever dreamed of, and now it seemed all that they'd worked so hard to build together hung in the balance. It was crazy to be waiting for the other shoe to fall. He knew he shouldn't be feeling that way, but if he lost this life that he and Ronan had been building, Ten wasn't sure he'd survive.

Ten was about to reach for his phone when the door alarm chirped out downstairs. He pulled up the clock and saw that it was just past midnight. *The witching hour*, Ten thought as a full-body shiver tore through him.

"Hey!" Ronan grinned, as he poked his head around the corner of the bedroom door. "Look what I've got!" The stuffed head of a monkey appeared above his own.

"Hmm, I can't tell who is who. Which one is my husband and which one is the monkey?"

"Funny, Ten." Ronan stepped into the room and sat on the side of the bed. He ran a finger down the uninjured side of Astrid's cheek. "How is she?"

"She's okay. It took a little bit to settle her down. She didn't want me to let her go. No bath time. I just put her in a pair of Bertha's pjs and we got into bed. Did you find what you were looking for?"

Ronan nodded. "Yeah. Lyric's phone was sitting on the passenger side floor of the car, just like Cisco said it would be. I dusted it for prints and lifted what was there. Then I logged into it using the passcode Katie gave me."

Ten was shocked to hear that Ronan dusted the phone for fingerprints. He didn't know why he was, God knows he shouldn't have been. "What happened when you logged into the phone?"

"There was nothing there. She hadn't sent any text messages or made any phone calls during the time of the accident. I also logged into the phone's app settings and none of them were accessed during the accident either. Lyric wasn't using the phone when the crash happened." Ronan leveled Ten with a serious look.

"Why don't you go grab a shower and we can get some sleep? Maybe now that she's asleep the baby will let me put her in the crib, which I couldn't even build earlier."

"Oh, I'll go grab one from the spare room."

Before Ten could stop him, Ronan darted out of the bedroom. They kept three pack and play cribs in the house for when Carson and the babies were over. It was just a matter of opening one up and setting the brakes and it was good to go.

Ronan rushed back into the room and had the small crib set up in no time. "Do you want me to take her from you?"

For some unknown reason, Ten held Astrid closer to his chest. "No, I've got her for now." He shut his eyes for a second and in his mind's eye could see Ronan leaving the house. "Where are you going?"

Ronan raised and eyebrow. "I thought you agreed to stay out of my head, Nostradamus." He wore a brittle grin.

"I wasn't in your head. I had a vision. I saw you walking out of the house." Tennyson knew now without a shadow of doubt Ronan was leaving the house.

"I'm going back to the hospital."

"Why?" Ten cringed at the hysterical tone creeping into his voice.

"Someone needs to guard Lyric. Jude is with her now. He's going to make arrangements with Hunter Conroy from Witch City Towing to have Athena's car towed to his lot with Lyric's so that we can have a look at them in the morning. Tobin's coming too."

Ten shook his head as if that might help him understand what Ronan had just said a little better. "What? Jesus Christ, Ronan. I don't understand any of what you just said. I mean, the words were in English, but they made no sense. Why does Lyric need a guard? Why are cars getting towed to Witch City Towing? Who the hell is Hunter Conroy? Why is Tobin involved? He has a day job you know!"

Ronan tilted his head and opened his mouth as if he were about to answer Tennyson's questions. Instead, he walked back across the room and pressed a gentle kiss against his husband's temple. "Lyric is the only one to have survived the attempt on her life. Maybe it truly was an accident, in which case, it won't hurt me or Jude to lose one night's sleep. If Lyric's accident wasn't an accident, she's our only living witness, Ten, since Jude still hasn't been able to get in touch with his grandfather about the charm that protects him from being read psychically. Hunter Conroy owns Witch City Towing, which is where Lyric's car was taken tonight. Jude, Tobin, and I are all car guys. We've all been grease monkeys since we were teenagers. We're going to go over both cars with fine-toothed combs tomorrow to see if either one was tampered with in any way. If they weren't, no harm, no foul, but if they were, then we have actual evidence to bring to Chief Jackson."

Tennyson sighed. Ronan was making sense. This wasn't some half-baked plan. It was well thought out and God help him, he couldn't find any flaws in it. "Okay. Just be careful."

"That was going to be my line to you. With Astrid here, that could put you in some danger. I could have Kevin come stay the night?"

Ten shook his head. "We've got the alarm and Dixie is here."

Ronan snorted and started to laugh. "All five pounds of Dixie will be sure to scare off the toughest witch hunter alive."

"Do you really think that's what this person is, a witch hunter?" Ten shivered again.

"Just because the actual 'witch hunt' here in Salem officially stopped in 1693 doesn't mean the persecution of witches actually ended. Tobin and I think it just went underground."

"Underground? What, it's living in the sewers with Pennywise the fucking clown?" Ten could feel his hysteria starting to creep back in again. "Ronan, this whole thing sounds insane, like you're turning into one of those conspiracy theory nut jobs."

"Right now, babe, the only one who sounds a little off the deep end is you. One of our best friends is in the ICU. She nearly bled to death, Ten. We could have lost her tonight. Seven women who belong to Lyric's same social group have died in the past two years. Now, maybe if they were members of the Daughters of the American Revolution or if they all went to the same pottery class my being asked to look into this odd set of coincidences wouldn't be such a big deal, but because they're members of the Salem Witches, you're losing your shit here." Ronan leaned forward to kiss Ten's rigid lips.

"Ronan, I..." Ten wasn't sure how to finish that sentence.

"Look, babe, it's been a long day. Why don't you get some sleep? I'm just going to sit in a chair outside Lyric's hospital room. Then I'll be across town looking at cars tomorrow. Everything's going to be all right. I promise. Love you!" Smiling, Ronan walked out the door.

It occurred to Tennyson after he heard the alarm beep to signal Ronan's departure that his stubborn-ass husband was due back at BPD headquarters tomorrow to work his regular shift. Fitzgibbon was going to lose his shit when Ronan asked to take another vacation day.

33

Ronan

Thankfully it had been a quiet night at the hospital. Ronan and Jude had taken turns sitting in front of Lyric's ICU room door while the other man napped in the main waiting room of the ICU unit. Guests of ICU patients needed to be on an approved list just to be buzzed in, but Ronan knew whoever was behind this plot to kill the Salem Witches had more than just luck on his side to have gotten this far undetected.

The plan for today was to have one of Hunter Conroy's guys from Witch City Towing go pick up Athena Mathieu's car from the lot in Somerville where it had been stored since her fatal accident last year. Thanks to Jude and his smooth moves, they'd gotten permission to use Hunter's garage to inspect both vehicles. The last step in pulling off his plan involved Fitzgibbon. To be honest, Ronan wasn't sure he had any leeway left with his boss.

"You look like shit, brother." Jude set a paper cup of coffee and a wrapped muffin in front of him and sat down beside him. "You didn't get bad news about Lyric while I was grabbing breakfast, did you?"

Ronan shook his head. "No, I was just thinking about having to call Fitzgibbon. It really is a world gone fucking mad, Jude. My husband and my boss are barely on my side and the witch-hater spent the night guarding the witch."

"Tennyson said something interesting to me the day we had lunch."

"Oh?" Ronan was curious about how Tennyson changed Jude's thought process around on the witches.

"Yeah, something about how I shouldn't hold all witches responsible for what happened to my father. You've told me so much about Lyric and what a great job she does in the BPD crime lab. She really stepped up and helped Niall and Tobin with all that shit going on at The Black Cat Inn a few months ago. Not to mention the fact that her sweet baby was in the car last night. I couldn't sit by and do nothing when there's someone out there deliberately trying to hurt these women." Jude shrugged before biting into his muffin.

Ronan made a mental note to thank his husband for those words of wisdom later. "No time like the present." Ronan pulled his phone out of his back pocket.

"What about that old saying, um, what is it?" Jude tapped his index finger against his temple. "Oh! It's easier to beg for forgiveness than ask for permission."

Rolling his eyes, Ronan punched Fitzgibbon's number on his call list. "Been there, done that. It might be easier in the short term, but it sucks donkey balls in the end." He hit the speaker button as the phone started to ring in his ear. Why should he be the only one to enjoy what was sure to be an epic ass chewing?

"Ronan, why am I not surprised to hear from you this morning?" Fitzgibbon's voice betrayed no hint of his current mood. Ronan hated that.

"Good morning, Cap. Jude and I spent the night guarding Lyric Vaughn's ICU room. She's still in the same condition as last night, critical, but stable."

"Shit. I'm glad to hear that she's stable anyway." Kevin muttered under his breath. "Did either of you sleep at all."

"We got enough. Thanks for asking."

"What did you find in the car?" Fitzgibbon was all business now.

"Lyric's cell phone was there, just like Cisco said it would be. I dusted it for prints and emailed them into your personal account."

"You did what? Jesus fucking Christ, Ronan!" Fitzgibbon bellowed.

Ronan had been expecting him to react that way. "I would have sent them to Lyric, but well, she's hooked up to a ventilator and might lose her spleen."

"Damn it, Ronan. How can you put me in this position? You know how much I love that girl. She's a bright light in our office and she's been so good to me and Greeley."

"Then help her now, Kevin! It might just be that the only prints I collected from that phone belong to her and the baby, but what if there's more? Right now, Lyric is the only member of the Salem Witches to survive an attempt on her life. That's the reason Jude and I stayed with her last night, so that whoever is behind this couldn't come back and finish the job they started. It's why I think Katie volunteered us to keep their baby, so that whoever did this would know they had to come through me to hurt Astrid."

Kevin sighed heavily. "You need the day off, don't you?"

"Yes. Do you want to know why?" Ronan half-hoped he didn't need to explain his plan to Kevin. It had been bad enough last night explaining it to Tennyson.

"No, the less I know, the better at this point. Don't do anything fucking stupid, Ronan. I'm warning you." The phone beeped three times and Fitzgibbon was gone.

Jude cringed. "I see what you mean about Fitzgibbon barely being on your side."

Ronan shook his head. He didn't have time to worry about Kevin right now. "Are you ready to go?"

Shoving the second half of his muffin into his mouth, Jude nodded.

Christ, with friends like that, who needed enemies? Ronan started to clean up the mess they'd made on the small table in the waiting room when a nurse he recognized from Lyric's care team approached them. Her nametag read. "Harlowe."

"Detective O'Mara, there's a young man wanting access to Ms. Vaughn's room, but he isn't on the approved list. He says he knows you. His name is Greeley Fitzgibbon. Can I let him in?"

Ronan started to laugh. It seemed they hadn't been abandoned by the entire Fitzgibbon clan. "Yes, let him in. He's close to Lyric and Katie. He's also my police captain's son."

Nurse Harlowe nodded and headed back to the nurses' station.

A moment later, the door buzzed and in walked a somber looking Greeley. The usual sparkle was gone from his green eyes, replaced instead with steely determination. "Dad's pissed. I walked out of the house when he saw your name flash up on the caller ID. Then, I called Uncle Ten from the car to see how his night with Astrid went and he sounded off too when I asked how you were. He said you and Jude spent the night at the hospital. I'm here to help with the half-cocked plan."

Ronan raised an eyebrow at the teenager. "What half-cocked plan?"

"If Dad and Uncle Ten are both pissed, whatever you're up to must be half-cocked. I'm in."

Ronan had to admit it felt pretty damn good to have someone asking to join his team, rather than walking away from it.

34

Tennyson

All in all, it hadn't been a bad night. Astrid only stirred once, crying out for her mothers. Tennyson had rubbed her back and put her stuffed monkey in her hand and the baby had gone back to sleep. He wished it had been that easy for him. He'd spent the rest of the night staring at the ceiling.

Now, instead of heading into work, he was taking a day off too. Just like his husband. They were turning in a couple of lazy-ass bastards.

"What the hell is *that* look for?" Truman asked, side-stepping his friend on his way to the coffee pot.

"I was just thinking that Ronan and I were turning into slackers." Ten had brought Astrid over to Carson and Truman's house so that she could play with the triplets and he could seek out some adult conversation.

"What? Are you kidding me, Ten? You and Ronan are two of the hardest working people I know!" Truman shook his head. He set a cup of coffee in front of Tennyson and sat down across the table from him. "Look, I know you're both in a strange place right now because of this situation with the witches, but keep in mind this is a temporary thing."

Ten sighed. He supposed Truman did have a point. One way or another this situation was going to resolve itself. "Maybe."

"I get that its hard to see a way out when you're standing at the bottom of it all."

"That's just it, Truman. This is the part that no one seems to understand here. We're not at the bottom. Not yet!" Ten threw his hands in the air.

Truman tilted his head, seeming to study Tennyson. "Explain that to me. Are you seeing something? Or is that a gut feeling." Truman shook his head. "I suppose it's the same thing, right? Your intuition is just as good as anything you see with your gift."

"Tru, Fitzgibbon keeps threatening to suspend Ronan and not in a teasing manner. He's said it twice now. Ronan's really on the edge here. We both know my husband isn't the kind of man to pull back and tiptoe around something like this until Kevin's anger or frustration blows over."

"Right, Ronan's more the type to drive an eighteen-wheeler through and blast the horn for spite." He huffed a dry laugh.

"Exactly. That's what scares me. He's so passionate about helping these women and don't get me wrong, I don't want to see anyone else get hurt or die, but at the same time, this is a critical spot for our family." Ten knew he sounded like a harpy going on and on about their baby-to-be, but damn it, this was important too.

"How do you see this playing out?"

"I don't. There's nothing. I keep reaching out with my gift and I'm getting nothing. Bertha stopped by to see me last night and she's got nothing either. She and Erin still can't reach the dead witches on the other side and Jude's grandfather hasn't been back in touch yet with a way that we can break the psychic block that Gideon Black has placed over this whole thing."

"Do you know for a fact that Black is the one behind all of this?" Truman's eyes narrowed.

"Black admitted to Ronan that he was coming after us again in this life, so I assume he's the one pulling the strings from the other side. He must have someone working with him here in Salem. A descendant of some sort."

"That should be easy then. All we needed to do is look up the family tree at the library and then we have his modern-day people."

Ten shook his head. "Ronan tried that and the computer database at the library is only updated through the 1940s. The librarian said something about the Baby Boomer generation being so big that it's taking a long time to get them all into the computer and lack of tax payer funding, blah, blah, blah…" Ten rolled his eyes. "All I care about right now, Truman, is that appointment at the clinic next week. All I want to think about is my daughter's conception. It's supposed to be this beautiful, magical moment and instead, my husband is out risking his career and his job."

Truman sighed. "Do you remember me and Carson on the cruise?"

Tennyson snorted. "The two of you were like the Titanic, sinking fast."

"You're right and let me tell you I still regret my part in that. I know Carson does too. You and Ronan both gave us excellent advice about making up for the sake of our babies and for each other. I wished to hell I'd listened to you and done my part to make it happen faster than it did. Listen to me, Tennyson. Take your own advice. Fix this thing with Ronan. Fix it now! You know damn well that you're crazy, stupid in love with him and that you're going to forgive him no matter what crazy, stupid thing he does. I know you're worried about him getting his impulsive ass suspended, so help make sure that doesn't happen! The two of you work so well together. Get in the middle of this thing and do what you do best. Help your husband. Hell, you're a consultant with the Boston Police. It's not like Fitzgibbon can suspend you too."

"I'll think about it, Truman. I really will." It was so unlike him not to be one hundred percent in Ronan's corner, but he needed to start thinking like a father even though their little miss was still days away from being conceived.

Tennyson needed to do what was in his daughter's best interests. He could only pray that would line up with what was also in his and Ronan's best interests too.

35

Aside from the fact that Hunter Conroy couldn't stop blushing every time Jude Byrne looked his way, the mechanic and business owner seemed like good people. As promised, he'd sent one of his guys to pick up Athena Mathieu's car from the lot in Somerville. The wrecked Ford Focus was waiting for them when they'd arrived. Hunter also hadn't blinked an eye when Ronan had arrived with an entourage of four guys.

"Why don't Jude and I take the Acura, and you, Tobin and the kid can take the Ford?" Hunter asked. His left side dimple was in full effect.

Ronan wanted to say, "Sure, just so long as Jude's dick doesn't slip into your mouth while you're at it," but Ronan was trying to be professional here, especially since Hunter was a friend of the police chief. He had to admit Hunter could give Jude a run for his money. Standing well over six feet tall with a broad chest and strong, heavily muscled back, he looked like the kind of man who could handle anything life threw at him. Throw in his electric blue eyes and shaggy blond curls, which reminded Ronan of a young Dierks Bentley, and the man was an absolute winner, but for the fact he was panting after Jude. "Sure thing. Let us know if you find anything suspicious."

"Kid?" Greeley muttered. "I'll show him."

"Come on, tiger. We've got work to do." Ronan slapped a hand on Greeley's shoulder.

"Where do you want to start, Ronan?" Tobin asked. He was wearing a ratty Red Sox cap on backward and a pair of old Wranglers which were hugging his ass in all the right ways. His black tee-shirt was stretched so tight over his chest that Ronan was half-wondering if Tobin bought them a size too small on purpose.

Ronan shook his head to get himself mentally back into the game. "Athena's accident report was very similar to Lyric's. Single car accident, that happened late at night. No signs of paint transfer or of another car being involved. There were no skid marks, which indicated to the investigators that she didn't even try to brake prior to impact. The assumption was that Athena fell asleep at the wheel."

Greeley was standing at the driver's side door with his hand hovering over the steering wheel. "I don't think that's what happened at all." He looked up at Ronan with a scared look on his face.

"What are you feeling, Greeley?" Ronan knew Greeley had a heightened sense of intuition. Nothing on the same level as Tennyson's gift, but he knew the teenager could be trusted.

"There's fear. It's like I can still sense it. Touch it, almost." Greeley looked puzzled.

Even if Ronan didn't believe in psychics or in intuition, he sure as hell believed in Greeley and in the look on his face. "Let's jack it up and look at the brakes. It's possible the lines were cut. If Athena was feeling fear before she died then it could have been because she couldn't stop the car."

"We're starting with the brakes too, Ronan!" Jude called from the other side of the garage.

"Why don't you try putting them on?" Ronan called back when he saw Hunter Conroy's left hand on Jude's right hip.

"Jealous?" Jude shot back.

Ronan wasn't going to dignify the question with an answer. Of course, he *wasn't* jealous. What he was, in fact, was stupid. While Greeley and Tobin used the hydraulic jack to hoist the two-ton car into the air, Ronan pulled out his phone to send a good morning text to his husband who had the patience of Job. He sent his love and asked how the baby was doing. His message concluded with a selfie of himself and the car up on the jack, so Ten would know he wasn't fucking around.

"See anything, Tobin?" Ronan asked, as he walked over to join them.

"No. The brake lines are intact. For a three-year-old car, the brake pads look practically brand new." Tobin shook his head. "These should have worked perfectly the night of the accident. We should check the pedal. Make sure there was nothing stuck under it and that it was working properly too."

"I'll get the lift," Greeley said.

Ronan frowned. This was all lining up with the accident report. Perfectly working brakes and no skid marks. If he'd been the officer responding to the accident, he would have thought it was a case of falling asleep at the wheel too.

Christ, what if Ten was right and there really was nothing going on here? What if the witches' deaths were really just random coincidence? Lastly, what if Gideon Black was just yanking his chain when he said there was a final battle coming? Shit, now that he was standing here, with his career and possibly his family on the line, that sounded like some melodramatic bullshit line he'd hear in a movie and groan over.

"There's nothing wrong with the brake pedal." Greeley called out from the driver's seat. "I can press it with no problem and it releases back when I take my foot off it. But..." Greeley trailed off.

Ronan walked over to the teenager who was sitting in the driver's seat with his hands just above the steering wheel as if he were afraid to wrap his hands around it. "What is it, Greeley?"

The teenager shook his head. "I can still feel Athena's fear, Uncle Ronan. I can sense it as strongly as if she were she were sitting here right now."

Tobin opened the passenger side door and got down on his haunches to peer inside. Ronan could feel Jude and Hunter coming up behind him. "Tell me what you're feeling."

Greeley shut his eyes and left his hands hovering over the steering wheel. They tremored slightly. "She's wide awake and thinking about her class tomorrow. She's a CNA but going back for her RN at Salem State. All she wants to do is help people. It's the day after Prince died and *Purple Rain* is on the radio. She turns it up and she's singing along." Greeley sang a few words of the chorus in a surprisingly deep baritone. "There's a curve coming up in the road and Athena taps the brakes. She knows she's going too fast, but the car doesn't slow down. She hits the brakes harder, but the car goes faster. She's panicking now. She tries to turn the steering wheel to manage the curve but it's too late. *Mom...*" Greeley's green eyes popped open. He scrambled to get out of the seat. Ronan had to catch him when his right foot got caught on the lip of the door.

"It's okay. I've got you." Ronan could feel the boy trembling and he held on as tight as he could.

"How is that possible? Tobin asked. "We checked the brakes. They were fine. The pads are practically new and everything was hooked up tightly. They should have worked. Athena should have been able to stop the car."

"Do you think someone messed with the car once it was in the lot back in Somerville?" Jude asked. He set a hand on Greeley's shoulder giving it a squeeze.

Hunter shook his head. "I don't think so. If someone is orchestrating these deaths, then that would be an awful lot of work and an awful lot of ways to get caught after the fact."

Pulling back from Greeley, Ronan turned to Hunter. "What do you mean?"

"If I was going to kill someone using a car as my weapon. I'd just fuck with the computer." Hunter held up his hands. "Not that I'd ever kill someone."

"The computer?" Ronan asked. He'd never thought of that.

Hunter nodded. "All of these new cars have computers on board. Most use them for diagnostic purposes, for the radio, Bluetooth, internet hotspots, security, and shit like that, but they run all the major systems now too, the brakes and acceleration being two of them. It's great from a diagnostic standpoint. All you do is hook the machine up to the car and the computers talk to each other and it tells you what's wrong with the vehicle. The bad thing is that those systems can all be hacked."

"I saw a story like that on GMA or something," Greeley said, sounding stronger. "I think someone was hacking cars on one of the California freeways by making cars accelerate uncontrollably."

"How do we find out if that happened here?" Tobin asked.

"Simple! We run a diagnostic. I'll go grab my tool." Hunter's blue eyes glowed under the fluorescent lights of the shop.

"I'll be grabbing his tool later." Jude waggled his eyebrows.

Ronan was so excited about Hunter being able to run a test to see if Athena's car had been hacked that he was willing to overlook Jude's overactive libido this one time.

"Seriously, asshole. You don't think he's hot?" Jude half-whispered.

Ronan rolled his eyes. "Seven dead women and one in the ICU, Jude. Now isn't the time to focus on your doorknob dick."

"What's a doorknob dick?" Hunter asked, looking confused.

"Everyone gets a turn!" Greeley and Tobin answered together.

"Okaaay!" Hunter shook his head. "Well, let's get down to business." He walked past Jude without making eye contact and knelt down by the driver's side door. Reaching inside he removed a panel and hooked his device up to the car. He tapped some buttons on the key panel and looked up at Ronan. "What was the date of the accident?" His voice was all professional now. Gone was the boyish flirtatiousness that had been there prior to Ronan's doorknob crack.

"April 22th, 2016," Ronan answered, but his eyes were on Jude. The man was looking like he wanted to kill Ronan. It wasn't his fault Hunter appeared to be looking for more than just a one-time ride on Jude's love train.

"Any idea on the time of day?" Hunter asked.

"Sometime around 1am. Athena was driving home from her shift at North Shore Medical Center." Ronan shook his head. She'd been a young woman with her entire life ahead of her. No one got into nursing for the paycheck or the prestige. They got into the field to help people.

"Oh, shit," Hunter whispered looking up at Ronan. "I gotta be honest with you, Ronan. I thought this whole thing was bullshit from the word go. Cisco said you were a bit of a Fruit Loop, but that you were with BPD, so humor you, but Jesus fucking Christ." He shook his head and looked back down at the diagnostic tool. "The car was hacked 1:04am on the morning of April 22, 2016. I can see that the brakes and the accelerator were both tampered with. The hack ended at 1:07am when the car went…" Hunter swallowed hard. His throat clicked.

"When the car went dead?" Tobin suggested.

Hunter nodded. He wore a shocked look on his face. "Ronan, I'm so sorry. I don't know what to say."

Ronan shrugged. "Who would believe a story like this, Hunter? A dark force bumping off witches in the dead of night. The fact that it went unnoticed by anyone for almost two years and the fact that it had its genesis *here*, in the most infamous place in the world for the mistreatment of witches? Not to mention the fact that I have been a bit of a Fruit Loop like Cisco said, so it's not your fault for thinking I was out of my tree."

"We need to check Lyric's car for the same thing. Now that I know what I'm looking for, it shouldn't take as long." Hunter detached the device and rushed off to the destroyed Acura.

"It seems you're making friends and influencing people." Jude frowned, slipping his hands into his back pockets.

"Don't tell me your pissed that Hunter doesn't want to boldly go where *every* man has gone before." Ronan smirked.

Jude shook his head. "Fuck, no. You know I'm not interested in anyone who's interested in me for more than one night. It's a shame though, he looks like he would have been one hell of a ride." He turned to where Hunter was working on Lyric's car. "No, what's got me upset is that you've been right about everything, Ronan."

"God, you're such a dick, Byrne. You don't get to be pissed off because I'm right about something." Ronan could feel his temper starting to rise. There were days when he swore he could punch Jude in the fucking throat.

"No..." Jude trailed off. The look on his face morphed from pissed off to guilty. "That's not it, Ronan. I lied to you and Tennyson about something and I'm not proud of it."

"You lied about something? What could you have possibly lied about?" Ronan studied his sometimes friend, all the time pain in the ass and then that's when the answer hit him. "Your grandfather. You never asked him about the psychic defense thing, did you?" Ronan took a step toward Jude. He felt his hands ball into fists at his sides.

Jude shook his head no. His eyes were on the concrete floor of the shop. "I never called him."

"Jesus fucking Christ, Jude! What the fuck is wrong with you?" Ronan thundered. His voice echoed throughout the garage. "Women are being murdered! Now this son-of-a-bitch is going after children too! How much longer were you going to let this go on? How much longer were you going to let us believe you were a good man?"

Jude's head popped back up at that last question. "I am a good man, Ronan. I saved your ass twice now. Took two bullets for you." Jude's right hand came up to absently finger the spot on his left shoulder where he'd been shot last November. "I'm also a flawed man." Jude sniffled loudly. "A witch murdered my father in cold blood, Ronan, killed him right in front of me. I was an orphan by the time I was thirteen years old. Maybe my life would have turned out differently if that hadn't happened. I'm not trying to be an asshole here, but I'm struggling with this case. My weakness and my own hate got the best of me and now Lyric's in the hospital and Astrid could have been..." Jude trailed off.

Ronan walked up to Jude, part of him wondering if he didn't deserve a left hook to the jaw, and pulled the man into a rough hug. "We're all flawed men, Jude."

"That baby could have died because of me, Ronan."

"Yeah, well my own daughter might not even be conceived because of what I'm about to do next, so hide your crazy and figure out how the hell you're going to stop me from getting my dumb ass fired." Ronan pulled back from their hug. "Hunter, did you find anything?"

"Same results." Hunter seemed wary of re-joining the group. "Lyric's car was tampered with at the time of her accident last night."

"How does that kind of evidence work? It there something you can print out or something that I can take to Chief Jackson about both cars?"

"Yeah, I can give you a printout of both diagnostic reports, but..." Hunter shook his head.

Ronan sighed. "But what, Hunter? Spit it out."

"I really don't know you all that well, but you seem to be pretty deep in the shit right now, Ronan." Hunter rubbed the back of his neck with his left hand. "Do you really think charging back in to the Salem P.D. is your best course of action at the moment?"

Ronan grinned at the mechanic. "Nope! I'm gonna make the Salem P.D. come to me."

"And he wants me to hide *my* crazy? Shit's about to get real now." Jude shook his head.

Ronan had to admit his plan was pretty ballsy. He just hoped to hell it worked.

36

Tennyson was getting used to pacing around the living room. He figured doing laps in front of the large picture window was so much more economical than buying a gym membership he was probably never going to use much anyway. The bigger problem with pacing today was the fact that a very pissed off Captain Fitzgibbon was sitting in the armchair opposite the window, fuming. Not even holding a cooing baby Astrid was helping to calm him down.

When Greeley called fifteen minutes ago from Witch City Towing saying he had some big news that he, Fitzgibbon and the chief needed to hear, Tennyson couldn't believe his ears. Greeley's next words, "You've gotta get them all to meet at your house," had been a bigger shocker still.

Ten had called Kevin, who'd barely been able to keep a leash on his temper after hearing that Greeley had gotten mixed up in this thing. Kevin had confessed later that Greeley was the only reason he'd made the call to Salem Police Chief Cisco Jackson. "He's here," Tennyson said.

"The chief or your husband?" Kevin sneered.

"The chief." Ten shook his head and hurried to the front door just as the doorbell rang. "Chief Jackson, come in. It's nice to see you again."

Cisco smiled at Tennyson. "I assume the same rules apply to this meeting as they did last night?"

Ten found a tight smile of his own as he led the cop into the living room. "I'd like to apologize for anything my husband is about to do before he does it, chief. I honestly have no idea what's going on right now."

"I believe you, Tennyson. Captain Fitzgibbon explained that Ronan is a bit of a wildcard which goes both ways."

"I don't understand," Ten said. He took a seat on the couch. The late night and then early morning wakeup call with Astrid were starting to take a toll on him. It wasn't even lunchtime yet and he already felt like he could use a nap.

Cisco grinned. "Well, when you have someone like Ronan working for you there are times you benefit from his fly by the seat of his pants way of doing things. On the other hand, there are also times when that look-before-you-leap way of doing things can bite you in the ass too."

"I have a feeling this is going to be one of those bite him in the ass days." Fitzgibbon stood up and handed Astrid to Tennyson. "I don't want to lose my shit with Lyric's baby in my arms."

"Now, Kevin…" Ten started when the captain moved toward the door.

"I don't mean at Ronan. My son seems to have thrown his lot in with your husband's impulsive, stupid ass too." Kevin stalked to the door and yanked it open. "Oh good, you're all here."

Ten could hear the venom dripping from Kevin's voice. This was going to be bad. He didn't need his gift to know that. He stood back and watched as Greeley, Jude, Tobin, and Ronan walked into the living room.

"Hey, babe." Ronan brushed a brief kiss against Ten's head and did the same to Astrid. "Thank you all for coming."

"You didn't give us much of a choice, asshole. Nice job using my son as bait." Fitzgibbon turned to Greeley, the heat in his green eyes only burned brighter. "We're going to talk later about just whose side you're on."

Greeley's eyes narrowed on his father. "There aren't any sides here, Dad. I don't know why you and Uncle Ten think that there are. Listen to what we found out at the garage today."

"I'm listening, Ronan," Cisco said.

"Both Athena Mathieu and Lyric's cars were hacked. Hunter Corwin gave me printouts of the diagnostics he ran on each of the vehicles that show that the hacks took place at the exact times of the accidents and that it was the brakes and accelerators that were messed with each time."

The room was dead silent. "What do you mean the car was hacked?" Ten asked. "Hacked like an email address?"

"Uncle Ten, don't you remember that crazy story a few months ago about cars that went out of control in California? They sped up but the drivers couldn't seem to slow them back down?" Greeley looked back and forth between Ten, his father and the police chief, seemingly looking for any signs of recognition.

Ten honestly couldn't remember a story like that, but Greeley looked like Tennyson should remember the story.

"Here are the reports from Hunter Conroy." Ronan handed the information to Fitzgibbon.

Cisco moved across the now cramped living room to look the documents over.

"Who is this Hunter Convoy?" Kevin asked.

"It's *Conroy*," Cisco corrected. "He owns Witch City Towing. Good guy. Trustworthy too." He took the pages from Fitzgibbon as Kevin handed them over.

"All this shows is activity in the accelerator and the braking systems at the approximate times of the accidents." Fitzgibbon looked up at Ronan. "Isn't that exactly what I should see when a car is involved in an accident?" Fitzgibbon sounded as if he thought Ronan had lost his mind.

"Look, Cap..." Ronan started.

"No! You look Ronan, I've had just about enough of your bullshit here! You're off the rails talking about past lives and a serial killer ghost killing witches who, incidentally, is coming back from beyond the grave for a final battle against you and Tennyson. Now you want me to believe that this printout of a car accelerating and braking before it was involved in an accident is proof that some outside source hacked it? No. I'm drawing the line. The madness ends here and now, Ronan."

"I have to agree with your captain, Ronan," Cisco said, his dark eyes pinning Ronan with a serious look. "There's nothing here in either of these printouts that comes remotely close to giving me any reason to think Athena or Lyric's accidents were anything more than that. Accidents. I appreciate all you've done here to help, but don't you think it's time you get back to your own cases in Boston? Why don't you grab a nap and I'll take over your watch at Lyric's hospital room?"

"Oh my God," Ronan gasped. "It's you! You're Gideon Black's descendant!" Ronan right arm came up to point at Salem's Chief of Police. "You said yourself last night that you're a Salem boy, born and bred. You're the one orchestrating all of this. It's why you refused to investigate Gia Gonzalez's murder. It's why you're refusing to see the evidence we've put before you now. All you have to do is call Hunter Conroy and he'll confirm everything I've just told you. It's *you*! You're the one killing the witches! And now you want to go stand guard over Lyric! Why, chief? So, you can finish the job? Over my dead body!" Ronan advanced across the cramped living room, but Fitzgibbon was quicker. He stopped Ronan dead in his tracks, sweeping his legs out from under him and slamming him to the floor with a loud crash.

"I hate to do this, Ronan, but you've left me no choice." Fitzgibbon panted, planting his left knee squarely on Ronan's chest. "As of this moment, you're suspended from the Boston Police Department. I'll need you to turn in your badge and gun."

"Hall table," Ronan wheezed, not bothering to make eye contact.

Fitzgibbon climbed off of Ronan's prone body. "We'll talk about this next week when you've hopefully come back to your senses. Until then, I don't want to see or hear from you. Understood?"

Ronan nodded, but didn't say a word. He also didn't bother to get up from the floor.

Tennyson stood rooted to the floor with Astrid in his arms. He watched, speechless as Fitzgibbon and Chief Jackson walked out the front door.

"Jesus, Ronan, are you okay?" Tobin bent down to the floor.

"No, I don't think I am. Knocked the wind out of me." Ronan's breath was coming in hitching wheezes.

Jude knelt down on the other side of him. "Take slow, shallow breaths." He looked up at Tennyson. "A little help here?"

"What the hell can I do, he's already dug his own grave." With those words, Tennyson headed up the stairs toward the bedroom. He didn't look back at his husband who was lying on the living room floor, struggling to breathe.

37

Ronan

Ronan didn't know how long he stayed down on his own living room floor with Tobin, Greeley, and Jude surrounding him. It was probably only a few minutes, but to him it felt like hours. He heard Tennyson stomp up the stairs and slam the bedroom door. It seemed to him such a final act, not that he was being melodramatic or anything.

Once he had his breath back, Ronan was finally able to sit up and haul his stupid ass up off the floor. Glancing around at his friends, no one seemed to know what to say. "Guys, it's going to be okay. It's not like the world stopped turning or anything."

"Do you really think it's Cisco?" Tobin shook his head as if he were still trying to wrap his head around the idea that the chief of the Salem Police Department could possibly be a serial killer.

"Let me ask you this, Tobin, if I'd laid out my case against him in the calm, cool manner I'm speaking in now, would you have an easier time believing it? I mean, he's been the one hindering my investigation at every turn, stopping me dead in my tracks by refusing to investigate my leads."

"You do have a point about the chief's behavior when you don't sound like a raving fucking lunatic," Jude agreed with a smirk. "So now what?"

Ronan rubbed a hand against the sore spot on his back. "Someone needs to be at the hospital with Lyric. We need a guard on her 24/7. With the chaos going on around me right now, I have no doubt this would be a prime time for the killer to get back in there and finish the job." Ronan hated the fact that they'd left her alone with only Katie all morning. Yes, she was a trained police officer, but she was also running on little sleep and a lot of emotion. She might not be at her best to recognize a threat.

"I'll call Niall." Tobin reached for his phone.

"I'm hoping that Carson and Truman might be willing to help out too." Ronan shrugged.

"You might end up bunking with them, Uncle Ronan." Greeley set a hand on his shoulder.

Ronan frowned at the teenager. "What about you, kid?" He couldn't help finding a moment of levity, remembering the way Greeley had bristled when Hunter Conroy had called him a kid. "I'm definitely at the top of your father's shit list now. You sure you want to throw your lot in with me here?"

Greeley nodded emphatically. "My Dad is always telling me to fight for what is right. Being on the side of the witches *is* what's right. There's going to come a day when my Dad and Uncle Ten are going to be very upset that they chose to sit on the sidelines for this fight."

"Is that so, Greeley?" Tennyson said from the stairs.

Greeley spun around to face a calmer sounding Tennyson. "Yes, that is so. I mean no disrespect here, but you and my Dad are wrong."

Ten raised an eyebrow. "Tell me how I'm wrong, Greeley." Ten's voice was quiet, but there was no anger in it.

Ronan knew that voice. It was the one that invited you to come closer by making you think Ten was calm and clearheaded, when in fact Ten was just gathering evidence to bury your stupid ass with later. Ronan, for once, was keeping his stupid mouth shut. Greeley knew what he was doing.

"When we were at the garage, I was sitting in Athena Mathieu's car. I could feel her fear and got an impression of what happened to her just before the accident. She wasn't falling asleep at the wheel or texting and driving or messing with the radio or daydreaming about some boy. Someone messed with her car, Uncle Ten. She kept trying to brake the vehicle, but it kept going faster and faster until it crashed and she died. Hunter Conroy had evidence that the car was hacked from the outside from a foreign IP address, but for whatever reason, Chief Jackson didn't want to hear that."

Tennyson's whole demeanor changed. "What do you mean the car was hacked from a foreign IP address?"

Greeley's lips quirked into a brief smile. "Your laptop has a unique IP address when you're on the internet here at home, but if you bring it to my house, let's say, and connect to our WIFI, your IP address changes."

"Okay, I get that, but what does that have to do with Athena Mathieu's accident?" Ten cocked his head to the side, appearing to focus completely on Greeley.

"Her car has its own IP address. That car was Bluetooth enabled and WIFI too. For the sake of my explanation let's say the car's IP address is 1234. All of the software downloads to the car and all of times she connected to Bluetooth all would have come from the 1234 address, got it?"

Tennyson nodded.

"On the night of the accident, the commands the car was getting to accelerate and disengage the brakes, those were coming from IP address 6789. This is why Hunter said the car's computer was being hacked." Greeley looked up at Ronan.

Ronan had been through a lot of proud moments with Greeley in the time he'd known the teenager, but this was his proudest moment yet. Ronan didn't think he could have explained the situation to Tennyson as well or as calmly as Greeley had just done.

"I don't understand." Ten shook his head. He walked slowly down the rest of the stairs and into the living room. "Why did Cisco refuse to look at the reports then?"

"Uh, maybe because *he's* the witch-murdering fucker Ronan accused him of being!" Jude rolled his eyes at Tennyson.

Ten sighed and sat down heavily on the sofa.

"Niall is already at the hospital. I'm going to meet him over there. We should probably set up a schedule for people to be with Lyric. I'll call Truman on my way to the hospital. See if he and Carson are interested in taking a shift." Tobin slapped a hand on Ronan's shoulder.

"I'll take the overnight." Ronan grinned at his friend.

"Come down to the Black Cat in the morning. I'll put you to work. My guys are getting $35.00 per hour. Since you have *other* unique skills, shall we say, I'll start you at $40.00. You buy the lunch, newbie." Tobin laughed and headed out the door.

"I'm gone too. Gonna jerk off and grab a nap." Jude shot a saucy wink at Ronan "I'll be at the hospital with you overnight." Jude turned to Tennyson. "I know this is none of my business, but cut him some slack. You have one hell of a man coming home to you every night." Jude looked like he was about to say something else, but he shut his mouth and walked out the door.

"And then there was one." Ronan shot Greeley a smirk.

"I need to go home and explain that IP thing to my father. I'm just so damned mad at him." Greeley shook his head. "He's always been on your side, Uncle Ronan. I just don't get why he's choosing now to turn against you."

Ronan laughed. "To be honest I was a bit of a dick today. Go home and talk to him, Greeley, but be calm like this, not all up in arms like I was earlier. Christ, the last thing we need is for him to take you down like he did to me." Ronan rubbed the spot on his lower back that had taken the brunt of the hit.

"That was pretty epic." Greeley snorted. "I mean, shit, my Dad's fifty years old. He took you down like you were a toddler."

"Gee, thanks, kid. Now scram. Don't ruin your relationship with your father over me. I'm not worth it." Ronan hugged the teenager. "Agree to disagree if you have to. Okay?"

"Same goes for the two of you." Greeley pointed back and forth between Tennyson and Ronan. "Later!" He headed out the door.

Ronan waited until the door closed behind Greeley before turning to his husband who was staring at him from the sofa. "Is Astrid asleep?"

Tennyson nodded. "At least someone in this house is getting some rest." He leaned forward, bracing his elbows on his knees. "Is this what you wanted, Ronan? Did you want Fitzgibbon to suspend you?"

"Of course not." Shit, is that what Ten thought? Tennyson, their daughter-to-be, this house, and his job were the most important things to him. He assumed his husband knew that, but maybe not.

"Then what was your game plan today? Because all I saw was my husband acting like a crazy person."

Ronan sighed. He slipped his hands into the back pocket of his jeans. "Is that really *all* you saw today, Ten? Did you really miss the fact that Jude, Tobin, Greeley, and I walked into this house with iron-clad proof that a woman was murdered and that a Boston Police Captain and the chief of the Salem Police Department ignored that evidence out of hand? I mean after what's happened with me over the last week or so, I could see Fitzgibbon dismissing any evidence I brought him, but Cisco trusts Hunter Conroy and Fitzgibbon trusts Jude and Greeley. Christ, both of them barely looked at what we brought them." Ronan sighed.

"Ronan, you accused Cisco Jackson of being a killer. You ranted and raved like lunatic. Then, as if those things weren't bad enough, you went after him." Ten shook his head. "You're damned lucky he didn't have you arrested and held on a 5150 psych hold. Jesus Christ, is this about the baby?" Ten asked.

"What?" Ronan had no idea what Ten was talking about.

"Are you scared about being a father and you're trying to get out of it and you don't know how to tell me? Because if that's what this *thing* is, then just tell me and we can stop the madness right now." The look in Ten's dark eyes was pure heartbreak.

"Tennyson, no. I want to be a father more than anything in this world." Ronan sat next to his husband on the sofa. "That little girl is everything to me, you both are everything to me, but how can we bring her into a world where women are being murdered like this and our friends are looking the other way? How can we let her live in a town where the chief of police could possibly be a killer?" Ronan's heart was broken at the thought that Ten believed that his helping the witches was an effort *not* get pregnant.

He had been in love with their daughter from the moment they'd started talking about her. He fell asleep every night reliving that moment from his wedding day when somehow Bertha Craig had made it possible from him to catch a glimpse of the young woman she would one day become. The thought of that little girl never coming into existence was almost too much to bear.

"I don't know what to say here, Ronan. I really don't. Fitzgibbon is pissed. You're lucky he didn't fire your ass on the spot." Ten scrubbed a hand over his weary-looking face.

"I don't mean to throw gasoline on the fire here, Ten, but I didn't do anything worthy of being suspended over. I didn't break any BPD rules of conduct. You know that, right?" Ronan offered his husband half a grin.

"What?" Tennyson shook his head as if Ronan had started speaking Greek.

"I don't know what the hell is going on with Kevin, but I sure as fuck wasn't about to ask with Cisco in the room. I don't like the idea that he took my gun, but I have others in the safe. Fitzgibbon knows that too." With everything that had been going on since the confrontation with his boss, Ronan hadn't had any time to think about what kind of game Fitzgibbon was playing.

"Are you serious? You didn't really deserve to be suspended?" Ten's eyes sparkled with hope.

"Being an asshole isn't an automatic red card, Ten." Ronan raised an eyebrow at his stunned-looking husband. "If it was, every officer in the BPD would be riding the bench." Ronan couldn't help snickering at the gobsmacked looked on Tennyson's face. "Maybe Fitzgibbon suspects Cisco of being the killer too and he was just playing the game. Maybe he really is pissed as fuck at me. I don't know and right now, I'm not in the mood to find out. He sure as hell isn't reaching out to offer his help in this thing, so I have to run on the assumption that he's out. Plus, if this suspension," Ronan made air quotes over the word, "is real, then I don't want to antagonize him into adding a second week to my sentence. But hey, at least I have a job in the meantime." Ronan offered Tennyson a smile.

"Your only job, so far as I'm concerned, is to jack off in a specimen jar next week. Got it?" Ten found a weak smile of his own. "Ronan, I get where you're coming from in this. I really do. I know someone is hunting and killing the witches. I know you need to stop them."

Ronan wasn't psychic, but he had a bad feeling in the pit of his stomach. "But?"

"But, I'm out. I can't step into the breech here. Astrid is my responsibility. Someone needs to be here standing up for her. I need to start thinking like a father and tonight, that starts with her." Ten looked at Ronan with glassy eyes. "With the psychic block Gideon Black has around this thing, I won't be any help to you in the fight at all. I'd just be one more person you'd have to protect. I'd be a liability."

Ronan nodded. He shut his eyes and rested his head against Tennyson's shoulder. He didn't want his husband to see the heartbreak in his eyes. He'd worked thousands of murder cases in the years before he'd ever heard Tennyson Grimm's name. So, why was the thought of working this one without him so daunting?

38

Tennyson

There might have been a psychic block surrounding the situation with the witches, but there wasn't a block surrounding Ronan's emotions. What he felt leaking out of his husband was grief. Ten hadn't been able to narrow down what the grief was in reference to, if it was about the accidents that killed Athena and severely injured Lyric or if it was about his being suspended from the BPD.

If Ten had to make an educated guess, it would be that Ronan was feeling grief over his refusal to join the hunt for the killer. There was really no other choice he could make here. Katie had trusted him with the care of her precious child. What was he supposed to do, hand the baby over to Truman or Fitzgibbon so he could hunt the witch-hunter with Ronan? Someone had to be the responsible adult here and Ten decided it had to be him.

He'd felt Ronan start to fall asleep soon after he'd told his husband that he was sitting out this case. He'd eased out from under his head and got him settled in with a pillow and a warm blanket. He did what he promised Ronan he wouldn't do and he read him quickly, but only to know how much his husband had slept last night. Ten saw that he'd only managed to grab a few cat naps through the night he'd spent in the hospital at Lyric's bedside.

One thing Ronan had said during their discussion had struck a chord with him. He didn't want their little miss born into a world where the chief of police was going around killing people. He'd liked Cisco Jackson. He really had. Ten had even had this bizarre moment where he'd seen the cop at their dinner table passing the pasta bowl to Kevin. How the hell was *that* possible if he was the one killing the witches? It was probably just his wild imagination getting confused with his gift. With all the shit going down with Fitzgibbon and Jace Lincoln, Tennyson had wanted to see their friend happy and settled. Cisco seemed like the kind of guy who would understand Kevin and his crazy hours. That was neither here nor there at the moment. All that mattered right now was keeping Ronan and the other witches safe.

There was a tiny cry from the baby monitor, Ten got up from the kitchen table where he'd been mulling over the situation with the witches, when he got dizzy. Reaching out for the kitchen counter, his left hand slid off the smooth granite and he felt himself falling to the floor. He could hear Madam Aurora screaming for help right before everything went black.

There was a baby crying. Why was there a baby crying? Their little miss hadn't been born yet. The second thing Tennyson realized was that his head was throbbing. What the hell had happened to him? Cracking open an eyeball, he realized he was looking at bottom of the kitchen island. Reaching out his fingers, they grazed against cold marble tile. Why the hell was he lying on the kitchen floor?

It all came back to him in a flash. The crying baby was Astrid Vaughn. She was upstairs in her crib. He was lying on the floor because he'd had a vision of sorts, an audio S.O.S from Madam Aurora. Ronan?

Where was Ronan? Would his husband even help after Ten refused to help him earlier.

Pulling his arms toward his body, Ten tried to push himself up into a sitting position. A flash of pain burst through his skull. He could hear Ronan's voice coming from the living room. Who was he talking to? Maybe he was on the phone with Fitzgibbon? Maybe the captain had called and explained why the hell he'd suspended Ronan for no reason this afternoon.

Tennyson gingerly climbed back to his feet, using one of the kitchen chairs to steady himself. A bolt of nausea caused him to grip the back of the chair a bit harder. Ten was pretty sure he had a concussion. He could still hear Ronan's voice coming from the living room, only there was something odd about it. It was monotone and not at all conversational. What the hell was going on?

He took a careful step away from the safety of the table and felt a bit dizzy, but nothing was going to stop him from getting to Ronan.

"NO!" Ronan shouted from the living room.

"Ronan!" Tennyson cried out. He forced himself to move faster. He could hear Ronan gasping for breath and tried to walk faster, but his vision was fuzzy and he kept feeling like he was going to lose his balance again.

"Ten?" Ronan's voice was filled with fear and something else Tennyson was too muddleheaded to place at the moment. "Jesus Christ, what happened to you?"

A second later, Ronan was scooping him up and bringing him back to the couch. Being held against Ronan's warm chest was a brief comfort, until he felt Ronan's heart hammering under his ear like a fleet of jackhammers. "What happened to *you*?"

"I asked you first! The side of your face is bruised." Ronan's fingers touched the right side of Ten's face.

"You were falling asleep on my shoulder, so I tucked you in and just let you sleep on the couch. I went into the kitchen to have some tea and think some things out." A bolt of pain ripped through his head. Ten shut his eyes against it. He took a deep breath before opening his eyes. "I heard the baby start to cry and when I got up to get her, I got this weird message from Aurora. I've never gotten a message like this before."

Ronan's eyes narrowed. "What do you mean by weird message?"

"She was screaming for help inside my head, but that's all I got. I didn't get a sense of why she was screaming or where she was. All I could hear was her voice. The message was so powerful that it knocked me out cold. I felt myself falling and barely had enough time to put my hands out in front of me to cushion my fall. The next thing I knew I woke up on the kitchen floor. I could hear the baby crying and you talking to yourself." Ten raised a hand to cup the side of Ronan's face. "You *weren't* talking to yourself, were you?"

Ronan shook his head no. "I wasn't talking to myself and I don't think it was Aurora's message that knocked you out, Ten. I think it was whoever took her."

"Whoever took her?" Ten was really confused now. He must have a worse concussion that he thought. Why the hell did Ronan think Madam Aurora had been taken?

"Gideon Black has Aurora. Well, not Gideon, but whomever his earth-bound agent is." Ronan sounded confident in his words. "I think Gideon Black sent you some kind of psychic attack, like the kind of thing Jude is always talking about and *that's* what knocked you out."

"Ronan, how do you know those things?" Ten asked curiously.

"You didn't hear me talking to myself. You heard me talking to that fucker. To Gideon Black. He visited me in my dream while I was visiting our little miss." Ronan's eyes turned misty. He blinked rapidly to keep them from falling.

"What?" Fear like Tennyson had never known in his life gripped his heart. Gideon Black had been near their child's spirt? He'd kill the motherfucker himself, if the bastard weren't already dead.

"Every once in a while, I visit her little soul in my dreams. I almost never remember it, but when I wake up, I have this feeling like she's right here in the room with me like you are now. We were walking together and came around a bend and there was Gideon. I tried to make her get behind me, but she insisted she stand at my side." Ronan huffed a rough laugh. "She's a brave girl, just like her fathers. Anyway, Black said she'd burn too. You know what our daughter's response to him was?"

Ten shook his head. Tears cascaded down his cheeks. He couldn't imagine what his bright light's reaction to such a vile creature could possibly be.

"I'll bring the marshmallows!" Ronan shook his head. "She's fearless, our girl. Black said he had a little preview of her future, a bonfire and witch roast in her honor that I wouldn't want to miss. He said I'd know exactly where to go and I do. I know where to find Aurora."

"Black has Madam Aurora and is going to burn her alive at the stake?" Ten's mouth hung open. He couldn't believe the words that had just come out of his mouth. This just kept getting worse.

"Yes, that's what I think. When he said I knew where to go, I assume he meant to that clearing in the Salem Towne Forest where you, Wolfgang Grimme, rather, met his end." The look in Ronan's eyes was dire. "That place obviously means something to him."

"What are you going to do, Ronan?" Even as the words left his mouth, Tennyson already knew what Ronan was going to do. He was going to rescue Aurora and put an end to this whole thing.

"I'm going to call Jude. Tobin too, and get out there. See what I can do to save Aurora and stop the fucker who's hurting her. I want you to grab Astrid and go stay with Truman and Carson."

"What about Fitzgibbon?" Tennyson's heart pinched hard in his chest. He should be going with Ronan. He should be the one standing at Ronan's side in this fight.

Ronan shook his head. "He's too much of a wildcard right now. He might go to Cisco and we can't afford to have him alerted."

"But if he's the killer, he already knows you're coming. What about the police? I mean if you stop this thing from happening by yourself doesn't that make you a vigilante? You can go to jail for that, can't you?" Ten could feel his own anxiety starting to ratchet up.

"Nah, I'm just going rogue. Everything will be fine." Ronan pressed a kiss to the side of Tennyson's head. "Pack up the baby. Go stay with Carson and Truman. Make sure they set the alarm. I'll see you later. I promise." Ronan kissed him again and bounded up the stairs.

Tennyson knew he was headed for the gun safe Ronan kept in his bedroom closet. He opened his sixth sense wide, trying to get a view of Aurora, Black, Cisco, of anything connected to the witches or this night. All he was getting was darkness. It was all black, like the dead of night.

39

Ronan

Ronan was strapping on his leg holster when the doorbell rang scaring the shit out of him. "Relax, asshole. It's not like Gideon Black is going to ring the bell like the fucking Mormons." Rolling his eyes at himself Ronan looked through the peephole and was just as surprised at who *was* standing on the other side of his front door: Callum Churchill. Ronan yanked the door open. "I'm surprised to see you here. I thought you were a writer, not a fighter." Ronan raised an eyebrow at the man who was dressed all in black and looking like Johnny Cash, somber and somehow repentant.

"Aurora's been taken." Callum offered a grim look. "I don't have a green hood or a bow and arrow, but will a black hoodie do? I've gathered the others. Our own little team of superheroes."

Ronan looked past him to the sidewalk where he saw Tobin, Jude, Hunter, and Greeley, all dressed in black and looking ready to go. "Are you sure about this Callum? I don't have my badge anymore and even if I did, I don't have any jurisdiction here in Salem as you were so kind to point out."

"Look, they have Aurora. Lyric is in the ICU fighting for her life. Hunter told me that that Cisco all but ignored the proof you and the others gave him this morning. All we have to rely on now are the five of us. We're stronger together than we ever could hope to be alone."

"Spoken like a true word scribe." Ronan rolled his eyes. "Stay here." He walked across the room to where Tennyson was standing with Astrid in his arms. "Callum brought the other Ninja Turtles. We're going to go kick some ass now and try to get Aurora back." He pressed a gentle kiss to Tennyson's shocked lips. "When I get back we'll order Chinese. I think I deserve a treat after this. Egg rolls and shrimp lo mein."

"A treat?" Ten barked out a surprised laugh. "You got suspended from your job and you're off to fight a three-hundred-year-old ghost who's about to murder another one of our friends."

"That kind of night works up an appetite." Ronan pecked Ten's cheek again. "I love you, Nostradamus. Don't ever forget that."

"Don't you dare make me have to remember it, Ronan Michael O'Mara!" Ten sucked in a ragged breath. "You'd better come back here in one piece, ready to do your business in a jar next week."

"I can do it now if you like." Ronan waggled his eyebrows at Tennyson. At least if he left his donation, Ten would have their baby to remember him by if things went wrong tonight.

Ten shut his eyes and when he opened them again had a look of determination on his face. "You go out there and do what you have to do and then you come home to me. Got it?"

"Got it. I know you love me too." Ronan kissed him again and headed toward the door.

"I love you!" Tennyson shouted as Ronan started to shut the door.

"Set the alarm. This could be a trap to get me away from Astrid." Ronan shut the door before he could get any more emotional about leaving Tennyson behind than he already was.

"How are we going to find Madam Aurora?" Callum asked. "I've had my gift wide open and I'm not getting any clues about where she is."

"I know where she is," Ronan said quietly. "Gideon Black came to me in a dream and told me where he was holding her."

"Gideon Black?" Hunter Conroy asked on a shocked laugh. "The preacher who hanged the witches in the Witch Trials? *That* Gideon Black?"

"You catch on fast." Jude grinned at the mechanic. "You wanna grab some breakfast when this is over?" He held open the passenger door to his black 1969 Ford Thunderbird.

"This your car?" Hunter asked, sounding impressed.

Jude nodded. "Found her in a salvage yard. Put her back together piece by piece."

"Yeah," Hunter grinned. "I'll have breakfast with you, but my sausage isn't on the menu. Got it?"

"No, obviously, I'm not *getting* it, but fine." Jude sighed, shutting the door once Hunter was seated.

"Jesus Christ, we're about to go up against a vengeful ghost who wants to fucking kill me and roast Aurora like a pig on a spit, and that one's making a date, while this one's playing hard to fucking get." Ronan looked up at the starlit sky hoping for divine intervention.

"Come on, Ronan," Tobin led him toward his truck. "I'll drive. You too, Callum, Greeley. Come with us."

"Thanks, I don't want to watch," Greeley waved a hand toward the loudly idling Thunderbird, "that. Whatever *that* is."

"Do you know how to get where we're going?" Ronan asked Tobin.

Tobin nodded wordlessly and started the truck.

There was something about that wordless response and the fact that Tobin was the Woods family historian that got Ronan thinking. There had been so much going on in his life back in April that he hadn't put two and two together back then. "You lost a family member in the original Witch Trials, didn't you?"

Tobin looked over at Ronan in shock. "Yeah, Susannah North was my great-grandmother ten times removed.

"*That's* why you're the family historian," Ronan concluded.

"The family historian doesn't just keep records, they don't just keep the memory of what happened alive, Ronan. We're supposed to keep it from happening again." Tobin shook his head. "How the hell did I *not* notice this happening? Seven women over two years are dead and it took a random visit from you for the truth to finally dawn on me."

"It's not that, Tobin. Whoever is behind this is doing it in a way that no one could put the pieces together. Obviously, their work isn't finished yet because all of the witches aren't dead." Tobin couldn't take this personally. The plan depended on being able to operate completely under anyone's radar.

"Hey!" Callum Churchill squawked from the backseat.

"This isn't the time to be thin-skinned, Callum. Whoever kidnapped Aurora is going to take a shot at you tonight too if you're not careful. Do you have any weapons on you?"

"You mean besides my acerbic wit?" Sarcasm dripped from the warlock's words.

"Yeah, besides that." Ronan rolled his eyes. "The last time I checked, words weren't a shield against bullets, knives, or what-the-hell-ever else Gideon Black's proxy plans to hurl at us."

"Words might not be a shield, but they can be weapons," Callum said quietly.

Ronan couldn't help remembering that Navajo weapon-word Jude had hurled at the witch spirits who'd been trying to harm Niall out at The Black Cat Inn. From the look Tobin was shooting him, he was remembering the same thing.

"Okay, boy-witch, load your quiver. We're here." Ronan unbuckled his seatbelt and pulled his gun out of its shoulder holster, tucking it into the back waistband of his pants. He had a second piece strapped to his ankle and a knife strapped to each thigh. He was armed to the teeth and he still felt naked, as if he were walking into this situation underprepared for whatever was to come. Looking up at the full moon, he whispered a silent prayer that he would make it out of this forest alive.

40

Tennyson

"I really think we need to take you to the emergency room, Tennyson." Carson said for the third time in the last half an hour.

"I'll be fine, Carson," Ten muttered. He wasn't fine. His head was pounding and he was seeing three of everything.

"Oh yeah, then why are you looking to my left every time you speak to me? I'm over here!" Carson waved a hand. "That's it. I really think we need to go! Now!"

"Where you both need to go is the Salem Towne Forest and you know it!" Bertha Craig was standing with her arms folded over her chest looking angry enough to wrestle a mother grizzly bear and win.

"Hi, Mom." Carson raised a hand.

"Don't you, 'Hi, Mom' me, Carson Cornelius Craig. You get your fancy ass out to those woods and help Ronan this instant. I can't believe the two of you are sitting here like bumps on logs while Ronan is risking his life."

"Mom, he has Tobin, Jude, Greeley, some warlock and a mechanic with him." Carson looked confused over the last two members of Ronan's team.

Bertha raised an eyebrow at him. "I don't care if he has an entire platoon of Navy SEALs. Move your ass, Carson!"

Tennyson didn't think Navy SEALs roamed in platoons, but he wasn't about to bring that up to Bertha now. "Is Ronan in danger, Bertha?" Ten asked. He wasn't getting any kind of psychic messages about his husband at all.

"I don't know, Tenny. I'm here with you and not there with him." Bertha looked more serious than he'd seen her in a long time.

"Get back to him then. Carson and I will get there as soon as we can." Tennyson was hoping his battered brain could hold on long enough to stand up to whatever was going to happen when he got to Ronan.

"I know where you're coming from, Tennyson. Putting your child before anything else, because that was never done for you, but Ronan has to factor into that equation too. You aren't going to get your daughter without him."

Ten nodded. He could see his mistake now. "Thanks, Bertha. Keep him safe for me."

She nodded and disappeared.

"Tennyson, are you sure about this?" Truman asked walking into the living room carrying Astrid. "Your brains are pretty scrambled."

"He's my husband, Truman. I never should have let him go without me in the first place. I thought I would be a liability to him out there, but we work better as a team."

"You do," Truman agreed. "What about calling the police? I know you think Cisco is the one leading all of this, but the whole department can't be in on it. Can they?"

"I don't know." Ten shook his head, causing him to wince. "For right now, the best thing to do is get to Ronan and we'll go from there. If you don't hear from one of us in two hours, call Fitzgibbon. I know he's pissed as hell at Ronan, but Greeley is with them."

Truman grimaced. "Jesus. That should motivate him. If anything happens to that boy Ronan's gonna end up cleaning the toilets at BPD until it's time to retire."

Ten snorted. "At least people won't be shooting at him in there. Thanks for your help, Truman."

"Okay, I'm ready to go." Carson walked out of the bathroom, looking a little paler.

"Why are you so scared, Carson?" It wasn't like Carson to back down from a challenge.

"Ronan isn't a cop anymore."

"Of course, he is. He's just suspended. The only difference is that Fitzgibbon confiscated his department issued gun and his badge. It's just a hunk of metal."

Carson shook his head. "It's his talisman, Ten. You know how powerful symbols of magic are. Let's go before I lose my nerve."

Tennyson hadn't thought about it like that before. He hoped to Christ Ronan hadn't either.

41

Ronan

Ronan could smell woodsmoke when he climbed out of the SUV. If there had been any doubt in his mind that he wasn't in the right place before, that was gone now.

"Shit, do you think we're too late?" Jude asked, running up Ronan.

"No. Black wants me here for whatever little game this is. He won't hurt Aurora until I'm here to see whatever it is he wants me to see. Just be on your toes everyone, especially you, Callum."

"You almost sound like you care, Ronan." Callum's lips quirked into a brief smile that was illuminated by the moonlight.

"Black wants all of the witches dead. Not only are you a warlock, Callum, you're a legacy witch with roots dating back to the original Witch Trials. He's going to want to sink his teeth into you something fierce. Maybe even more so than Aurora. She doesn't have the history that you do, but Black likes to torture women."

"I'll stick by him, Ronan," Jude offered. "I'm armed to the gills. Come on, boy-witch. You're with me."

"I don't see a gun or a knife," Callum squeaked when Jude roughly grabbed his arm and pulled him toward the forest path.

"I don't either," Hunter said from behind Ronan.

"His gun is in his underpants and his weapon is his brain." Ronan grinned at the mechanic.

Hunter shook his head. "I can't get a read on that guy. One minute he's trying to get into *my* pants and the next minute he's..." Hunter trailed off.

"He's what?" Ronan grinned. He had a feeling he knew what Hunter was going to say. Ronan started walking toward the forest path. He saw Tobin and Greeley were bringing up the rear.

"Jude's acting like a hero." Hunter sounded surprised at his own words.

Ronan snorted. "Yup, that's our Jude in a nutshell. Horny dick with a side dish of hero."

"Thanks for the warning." Hunter chuckled.

"He's a good guy, Hunter. We just keep hoping he'll settle down his horndog ways." Ronan wasn't betting on that any time soon.

Nodding, Hunter pointed ahead to the reddish glow they could see in the forest. "I think maybe it's time to focus on that, huh?"

His heart started hammering in his chest. Ronan nodded, wishing again that Tennyson was here with them. As they got closer to the clearing, Ronan could hear the crackling of the bonfire. It was just like his past life flashback, only he knew when he reached the bonfire, it would be Madam Aurora lashed to the stake instead of Tennyson.

The scene did not disappoint. It was just as Ronan knew it would be. The bonfire was roaring. The tips of the flames were licking toward the nearby trees. Aurora was tied to a wooden pole driven into the ground. She was standing stoically and not resisting her bindings. Ronan was proud of her defiance.

There were two hooded figures standing off to the side of the fire speaking to each other in low tones. Ronan couldn't hear the words, but they were unimportant at this time. He knew one of the hooded figures was Gideon Black. There was no way the long-dead spirit wasn't going to find a way to manifest himself for the final battle, as he called it. He was too proud to allow his words to be translated through a psychic like other spirits did. No, Black would use all of his power to be here in person. The real question was who was wearing the other hooded robe? Was it Chief Cisco Jackson? Ronan actually had a crazy moment back at the house before the doorbell rang, that the person behind it all was Callum Churchill. Who better to infiltrate and then betray the Salem Witches than a member of their own inner circle?

Now that he knew Churchill was innocent of betraying his sisters, it was time to find out who was behind the hood. "Black!" Ronan shouted. "Show yourself!"

A venomous laugh started low and grew as the seconds passed. One of the two hooded figures turned. "Ronan! So good to see you!" Gideon Black pushed back his hood. His dark eyes danced as they moved over the group assembled beside Ronan. "You brought me presents and I don't have anything for you! Look at this! A legacy warlock! I've never burned a warlock before. I wonder if they scream like the bitches do? And what do we have here?" Black looked Jude up and down. "You're not like the others, no, not at all. You should join me. We have a lot of important work to do."

"Fuck off, Darth Vader." Jude took a step away from Gideon Black. "I might not like witches, but I like fuckers who hurt innocent women even less."

"There's such drama in today's youth." Black rolled his dark eyes. He stepped up to Greeley next. "You have a touch of magic in you, little one. A touch of darkness as well. You will be useful."

Greeley started to laugh. It sounded to Ronan like the kind of laughing fit that always seemed to overtake you in the middle of church.

"What the hell could possibly be funny now?" Ronan half-whispered.

"That he thinks I'd join his merry band of beyond the grave Jedi Knights in training."

"You'll change your mind soon enough." Black grimaced at the teenager before stopping in front of Tobin. "You are the one who ruined everything with Mariah and the others, sending them into the light. They were mine to control and you set them free It's going to be a joy watching you suffer and die."

Tobin locked eyes with the crazed spirit. "You're welcome to try."

Gideon cackled. "You saw what my witches did to your boy. All I have to do is think the words and you'll be down on your knees suffocating."

"But I'm not." Tobin stood taller.

Black's eyes shifted from Tobin to Hunter. "What are you?"

"Just a concerned citizen of Salem who thinks you need to step the fuck off." Hunter's entire body tensed when Black moved closer to him.

Ronan exchanged a look of surprise with Jude. Black hadn't asked *who* Hunter was, but rather *what* he was. He hoped the fuck he survived what was to come just so he could ask Hunter what the hell Black meant.

Gideon looked unconcerned. "No matter, you'll burn like the rest."

"Enough of the theatrics, Gideon. Who's your sidekick in the hood? That's why we're here. To rescue Aurora and take your partner into custody."

"Rumor has it you're not a real cop anymore, *Mr.* O'Mara." Black cackled.

"That doesn't matter. You're partner in crime kidnapped Aurora. She'll be able to tell someone at the Salem P.D. what happened to her. They won't care that I'm on suspension. All they'll care about is that the dirtbag who took her is in custody." Ronan really hated this spirit, which, he supposed was exactly what Black wanted. He needed to calm down and try to find some Zen in this situation so he could think more clearly.

Gideon laughed again. "Oh, that's right. You think my grandchild is your chief of police. Maybe it's time for the grand unveiling."

The second hooded figure stepped forward. Their head was down as they walked forward to join Gideon.

Ronan studied the person as he walked forward. It was dark and the shadows cast from the fire were making it hard to discern any details. Anyone could be under that cloak. Hell, for all he knew, it could be Cisco. Or Fitzgibbon.

A full body shiver tore through Ronan as the sidekick lifted their hands to push back the hood. Ronan blinked twice, while the others around him gasped in surprise. "Lydia?" Ronan shook his head. "The genealogy librarian? *You're* the one who's been killing the Salem Witches? *You're* Gideon Black's descendant?"

"You were so close, dickhead, and you never had a clue." The tiny librarian smirked at him.

Ronan bristled. "There's no need to be rude, Lydia." He reached behind him to pull out his handcuffs. "Let's go."

Everything happened at once. Ronan felt himself flying backward and he wasn't entirely sure, but he could have sworn he heard Jude and Callum shouting in foreign languages. He landed hard against the trunk of a tree, seeing stars, when he finished up flat on his face.

When Ronan looked up from his place on the ground, he saw Tobin lying a few feet away from himself, holding his right arm gingerly. "You okay?" he shouted.

"Think it's broken, but it's gonna take more than that to stop me. What the hell just happened?" Tobin was trying to get his feet back under him.

"Felt like a shock wave. Like what happens during an explosion, only I didn't hear or feel anything blow. Did you?"

Tobin shook his head. "Must have been Black. Dark magic or some shit."

Ronan had no idea what it was. What was worse, he had no idea how to fight it either. He turned his attention back to Callum and Jude who were standing back to back shouting up at the sky. Callum had his hands poised in the air looking and sounding like something out of *Harry Potter*, while Jude sounded like he was shouting more words in Navajo. If Ronan survived this fight, he was going to have to remember to ask Jude what the hell was up with *that*.

Looking around, he couldn't see Greeley or Hunter. "Shit, Tobin! Where are Greeley and Hunter? Do you see them"

"I don't know where they are." Tobin staggered back to his feet, still cradling his right arm.

"Looking for this, asshole?" Lydia screeched from twenty feet away. She was holding a dagger to Greeley's throat.

"Let me go, bitch!" Greeley gritted from behind his clenched teeth.

"Do what he says, Lydia. He isn't what you came here for. We both know it's me you want." This wasn't good. It was too dark to get off a clean shot even if Ronan could get to his gun before Lydia used the wickedly sharp dagger on Greeley. He was wishing now that he'd left the kid at home. This was no place for an eighteen-year-old boy who was just starting his life.

"Just starting his life out?" Lydia cackled. "This little whore? He's gotten more ass than a public toilet. Give me one good reason why I shouldn't slit his worthless fucking throat right now."

"Because it's the last thing you'll ever do," Ronan spat from behind gritted teeth. "Kill him and I'll shoot you on the spot, even if it's the last thing I ever do. I'll die knowing my last act on earth was a heroic one." Ronan had no desire to die here in the middle of this forest, but he would do it without hesitation to save Greeley.

"Save me the fucking melodrama, Ronan. We both know that all you want to do is get home to your precious Tennyson so you can jizz in a jar and make your spawn with a turkey baster."

Lydia had a point, but there was no way in hell Ronan was going to let her see that she'd hit a nerve. "Let Greeley go, Lydia. You've got me."

"What makes you think you have any power at all here, Ronan?" Gideon Black's voice boomed.

Ronan opened his mouth to answer the mouthy spirit when he felt himself lift into the air. At the same time realizing he couldn't breathe. Looking to his right, he could see that Jude and Callum were also suspended in mid-air. Callum was clawing at his neck in an obvious attempt to breathe, while Jude hung limp, as if he'd given up the fight or wasn't giving Black the satisfaction of seeing him struggle against whatever force was doing this to them.

His lungs were starting to burn from the lack of oxygen while his vision was starting to grey out at the sides. Ronan knew that he wasn't going to be able to survive much longer like this. His thoughts turned to Tennyson and the life they could have lived together with their little miss. He sent up a prayer that their friends would be able to comfort him after Ronan was gone. The last thought Ronan had before the darkness swallowed him was that at least Tennyson would survive in this life.

42

Tennyson

Carson Craig drove like Tennyson's grandmother. At least it felt like he did. It was only a fifteen-minute drive across town from where they lived to the Salem Towne Forest, but God Almighty, it seemed like they'd been driving for an hour.

There had been a burst water main near Essex Street that had traffic detoured for three city blocks around the mess. Plus, there was the curiosity factor that had everyone slowed down to look at what was going on.

Now, it was smooth sailing and Tennyson was getting more and more nervous by the minute. "Jesus Christ, are we there yet, Carson?"

"I think this left turn up here is it." Carson turned the minivan into the dim parking lot. "Look, isn't that Jude's Thunderbird?"

"Yeah, and that's Tobin's truck over there. Thank God, because I wouldn't have known where else to go."

"I think Mom would have helped us out." Carson scrambled out of the minivan.

"Come on, let's go. This way." Tennyson pointed to the well-worn path leading into the woods. His gift was of no use to him at this time. He knew Gideon Black had blocked the whole area, so all he had to go on were his five senses and with his concussion, they all felt dull and muddled. He should let Carson lead the way, but his gut instinct was telling him to get to Ronan now and he couldn't ignore that feeling.

Running as fast as his aching head allowed, Tennyson could see the glow of the fire up ahead. He knew that was where the action was happening. He slowed to a stop when he realized the only thing he could hear, aside from the slap of his shoes against the forest floor, was the crackle of the fire. There was no sound of a fight. There was no grandiose speech coming from Gideon Black. There weren't even cries for help from the wounded. What the hell was going on?

"What?" Carson panted, bending double to catch his breath. "What is it?"

"Nothing. I can't hear anything, aside from you gasping for breath."

"I chase three toddlers through the house. I'm not built for long-distance running." Carson managed a brief smile. "What's our plan here?"

"We need to get in there and find out what's going on. It's too quiet." Tennyson's stomach was pitching and rolling in concert with his aching head.

"It's probably a trap." Carson sounded pretty certain.

"I know, but what choice do we have? Let's go." Tennyson started off again, heading toward the clearing. The closer he got, the louder the roar of the fire became and the creepier the silence of the forest was. Tennyson should hear Ronan's big mouth somewhere.

Running the last few feet into the clearing, Tennyson stopped short when he saw the raging bonfire and Aurora lashed to the post in front of it. He was about to run to her and set her free when Carson grabbed him from behind and gave him a hard yank. Ten knew Carson wanted him to see something behind him. The problem was, Ten wasn't so sure he wanted to see it.

Right now, his life was fine. Ronan was fine. All of his other friends were fine. Once he turned around, that would all change and not for the better. Taking a deep breath, Ten slowly spun around and gasped at what he saw. Ronan, Jude and Callum were all suspended in mid-air. Reminding him of what happened to Niall Gallagher a few months back. Tobin was sitting on the ground cradling his right arm and some woman was holding a knife to Greeley's throat. Doing a quick count, Ten realized Hunter Conroy was missing. "Shit, where's Hunter?"

Carson shot him a confused look. "The tow truck driver? How the hell'd he get mixed up in this?"

"I'll explain if we survive." Tennyson rolled his eyes. He wished to hell he remembered the Navajo weapon-word Jude had hurled at the spirits haunting The Black Cat Inn when they were doing this exact thing to Niall Gallagher.

"I'm so glad you're here, Tennyson. Just in time to watch Ronan die. I'm enjoying the little role reversal this time around, with Ronan dying and you living." Gideon Black laughed. "The only problem with that little scenario is that it's wrong. I'm going to kill you too."

Ronan let out a strangled moan.

"Oh, isn't that cute, your husband is reaching out for you," Black snarled.

Ten locked eyes briefly with Ronan before turning back to Black. "What do you want, Gideon? What's your end game here? Something keeps going wrong, otherwise we wouldn't keep doing this over and over again throughout time."

Black's eyebrows knit together. "What are you talking about? I'm chasing you and Ronan through time and my descendants and I are enjoying the hell out of killing you and the witches. Aren't we, Lydia?"

"Yes, we are, grandfather!" Lydia shouted. The knife jiggled against Greeley's throat, drawing a thin line of blood.

Tennyson turned his focus back to Gideon Black. If he kept looking at Greeley, he wasn't going to be able to think straight. "See, that's where you're wrong, Gideon. History keeps repeating itself and putting Ronan and me back together again, not so that you can keep killing one of us or both of us, but so that we can finally beat you. Today's the day."

There was a presence behind him. Something he'd never felt before in the eighteen years since he'd been given his gift. It wasn't entirely human and whatever is was, was somehow able to slip beneath the psychic block Gideon Black had over this area. The only thing Tennyson knew for sure at the moment was that whatever was standing behind him was on his side.

Gideon Black laughed again. Lydia joined in. "Today's the day. Is it?"

"Let them all go, Black. This is your last chance!" Tennyson demanded.

"No, Tennyson, It's yours." Black raised his hands as if her were about to cast a spell on Tennyson when there was a blur of movement behind Lydia. Something snatched Ronan out of the air and disappeared with him. Gideon Black let out an ear-piercing scream.

"Jesus Christ, Ten. Did you see that? Where's Ronan?" Carson sounded more shocked than panicked.

Ten had seen it. "I don't know where he is, but I think he's safe."

That same blur of movement sped by again, snatching Greeley from Lydia.

"Holy shit!" Carson exclaimed. "It's The Flash!"

"The what?" Tennyson asked. He still had no idea what was going on and couldn't concentrate with Gideon Black screaming like something was killing him which was impossible since he was already dead.

"You heard the man, Black. Let Jude and Callum go. Unless you want more?" The figure who had been standing behind Tennyson stepped out of the shadows. His left hand was raised in the air in a "stop" gesture. His right hand rested benignly at his side.

 Tennyson chanced a look away from Gideon Black to gaze up at the creature standing beside him. He was well over six feet tall and so dark that he could melt easily back into darkness. Ten thought the voice sounded a bit familiar, but there was no way the…the being standing next to him was Hunter Conroy. Was it?

"What are you?" Black whimpered.

The creature grinned, taking a step forward. "Let them go. Last chance." His right hand twitched and started to rise.

Black screamed again.

Jude and Callum started to fall back to earth. A blur of color shot out managing to grab them both and set them gently back on the ground.

"Now back to hell with you, where you belong." The creature commanded.

"I'll be back!" Black howled.

His dark hand twitched at his side. "I'll be waiting."

Gideon vanished, leaving only his robe behind.

"Tennyson!" Ronan's voice boomed through the forest.

"Here!" Ten shouted. The pain in his head ramped back up now that everyone was out of danger. He turned to his right to look at the man standing next to him. "Who are you?"

The man grinned. "You know who I am, Tennyson."

Ten's eyes narrowed. "I think you're Hunter, I'm just not sure what form you're in at the moment."

The man nodded. "Hunter Conroy at your service. You're gonna want to keep this under your hat, but I'm a-"

"Tennyson, look out!" Ronan bellowed from a distance.

Tennyson screamed in pain as the dagger Lydia had been threatening Greeley with was now embedded in his left shoulder. "Ronan?" Ten said weakly before being claimed by the darkness. The last thing he saw, was the dark face that belonged to Hunter Conroy.

43

Ronan

Ronan felt his heart stop beating in his chest when he saw Lydia raise her arm and throw the dagger at Tennyson. A second after the weapon left her hand, something tackled the librarian to the ground. Lydia screamed either in terror or pain. He hoped it fucking hurt.

Running as fast as he could to Tennyson, Ronan tried to put the fear he was feeling out of his mind for the moment. Ten was going to be fine. Everything was going to be fine. "Ten?"

"It caught him in the shoulder," Carson said. "He's bleeding like hell, but we shouldn't take it out, right?" He sounded like he was getting hysterical.

"That's right. Don't pull the dagger out. Just keep steady pressure on the wound." Jesus Christ what an epic cluster fuck this had turned into.

"Greeley?" Ronan called out.

"Calling 911!" Greeley shouted back. "Already called my father."

Ronan loved it when the kid read his mind. Thankfully Greely was unharmed, but for the superficial cut on his neck. He knelt down beside his husband. "How you doing, babe?"

"Been better, asshole." Ten rolled his eyes. "Gotta concussion and a fucking knife in my arm, but other than that, Mrs. Lincoln…"

"Keep him talking, Carson." Ronan stood up, looking around. "Lydia?" He bellowed.

"Uh, I've got her right here, Detective O'Mara," a strange voice called out.

Ronan looked over at Jude and Callum, who were making their way over to him with Madam Aurora who aside from a black eye, didn't look any the worse for wear. "You okay, Aurora?" Ronan asked.

"Nothing a few days in Key West won't cure. Aurora managed a week smile.

Ronan knew Aurora would be just fine. He turned his attention to the stranger who had Lydia. "Who are you?" Ronan called back.

"Luca Pennington, sir. I was out for a walk when I heard what was going on. I couldn't leave without helping. You and Tennyson have done so much for Salem, so I figured I should give back." The young man shrugged his thin shoulders. He stood about 5'9" tall with a slim build and shaggy dark hair. In the darkness, Ronan couldn't tell what color his eyes were.

"I don't mean to be rude, kid, but *what* are you?" Ronan couldn't believe he was asking the question, but when a kid who maybe weighed a buck fifty soaking wet somehow managed to fly through the air, breaking whatever spell Gideon and Lydia had put on him and then somehow managed to land him safely on the ground as if he were Lois Lane to the kid's Superman, then the question bore asking.

Luca ducked his head, his left sneaker digging into the forest floor.

"He's a vampire." Callum Churchill said with a grin. "What else would explain his superhuman strength and the way his eyes are glowing from within as if they were lit from his very soul?"

"Jesus Christ, Wordsmith!" Ronan groaned. He could hear sirens coming from a distance. He turned back to the kid. "Is that true?"

Luca gave a brief shrug in response.

"Everyone keep this under your hat." Ronan turned back to Luca. "Thank you for saving me and my friends tonight. If there's ever anything I can do for you in return, all you have to do is ask."

"There just might be…" Luca trailed off as shouts and flashlight beams started making their way through the woods.

"Now you," Ronan turned to Hunter Conroy, who somehow looked the same as he had when they'd gotten here. "Same deal of secrecy."

Hunter raised an eyebrow as he looked around the group of people.

"For the love of Christ, Hunter!" Ten wailed. "I've got a fucking knife in my shoulder, we just met Dracula and you somehow managed to send Gideon back to hell. Telling me you're a griffin or a sphinx right now wouldn't surprise me."

"Not a griffin. Try gargoyle," Hunter said softly.

Callum sucked in a harsh breath. "Legend has it that only a gargoyle has the power to banish evil spirits to another realm. You are a true hero."

Hunter blushed. "Guys, I'm a tow truck driver and a mechanic. That's it."

"Not true," Jude grinned. "You're also my breakfast date."

Jesus Christ, leave it to Jude to think with his dick at a time like this. Ronan stifled the laugh that was bubbling up his throat.

"Greeley!" Fitzgibbon roared.

"Here, Dad! Tennyson's got a dagger in his shoulder, but I'm fine."

"The EMTs are right behind me. How's everyone else?" Kevin shouted.

"Tobin's got a broken arm from when Gideon Black threw him against a tree and Aurora got a black eye from when Lydia kidnapped her. Other than that, she's fine," Ronan said.

"Why do you sound hoarse?" Fitzgibbon narrowed his eyes at Ronan.

Ronan narrowed his own right back. "I'm not sure you'd believe me, captain. Weren't you the one who told me you didn't believe Gideon Black was coming back for me and Tennyson, that there *wasn't* going to be a final battle? Well, guess what? There was a fucking final battle! It looked like something out of fucking Harry Potter with the reanimated spirit of Gideon Black Force-choking me, Jude, and Callum. We were all suspended thirty feet off the ground. Lydia had a dagger to Greeley's throat. I don't know what the hell would have happened if it wasn't for Luca and Hunter saving the day."

"Who's Luca?" Cisco Jackson asked. He'd been standing behind Fitzgibbon listening to Ronan yell.

"Me." Luca waved. "Just happened to be in the right place at the right time."

"In the Salem Towne Forest in the middle of the night?" Cisco's dark eyes narrowed on the young man.

"I'm a college student at Salem State and I tend bar at Spellbound. I like to walk through the woods after a shift to cool down before going home."

"I know you!" Tobin called out. "You're the body shot kid from Spellbound!"

"Hey, Tobin!" Luca waved. "Long time, no see. Rumor has it you got yourself a boy-toy."

Tobin laughed, wincing in pain. "He's my future husband now."

"Good for you man. Spellbound was never your jam anyway." Luca's smile was genuine.

"Body shot kid?" Cisco asked. "Do I even want to know what that is?" He walked over to the boy and sniffed him. "I don't smell pot or booze. You can go home, kid. Keep a lid on what you saw here, huh?"

Luca nodded. He moved to head off, but not before Ronan handed him his business card.

The EMTs swooped in and loaded Tennyson onto a gurney. Ronan started to follow them out. He could see more medics attending to Madam Aurora and Tobin. He was glad his friends were getting attention, he had a million questions about what happened here tonight and what came next, but all he wanted to do right now was go with Tennyson to the hospital.

44

Tennyson

Tennyson felt like he was on top of the world. He had one hundred and twelve stiches in his left shoulder, which made him look a little like Frankenstein's monster, and a whole lot of morphine coursing through his system, which meant he was feeling *no* pain.

Ronan was around here somewhere, but at the moment, only Erin O'Mara was sitting in his curtained off emergency room cubby with him.

"How's my boy doing?" Erin ran a hand through Ten's limp hair.

"I'm okay, Mom. Did you see how brave I was? Well, up until that bitch threw her knife at me." Ten frowned, "but I was *real* brave until then." He started to giggle. Damn, this morphine was something.

"Are you losing your marbles, babe?" Ronan asked as he slid back the curtain. He was carrying a paper cup filled with ice chips.

"Your Mom is here and I was telling her how brave I was." Ten smiled at his husband, who was thankfully all in one piece and able to make his baby-juice donation next week.

Ronan handed him the cup. "You were very brave. I was so angry when I saw you though. I thought it was going to be me who died in this life and then there you were telling Gideon Black today was the day we were going to beat him."

"Well, it was," Tennyson grumped, chewing on a piece of ice.

"Not without a little help." Ronan sighed. "Thank God you brought Carson with you."

Tennyson opened his mouth to broach something with Ronan, when he was stopped in his tracks.

"Knock, knock." A familiar voice called out. Seconds later, Fitzgibbon's face appeared around the curtain. "Am I welcome here?"

"That depends, you gonna suspend Ten now too?" Ronan's tone was pure ice.

Ten giggled again. "He can't upend me, Ronan! I'm just a consultant." That didn't sound right either. Not that Ten cared. He was on top of the world.

"Maybe I should place him on injured reserve until he's off the sauce?" Fitzgibbon offered a smile.

Ronan didn't smile back.

Fitzgibbon cleared his throat. "Is he going to be okay?"

"He'll be fine. We just have to watch the stitches for signs of infection and his concussion is only a slight one. He can go home soon." Ronan glanced back to Ten who was giving him moon eyes.

"I'm fine, Kevin. I'd be better if you'd un-pretend my husband, so we can make our baby in peace next week." Ten huffed.

"I wanted to talk to you about that, Ronan." Fitzgibbon sighed.

"Are you adding more time to my sentence, *warden*?" Ronan asked.

"I wish you'd shut the hell up and listen to me." Fitzgibbon reached into his back pocket and pulled something out. "Here." He handed Ronan's badge back to him. "You weren't really suspended, Ronan. I never put the paperwork in. Your gun's in my safe at home."

"I don't understand." Ronan held his badge in his hand. He had a look in his eyes like he never thought he'd see it again.

"You are your own worst enemy, Ronan." Fitzgibbon dropped himself into a plastic chair next to Tennyson. He looked worn to the bone.

Ronan opened his mouth, presumably to contradict his boss, but Tennyson shot him a look to shut the hell up. Surprisingly, Ronan obeyed.

"I might not have believed that Gideon Black was coming back from beyond the grave, but I sure as hell believed there was something going on with the witches. I could see where you were going with Cisco Jackson as your lead suspect too, but Jesus, Ronan, to come out and accuse him like that, with no evidence and then to charge at him like a raging bull? I had to stop you before you ruined your case and your career. I had to save you from yourself."

"Did you have to do it with a body slam? I'm not a twenty-something anymore. My body doesn't bounce back like it used to." Ronan shot Kevin and ugly glare.

"As long as your jewels are okay, babe, who cares how he did it?" Ten rolled his eyes.

Kevin snorted. "Be mad at me all you want, Ronan. I did it because I love you. I don't say that often enough, but you're like a son to me. If I didn't care about you, I'd let you run wild. Now, you're on leave until next Wednesday. Take care of your husband and yourself. Do everything the fertility clinic doctors tell you so that you make the most beautiful baby next week. Take good care of Emilyn too. She let it slip on the cruise that her favorite ice cream is rocky road. So, start stocking up. I sent the PDF application for the July sitting of the Sargent's Exam to your work email. It had better be sent back to me for my approval by noon on Wednesday or I'm suspending your ass for real this time. Don't test me, Ronan."

"I won't." Ronan walked to his boss and pulled him out of his chair for a hug. "Thanks, Kevin. I owe you."

"Yeah, well you also owe Cisco Jackson. Send the Salem P.D. a fruit basket or a couple dozen muffins or cookies from Cassie's bakery. That man has the patience of a saint and an O'Mara-sized ulcer thanks to you." Fitzgibbon grinned. "I'm going home. My boy and I need to have a discussion about the merits of vigilantism just days before he applies to the police academy. I swear its like running a daycare with you people." Fitzgibbon stepped out of the curtain.

"All's well that ends well." Ten grinned goofily at his husband.

"Maybe not quite." Ronan dragged Fitzgibbon's chair close to Tennyson. "Now might not be the best time to talk about this, babe, but did we really meet a vampire and a gargoyle tonight?"

Tennyson had a feeling this topic of conversation was going to come up sooner rather than later. He was glad Ronan was the one bringing it up because he wasn't entirely sure how to broach it himself. "I've encountered things, beings, I guess you could say since I've gotten my gift, that I haven't been able to identify. I know now what spirits, angels, and demons are, but there are still some things I come across in readings and in life that I can't quite put my finger on."

Ronan's brows drew together. "You're serious? This you and not the morphine talking here?"

Ten nodded. "We hear about things like vampires and werewolves all the time in pop culture, right? All myth is based in fact somewhere, but there's always something attached to that myth to explain the magic away. Like medical conditions that explain the human need to consume blood or that it was manatees or some other kind of sea creature that sailors saw instead of mermaids, right?"

"I get that, but an actual vampire? Here in Salem?" Ronan shook his head.

"What better place for one to be, Ronan, with all of the bizarre things that go on in this city and its open arms of inclusion to the LGBTQ community? Plus, it's a college town, so there's a lot of young people. Salem is the place to be if you're different or a misfit of any kind." Ten shrugged, pointing to himself.

"Why didn't you tell me about these kinds of beings before? Gargoyles are real? Not just the stuff of lame B movies? And Disney cartoons?" Ronan shook his head.

"Babe, you're still getting used to the idea of psychics and spirits. I didn't want to add to your burden by telling you that sometimes I encounter things that scare me or things that don't make sense to me."

"So, we could have other things here in Salem? Werewolves? Kraken? Giant spiders? Jude? What the hell is Jude?" Ronan's eyes widened more with each thing coming out of his mouth.

"Werewolves are a possibility. Kraken, maybe? You won't catch me in the ocean past my ankles because of the great white sharks down the Cape alone, that's for damn sure! Giant spiders are a definite no. Jude's a question mark since no one can read him." Ten shrugged.

"Yeah, but what about Hunter Conroy? Did you know about him?" Ronan settled back into his chair, looking a bit calmer.

Ten shook his head. "I never tried to read him before. While he was standing next to me and was shifted into his gargoyle form, I couldn't identify him. I did know that he was on our side and that Gideon's block didn't affect him." Ten grimaced, rolling his left shoulder.

Ronan nodded. "The morphine wearing off?"

"Yeah, but don't hit the button. I want to talk to you while my head is still somewhat clear." Ten reached out for Ronan with his good hand. "I was so scared when I saw you dangling in the air like you were caught in some kind of spider's web."

Leaning over the bed, Ronan pressed a kiss to Tennyson's temple. "I'm so sorry you had to see me like that."

"What you went through in all of those past lives, having to watch me die, Ronan, finally hit home. I never really got what you had to go through until that moment. I'm sorry it took me so long to understand why helping the witches meant so much to you." Ten could feel his emotions starting to get the best of him.

"I understand that you were just trying to keep me and our family safe, Ten. It's just that sometimes there are things that come up in my life that are bigger than us. You talking about having to think like a father made me realize that I need to re-evaluate those things too. I can't leap before I look anymore. I should be considering you and our child first, then leaping. Or not."

"That impulsiveness is one of the things I fell in love with." Ten squeezed their joined hands.

"Maybe now I'll only be impulsive in the bedroom?" Ronan winked at his husband before he pressed the button on Ten's morphine pump.

Ten giggled. Christ, he sounded like a schoolboy to his own ears. Who cared? He was safe. His husband was safe, as were his precious jewels, and said husband was flirting with him even though his brains were scrambled and he looked like something out of Mary Wollstonecraft Shelley's imagination. Life might not be perfect, but it sure was good!

EPILOGUE

Ronan

Three weeks later...

Ronan was pacing around in the waiting room like an anxious father-to-be. As far as fertility clinics went, he had to admit this place didn't look particularly fertile. It looked like the waiting room of any other doctor's office that he'd ever been to in his life.

A few weeks back, he'd been led into an examination room where he'd been given a specimen cup and been shown the extensive collection of arousal materials, i.e., porn, should Ronan's soldier need any help in rising to the occasion.

The nurse, in a very soothing voice, had explained to him that sometimes men, under this kind of pressure, suffered from performance anxiety and had a hard time depositing their funds into the bank, as it were.

Being the world-champion monkey-spanker he was, Ronan had known making his *deposit* wasn't going to be a problem. He'd simply shucked his jeans to his feet, pictured that time he and Ten had gotten jiggy with it on the balcony of the cruise ship, and before you could sing the chorus to *The Love Boat* theme, he'd been screwing the cap back on his jar and had been pulling his pants back up to full mast.

Now was the hard part. Waiting. Ronan and the whole gang were at the clinic waiting for news on Emilyn's pregnancy test. Cassie had gone into the procedure room with her. Both Ten and Ronan had offered to go, but in the end, Emilyn had chosen the only other women in the group to hold her hand. It was no surprise considering the fact that both of the fathers-to-be were acting like they were about to deliver a litter of kittens themselves at any second now.

"Shit, was it like this for the two of you when you got pregnant with the triplets?" Ronan asked Truman and Carson.

Carson snorted. "We didn't have an audience for starters."

Truman was shaking his head. "Carson had seen that we were having these babies, so there was nothing to worry about for me, which is why I don't understand why you're practically climbing the walls here, Ronan. You're usually so calm, cool, and collected."

Jude burst out laughing. "Yeah, and I'm the Queen of England."

"You're a queen all right." Ronan rolled his eyes and slumped down into the seat next to Jude. "How'd things go on your date with Hunter Conroy anyway?"

"He's a nice guy. Way too nice for the likes of me. Interesting too, what with his *situation*..." Jude shrugged.

Ronan knew what Jude was referring to was Hunter's shifter side and was curious what his friend had been able to learn about that. "You gonna see him again?"

Jude shook his head no. "He's a little virginal for me, plus he's got shit going on that I don't think he wants anyone involved in."

"Or maybe he only wants Mr. Right involved in his shit. You ever think of that?" Ten asked.

Jude frowned. "You people and your idea of fated mates and forever loves and little misses."

"Gee, Ronan, maybe we shouldn't have made Jude one of her godparents. Is it too late to change our minds? I don't think our *little miss* should have a cynical son-of-a-bitch as such an important role model in her life. Do you?" Ten was shaking his head.

"What?" Jude squeaked. "Godparent? *Me*?"

"You might be right, Ten. I wouldn't want him to give her lessons on how love sucks." Ronan laughed at the comical look on Jude's face.

"Or on how to be a gigolo," Ten added.

"Now hold on a minute!" Jude sounded like he was getting all wound up. "I would never teach her *that*!"

Ronan shot Tennyson a silent look. "What would you teach her?"

Jude was quiet for a minute, as if he were really thinking about the question. "How to change the tires on the Thunderbird. How to execute the perfect roundhouse kick. How to sit still enough so a butterfly will land on your hand. How *not* to take shit from any man and most important of all, how much her Uncle Jude loves her."

"Damn it, Jude," Fitzgibbon grumped, swiping at his eyes.

"After a speech like that, we have to keep him, don't you think?" Ten asked.

"I guess so." Ronan shrugged.

"You *guess* so?" Jude all but roared.

Ronan burst out laughing. "Of course, we're keeping you, Jude."

"You asshole! Just for that, I'm gonna teach her all the best curse words and hop her up on sugar too!" He crossed his arms over his broad chest and shot Ronan a dirty look.

"You're gonna have to stand in line for that. Ronan's got first dibs, then Fitzgibbon." Carson laughed.

"Hey! I'm not that bad. Am I?" Fitzgibbon looked around the room.

"No." Truman shook his head. "Fuck is only going to be my kids' first word because of your delicate nature."

"Shit! Is it?" Kevin looked shocked.

"I think you answered your own question, Cap." Ronan snorted.

The door to the exam rooms opened and Cassie walked out. "Emilyn is ready for visitors, guys."

Ronan picked up the bouquet of blue roses he and Ten had grabbed at the florist on their way to the clinic and linking hands, headed toward Cassie. "Is she okay?" Ronan whispered.

Cassie nodded. "Everything went fine." She patted Ronan's shoulder.

Walking hand-in-hand down the hall, Ronan could feel his heart thumping against his ribcage. After all the planning and worrying and the tears and the laughter, they were finally here. He lifted his hand to knock on the door.

"I love you, Ronan," Ten whispered.

"I love you too, babe." Ronan pressed a kiss to Ten's head.

"Come in!" Emilyn's cheerful voice called out.

Ten pushed the door open to see Emilyn lying in the procedure chair wrapped in a warm blanket.

"Hey, Dads!" She was all smiles. "The pregnancy test was positive! We're pregnant!"

That did it for Ronan. He felt the first of what he knew would be many tears trickle down his face.

"We're pregnant?" Ten asked, taking a seat next to Emilyn.

"It all went perfectly. I can already hear her speaking to me." Emilyn's smile was watery.

"You can?" Ronan asked, swiping at his eyes. "What's she saying?"

"That she loves you to Dublin and back, Ronan." Emilyn reached out for his hand.

Ronan felt a fresh wave of tears threatening to spill down his face. That was always the line he and his mother used to exchange with each other.

"She also has a request for the both of you." Emilyn looked back and forth between Ten and Ronan.

"What's that?" Ten asked. He wore a look on his face like their little miss's request was as much a surprise to him as it was to Ronan.

"She wants you both to start using her name." Emilyn grinned at them both. "It's time that the whole world knows her name. She's standing with both arms crossed over her chest and she's wearing a crown."

"Well, there's a surprise!" Tennyson burst out laughing. "Our daughter acting like a queen."

"I always said whatever Everly Erin O'Mara wanted, she'd get." Ronan could feel those fresh tears getting ever closer to falling. It was both shoulders getting a bit warmer that sent them cascading down his face. "Mom and Bertha are here loving on me, aren't they?"

"No," Ten said on a laugh. "Whenever you say her name, there she'll be."

Ronan shut his eyes and focused on the spirit of his daughter. He could feel her warmth, her light and he swore he could hear her musical laugh.

He knew he was flawed man, impulsive, suspicious, and given to a quick temper on occasion, but he was determined to be the best version of himself he could be for her.

For his little miss.

For Everly.

THE END

COLD CASE PSYCHIC BOOK NINE, DEAD MAN WALKING, IS AVAILABLE FOR PRE-ORDER! GRAB YOUR COPY TODAY!

Cold Case Detective, Ronan O'Mara is stunned to see the breaking news that a well-known mobster he helped to put behind bars, Vito "The Dragon" Dragonni, has been released from prison after his life sentence is overturned on a technicality. When prominent members involved in the original case against The Dragon start turning up dead, Ronan starts to wonder if he's next.

Psychic, Tennyson Grimm starts having visions of dead men with The Dragon's signature kill shot: two bullet holes to the forehead. The men in the visions are strangers, but when he learns from an undercover agent that Dragonni has compiled a hit list with Ronan and his ex-partner, Tony, at the top, he fears a day will come when he recognizes the murder victim in his vision.

Tony Abruzzi has been a broken man since the tragic death of his adopted son, Mark. Refusing the offer of protective custody until Dragonni and his hit squad are off the streets, he seems to be daring the mobster to come after him. Despite the fact that they've been estranged since the case that cost Tony's son his life, Ronan decides to stick to his former partner's side as his personal bodyguard, whether Tony wants his help or not.

Can Ronan and Tony find a way to work together to stop The Dragon before he can cross more names off his hit list or are both detectives dead men walking?

I HOPE YOU ALL ENJOYED MEETING LUCA PENNINGTON! HIS STORY, BLOOD SONG, IS AVAILABLE NOW!

College senior, Luca Pennington, answered an ad to participate in a medical trial to help pay tuition, only to develop an allergy to the sun and an alarming craving for AB negative. Salem Police Chief, Cisco Jackson, catches Luca stealing blood from a university medical lab. Sparks fly when the rookie vampire refuses to feed from the veteran cop in a Meals-On-Wheels-with-benefits exchange, things really start to heat up with Cisco threatening to arrest Luca if he catches him stealing blood again. Luca's response to the sexy, older cop is, "Catch me if you can!" Are Cisco and Luca fated mates? Or fated to cross swords over the proper way to feed your vampire.

THAT OLD MAGIC, CAPTAIN KEVIN FITZGIBBON'S LONG-AWAITED SPIN OFF IS NOW AVAILABLE! GRAB YOUR COPY TODAY!

Boston Police Captain, Kevin Fitzgibbon thought he'd found the missing piece of his heart when psychic Madam Aurora prophesied the love of his life was philanthropist, Jace Lincoln. After spending months as on-again, off-again boyfriends, the pair are off again, perhaps for good, leaving Kevin distraught and grumpy.

Jace Lincoln is still trying to put his life back together after Fitz dumped him on Valentine's Day. While getting back into the swing of things with a new man, a drunk Fitzgibbon barges in on their date like Godzilla destroying Tokyo. Listening to Fitz carry on about how much he misses what they had together makes Jace wonder if they still have enough of that old magic left to try one last time.

Through a series of dates ranging from ridiculous to right on the money, Fitz and Jace reconnect and find that the things keeping them apart might not be so insurmountable after all. Deciding to give their relationship another try, they start planning a bright future together.

That future is stopped dead in its tracks when tragedy strikes at a party celebrating the tenth anniversary of Jace's homeless shelter. Will Kevin and Jace survive to begin a new life together or have they lost their last chance at happiness for good this time?

IF YOU ENJOYED MEETING HUNTER CONROY, HE'S GOT HIS OWN BOOK. HUNTER'S CURSE IS AVAILABLE NOW!

1418, Wales: Hunter Conroy, the youngest in a family of powerful demon slayers, is captured by the evil warlock Osian. Young Hunter is given a choice: join forces with his enemy and kill his own family, or be cursed to live through the ages as a stone gargoyle. Once a century, Hunter is released from his prison, and tempted with the chance to build a life for himself. At the end of a decade of freedom, if Hunter does not choose to become one of Osian's minions, he is again remanded to the cold, lonely rock.

Fast forward six hundred years, and Hunter finds himself in Salem, Massachusetts. He has forged a quiet life, knowing that at the end of this latest cycle, Osian will once again return, and Hunter will decline his offer. He is content to live out the last few months of this round alone, until he meets Walker Harmon.

ER Doctor Walker Harmon had expected to be married with children by now, but so far has been unable to find the man of his dreams.

Hunter Conroy sparks his interest until he sees the handsome tow truck driver throw a man across the room without even touching him. When Hunter reveals the source of his powers, telling Walker that his days in Salem are numbered, it's a story beyond belief. Realizing he's in love with this cursed man, Walker is willing to risk everything to fight for Hunter.

With time running out, Hunter amasses a dream team of witches, psychics, and a mysterious wizard to help him break the warlock's curse. Will their combined powers be enough to free Hunter, or will the gargoyle reclaim him for another century?

Made in United States
North Haven, CT
19 July 2022

21584040R00236